SNAKE-EATER

ALSO BY T. KINGFISHER

Horror

The Twisted Ones

The Hollow Places

A House with Good Bones

What Moves the Dead

What Feasts at Night

Fantasy

The Seventh Bride

Swordheart

Nettle & Bone

Thornhedge

Paladin's Grace

Paladin's Strength

Paladin's Hope

Paladin's Faith

A Sorceress Comes to Call

SNAKE-EATER

T. KINGFISHER

This is a work of fiction. Names, characters, organizations, places, events, and incidents are either products of the author's imagination or are used fictitiously. Otherwise, any resemblance to actual persons, living or dead, is purely coincidental.

Published by 47North, Seattle
www.apub.com

Amazon, the Amazon logo, and 47North are trademarks of Amazon.com, Inc., or its affiliates.

EU product safety contact:
Amazon Media EU S. à r.l.
38, avenue John F. Kennedy, L-1855 Luxembourg
amazonpublishing-gpsr@amazon.com

ISBN-13: 9781662525094 (paperback)
ISBN-13: 9781662525100 (digital)

Cover design by Logan Matthews
Cover illustration by Tristan Elwell

Printed in the United States of America

This one's for the whole Bubonicon crew.

Chapter 1

Selena picked her new home for no better reason than the dog laid down on the porch.

The dog was a middle-aged black Lab, though her Labrador-ness had been diluted by a fence-jumping father of questionable ancestry. Whatever he had been, his genes had helped temper the breed's boundless energy. She still worshipped chasing tennis balls as the highest form of canine endeavor but wanted a long nap afterward, and ideally a long nap beforehand as well.

Selena named her Copper, which Walter said was a stupid name because there was nothing copper colored about her. Selena felt guilty when he pointed that out, but Copper had already learned her name by that point, so she put a collar on the dog with bright copper tags. Walter rolled his eyes, but Selena was pleased with herself for having set things right again.

The dog, it must be said, never seemed to mind either way.

Selena had ridden out on the train, two and a half days to get there, and she'd been afraid the whole time that somebody'd tell her she couldn't have a dog on board. She didn't know what she'd do. Fortunately Copper had excellent travel manners and mostly lay under her seat and let out the long sighs of an old dog at peace with the world. The rocking of the train seemed to agree with her. She squatted obediently at every stop and was extremely pleased to share the sandwiches that Selena passed down to her.

At the second-to-last stop, the conductor bent down and scratched Copper behind the ears, and Selena was so relieved that she nearly cried.

When they reached the final stop, Copper stood up and stretched. Her muzzle had begun to go white, but her eyes were clear. She glanced around the train platform and then up at Selena, as if expecting orders.

Quartz Creek was painted on the platform wall, in faded blue. The train platform was cinder block and adobe. It could have been ten years old or two hundred.

There were no gates or turnstiles, no ticket takers. Also no taxis. Selena knew that the area was a historic zone, which meant that you couldn't put developments up all over the place and drones were banned, but she hadn't expected a lack of taxis. Or maybe there just weren't enough people around for taxis to make any money, which was a somewhat alarming thought.

"I guess we just go?" Selena asked empty air. She wrapped the leash around her right hand and gripped her suitcase handle in her left.

The station was nearly deserted. Two men in faded jeans unloaded several boxes from one of the cars into the back of a battered pickup truck. The conductor went over and had them sign a sheet of paper, then said something that made the others laugh.

Selena stole a glance to make sure that they weren't laughing at her. They didn't seem to be.

There was a drinking fountain against one wall. The water came out lukewarm and tasting of metal. She filled her water bottle and let Copper drink her fill from the little metal dish in her backpack.

There was hardly anything else to the station. Two small shelters with benches, the drinking fountain, and a list of timetables under glass. The stairs down from the platform ran directly to a rutted dirt road. Selena stared down the road in mild disbelief, then slowly lifted her eyes.

The town was visible a long way in the distance. There was a hill behind it, or maybe a mountain. Between town and station stood two or three miles of desert, full of scrubby little bushes and big gray-green saguaros, and dozens of plants that she didn't know the names of. One long, serpentine thing might be ocotillo, but then again, it might not. Whatever it was, it had thorns. So did most of the other plants.

The dirt was bone white and the sky was hard blue. It was only midmorning, but heat was already making long squiggles in the air.

She'd expected the town to be closer, or for there to be taxis or buses or something. She hadn't expected a hike from station to town. Aunt Amelia would probably have come out to meet her, except that Amelia didn't know that she was coming. They corresponded by erratic postcards and neither had ever included a phone number.

Even if she'd known the number, she didn't dare turn on her phone. The location tracker that had seemed like such a sensible precaution when Walter explained it would give her away, and she just wasn't ready to deal with that yet. Which also meant that she couldn't use a rideshare app, assuming there were any way out here.

Selena picked up her suitcase and let the dog lead the way.

Behind them, the train let out a long whistle and began to chug away.

The black dog kicked up little puffs of dust as she trotted along, occasionally reaching the end of the leash and pausing for her human to catch up. Selena studied the verge of the road. She had expected deserts to be full of sand, but the earth here looked more like talcum powder mixed with rocks. The shrubs along the road had gray bark and grew sideways, split, grew sideways again.

There was so much sky that it was hard to think. In the city, there were walls you could put your back against, doors to shut, places to hide. To hide out here, you'd have to crouch down and worm your way under one of the scrubby little bushes, and you'd probably get a faceful of spines for your trouble. Even the shadow of the Scottsdale arcology had faded away into the endless blue.

Selena wiped her forehead, where beads of sweat were already beginning to form. She was very tired. Unlike Copper, she hadn't slept well on the train. Dragging her suitcase wasn't helping. The wheels on the bottom were made for flat surfaces, not dusty roads with washboard ruts. The rattling went all the way up her arm and into her skull, setting her back teeth clattering against each other.

I shall invent an all-terrain suitcase and make a fortune. With giant wheels, and a handle that doesn't try to twist out of your hand when you hit a rock.

She had dragged the suitcase perhaps a quarter of a mile when the battered pickup from the station rumbled up alongside them. It stopped by the side of the road.

"Need a ride in?" asked the driver. He was an older Latino man with a lean, angular face covered in narrow wrinkles. "It's a short drive but a long walk."

Selena's first instinct was to refuse. You didn't take rides from strange men—that was asking for Bad Things to happen. They could kidnap you and dump your body somewhere in the desert where you'd never be found.

Then she had to laugh at herself. There were no other people around and nowhere to hide. If they were planning on kidnapping her, it didn't matter whether she climbed into the truck or not.

Besides, if I have to walk the whole way, my body may end up somewhere in the desert anyway.

"Thank you," she said. *Was that enough? Probably not.* "I'd appreciate that a lot." *There, that should be good. Just enough, not too much.*

"Hop in," said the old man, jerking his thumb toward the back.

The other man was riding in the back alongside the crates from the train. He lowered the tailgate and Copper leapt up. "Hey girl," he said to the dog, and she thumped her tail twice, then settled at Selena's feet. "Ma'am," he added, dipping his head to Selena, and helped her settle her suitcase.

It was too loud in the back of the truck to talk, for which Selena was grateful. She gave the man a quick smile and then looked away, at the desert. Copper was a reassuring weight against her shins.

She wondered if the men knew her aunt. She could ask. What little she could see of Quartz Creek looked too tiny for anyone to be a stranger. Aunt Amelia had always said it was a small town, but she hadn't realized quite *how* small.

She practiced what to say to the driver in her head. *Thank you for the ride. You were right, it would have been a long walk.* That sounded pretty good. That was a normal thing somebody would say, right?

Thank you for the ride. You were right, it would have been a long walk.

She ran it through a couple of times, staring at the landscape bouncing over the side of the truck bed. The dust cloud that rose up behind them was four or five times the height of the truck and looked like a plume of ash.

Was the desert beautiful? It would be hard to tell. It was hard and dry, which Selena had expected, and *intricate*, which she hadn't. She'd been picturing sand and stone and scouring winds. Not the little bushes fitted all together with strips of dust in between, not the stacked paddles of prickly pear. It looked like a complicated mosaic with white mortar, or one of those paintings made out of hundreds of dots. If she were far up in the hard-blue sky, would the desert resolve into a picture?

Thank you for the ride. You were right, it would have been a long walk.

Lord, I must be tired. She almost always had to repeat a script in her head, but not so many times, and not such a simple one. Most of her scripts had been memorized long ago. It was only lately, with the funeral and wrapping everything up—and now the train—that she'd had to make so many new ones, and maybe they were crowding out old ones, like how you thanked someone for giving you a ride.

The truck rattled and cracked down the dry road, the wheels fitted into the ruts like train tracks. A line of fat, gray bodies ran alongside for a moment. Selena blinked, surprised, at a flock of plump little birds with black topknots and stubby wings.

Are those quail? *Real quail?*

She supposed she knew that quail existed somewhere, but she'd never expected to see them. They were creatures out of children's books, more like stuffed animals than real flesh and feather and bone. But here they were, plump and ridiculous and very much alive.

Selena realized that she was grinning foolishly. She darted a glance at the other passenger, and saw him smiling. He said something, but she couldn't hear it over the roar of the engine. She shook her head.

He was middle-aged, probably the driver's son. He wore a bandanna over his hair, and his skin was deeply tanned. There were thick silver rings on three of his fingers and black rings of grease under the nails.

When the truck slowed, entering Quartz Creek, and the wind died down, he leaned forward. "What brings you to town?" he asked.

Selena felt the little muscles along the back of her neck go wire tense. *It's a normal question. It's perfectly normal. You know what to say. You practiced this.*

She reached into her chest, and the words were there, just as she'd practiced them. "I'm looking for my aunt," she said. "She lives out here. I'm just not sure what her address is."

To her intense relief, he nodded, as if this wasn't strange at all. "Go up to the post office," he suggested. "It's right across the street. If you've got people here, Miss Jenny will know where they're at."

"Thank you," said Selena, although she had already planned to try the post office. "That's a good idea." Compliments were good, though not flattery. She thought she'd done it right. She had praised the idea, not him, and not extravagantly. She dropped her hand to Copper's collar, and the dog thumped her tail.

The town wasn't very large, a few dozen houses. They stood wide apart with ditches between them, and small roads arranged like the spokes of a wheel. The buildings were pale adobe with flat roofs, wide porches, and what looked like whole logs sticking out the sides. It was a very strange look, as if they'd built the rafters too long for the walls. One of the buildings was taller, an old Spanish Mission–style church, with double doors thrown wide.

Most of the houses had solar panels on the roof or the garage, the old, ugly kind—cheap and nearly indestructible. The sort that Selena associated with poverty one step up from corrugated-steel siding.

I've got twenty-seven dollars left to my name. I don't get to talk to anybody about poverty, I guess.

Did one of the houses belong to her aunt? Was one of those scruffy, speckled chickens hers?

Somehow Selena had never thought of her aunt as poor. *She has a house! People with houses aren't poor.*

At least . . . not in the city . . .

They passed an old garage, a temple to cars where mechanic-priests sat around in their overalls. There was a line of electric charging poles, but no stoplights. Chickens scattered along the road as the truck passed, and dogs lay panting in the shade. There were a couple of ragged pine trees, and some strange trees that Selena didn't know—one that was all green, even the trunk, with fine slender needles, and one with slick red bark that peeled like a burn.

The truck stopped.

Her companion unhooked the tailgate and jumped out. He reached up a hand to her.

Do I take his hand / you're not supposed to touch strangers / but he offered first and now it would be rude / no, it's like a handshake, that's okay, handshakes are okay—

She took it with, she hoped, no obvious hesitation. His fingers were dry and hard and had calluses like bits of gravel.

He helped her down from the truck and handed down her suitcase.

"Thank you," said Selena.

"No problem. Post office is right over there."

Selena took a step toward it, then stopped. *Don't forget.* She walked up to the cab of the truck and said, carefully, "Thank you for the ride. You were right, it would have been a long walk."

"Anytime," said the old man. He lifted a hand in half a wave, and Selena waved back.

She felt a bit giddy as she approached the post office. She'd done it right. She hadn't practiced getting a ride, but she hadn't said anything stupid. It was an unexpected victory.

The post office stood in the center of town. It was the same square adobe style as the rest of the buildings, but there was a metal sign over the door that said Post Office. Two of the strange green trees grew out in front, their leaves buzzing with cicadas.

Selena tied Copper's leash to one of the porch posts and said, "Stay." Copper fell over on her side with a drawn-out groan, the world's most put-upon dog.

Next to the door was a little wooden sign with letters burned into it that said Burnt Branch House.

Selena paused with her hand on the knob. Was that the name of the building? She'd seen named buildings in the city, but mostly they were named for historical figures. *Burnt Branch House. Hmm.*

She pulled the door open.

Inside it was all tile: red clay on the floor, bright blue for the counter. A line of painted sunflower tiles circled the wall. Even in the dim light, the room glowed with color. Selena had never seen a post office that was anything but industrial gray, and the sight made her want to grin in the same way seeing the quail had.

A stout woman sat behind the counter. She looked up and raised her eyebrows as Selena came in.

"Can I help you?"

Say it. Say it just like you practiced. It'll be okay.

"I'm sorry to bother you . . ." Selena reached into her backpack and pulled out the old postcard. The ink had blurred in a couple of places, and the stamp was half gone, but the name on the return was clear. *Amelia Walker.*

There was no street address, just the name of the town, which Selena had thought was odd until she came to Quartz Creek and saw how small it was.

"I'm looking for my aunt," she said and slid the postcard across the tiles.

The woman behind the counter picked it up, flipped it to the back. A line formed between her eyes, and she looked up.

Her broad face was sympathetic, and even before she spoke, Selena knew.

No. No. *She hasn't said anything, you're wrong, she hasn't said anything so it isn't real—*

"Oh, honey," said the woman. "I'm sorry. She passed away—only about a year ago. We didn't know how to find her next of kin, or we would've tried to get out a letter."

Selena was aware that she was staring straight ahead. Heat was rising up her face, to her eyes, and when it hit, she was going to burst into tears.

No, no, she can't be—I came all this way—I can't afford to go anywhere else—I can't even afford a ticket back—

And then the old anxiety came back, and she realized she'd been standing there for much too long and the woman was looking at her.

"Thank you," she said in a high, strangled voice. She might have said more, but she knew that it sounded like she was going to cry, and you did *not* cry in public, that was something you definitely did *not* do. Her mother had always been very clear on that. "You might as well wet your pants on the street corner!" she'd said.

Selena turned away and practically ran out the door.

Copper was waiting there. Copper, who was big and solid and made of fur and bone and muscle. Copper, who loved her even though she didn't deserve it. Selena crouched down and put her face in the black Lab's shoulder.

A year ago. A year ago. The phrase beat in her head like a pulse. *A year ago.*

Oh god, only a year. If she'd found her courage just a little bit sooner, if she'd gone only nine years instead of ten, she would have come out and found her aunt alive.

Whether her aunt wanted to see her—whether her aunt had any fond memories of the city or had sent the postcards purely out of loneliness and duty—those were hurdles she could have faced.

Now she couldn't.

Now she was in the desert hundreds of miles away from home, and there was nothing but strangers and heat and dead white dust.

Copper licked her face and wagged her tail, concerned that her human was making upset noises. That was okay. She could wipe dog slobber off her face and nobody would know she was wiping off tears.

The door creaked behind her.

"Oh, honey," said the post office woman. "I'm sorry." She sat down on the porch next to Selena, not touching, but close by. "Guess you were hoping for better news."

Selena had no scripts at all now, and only nodded.

Stupid, stupid, should have thought what you'd do if she was dead or even had moved, didn't think, didn't plan . . .

What she knew, down in her heart of hearts, was that she couldn't have planned. This had been her last thrash toward self-preservation. She might as well go lie down in the desert now and let the sun bleach her bones.

"I'm sorry," she croaked. Copper licked her chin again, worried.

"Nothing to be sorry about," said the post office woman. "We all ought to have somebody to cry when we pass on."

Guilt joined the lump in Selena's throat, because she hadn't been crying for her aunt at all, but for herself. *Callous* and *stupid.*

The woman held out her hand to Copper, who sniffed it and gave it a vague, meditative lick. Selena rested her cheek on the dog's warm, furry back and tried to think of nothing at all.

"What's her name?" asked the woman.

"Copper," said Selena. Her voice was still shaky, but that was a safe question and a safe answer.

"Good name." She scratched Copper behind the ears and was rewarded with an enthusiastic tail wag. Copper did not believe in disguising her emotions. "Black Lab?"

"Mostly." Selena wiped her face. "The rescue wasn't sure what the rest was. Some kind of hound, maybe."

"You're a pretty girl, aren't you?" the woman asked Copper. Copper gazed at her soulfully and attempted to convey that she had never been petted, not once, but would like to experience it.

The familiar conversation grounded Selena a bit. Everything was terrible, but she still had to do the next thing and the next thing after that. She couldn't just sit on the porch crying all over her dog.

"Is there . . ." She swallowed. *Twenty-seven dollars.* "Is there a motel or a hostel near here?"

"Can't say there is, no."

Selena hadn't expected there would be. Quartz Creek didn't look big enough to have a Dollar General, let alone a motel.

I'll have to get back on the train. Somehow.

She could call Walter, of course. Turn on her phone and call him. He'd wire her the money and she could get a ticket and go home.

If she did that, he'd explain to her that her nerves had just been disordered from grief over her mother's death. Or maybe she could say that she went to tell Aunt Amelia in person, and then he'd chide her for not having thought it through, but allow that it was perfectly understandable under the circumstances. Losing her mother had been a blow, and it was bound to dredge up lots of things. Anyone would act a little irrationally under the circumstances.

He'd be right, of course. And—Selena knew herself—she'd be grateful to him for being so understanding. She *would.* And then later he would refer to the time that she had hared off to the middle of nowhere without enough money to get home, and she would flush hot with shame at the memory.

It would become one more of the stories about How Selena Had Done Something Foolish and Walter Saved Her. The story might lie in wait for years, but then it would rear its head and strike. She'd never know when to expect it. During an argument. Or during a party, maybe, when Walter needed to top a coworker's story about something silly their spouse had done. Or maybe just in a moment when Selena wasn't sufficiently grateful for all the things he did for her.

The story would never go away. Walter forgave immediately, but he never, ever forgot, and so neither could Selena.

The thought was so exhausting that she felt like crying again. She drank some water to stave it off, swallowing down the lump in her throat.

The woman from the post office studied the postcard again. "Tell you what. The house is still there, you know. Amelia's house."

Selena looked at her blankly, one hand hooked under the dog's collar.

"Nobody's claimed it," said the woman. "She's got no kin around here, and it's not a big house. And you look about done in, if you don't mind me saying so. No reason you can't stay there for the night. Or however long you need."

Selena had to think for a minute, to put the words together. She tried them out in her head a few times, then said, "Is that allowed?"

"Sure," said the post office woman. "I said it was fine, didn't I?" She grinned. "I'm the mayor, you know. Also the postmaster, fire marshal, and the chief of police. My name's Jenny."

She stuck out a hand and Selena shook it. Shaking hands was polite, and if she was careful, she wouldn't start to overthink whether she'd been shaking too long or not long enough.

She didn't want to babble or dominate the conversation, but surely she could ask one more question. "You're sure no one will mind if I stay there?"

"Nobody around *to* mind," said Jenny. "Lotta places standing empty these days. Can't keep people in 'em. You know how it is."

Selena didn't have the least idea how it was and didn't know where to start asking, so she simply nodded and hoped that Jenny wouldn't have any follow-up questions.

"You're next door to Grandma Billy, out past the old well, and then there's nothing for a mile on. You'll have to check the old solars, but they should be working well enough to make tea, and you ain't gonna need heat for a couple of months yet." She leaned back on her hands.

"Give it a look over. If you're inclined to stay, just come by the post office and let me know. I'll make you out an address form."

An address form? For what? Is she suggesting I move in? I can't do that. Houses are expensive. People with houses are always complaining about it. You can't buy a house with twenty-seven dollars. Even if they gave it to me, I couldn't keep it. The roof will fall off and the walls will fall down and I'll have no money and they'll hate me for not taking care of it. And it's stupid to think anyway, because nobody gives away houses.

"I can't stay," said Selena. She had no money and apparently no family either. She'd have to leave, go back, deal with what she found in the city. With Walter. Running away hadn't solved anything.

"Up to you," said Jenny. "Train won't be back till tomorrow, though, so you might as well walk over and take a look." She pointed down one of the roads. "'Bout half a mile that way. Grandma Billy's the one with the blue door, and you're the one just past it."

"Thank you," whispered Selena, her store of words exhausted.

Jenny, the mayor and the postmistress and the fire marshal and the chief of police, smiled at her and said, "It's called Jackrabbit Hole House. You can't miss it."

Chapter 2

In the end, she went because the alternative was to sit on the post office porch until the sun went down. She had no real hope for Jackrabbit Hole House. (And what kind of outlandish name was that, anyway?)

Truth was, she had only met her aunt a handful of times, mostly as a teenager. She remembered a thin woman with a seamed face, wearing clothes that were too big for her, as if she was afraid that someone might grab her and she'd have to wriggle away. But she had a sharp, cutting sense of humor that delighted the teenage Selena, and over the years, postcards had come from a dozen places. It was only the last few that had come from the same place, as if she had been caught at last.

The last postcard was nearly three years old now. It had ended with "I hope you can come out and visit me sometime."

Selena had been putting all her faith in those ten words.

What am I going to do now?

There were no answers on the post office porch, and if she kept sitting there, Jenny was going to keep sitting with her. Someone who had so many jobs was undoubtedly busy, even in a town as small as Quartz Creek, and Selena had taken up enough of her time.

"Straight down that road," said Jenny, pointing again. "If you don't like what you see, come on back. There's a potluck at the church Wednesdays and Saturdays, everybody welcome."

Selena nodded. "Thank you," she said. That was about all she could trust herself to say.

People are telling me where I can get free food. Oh god, how much farther can I fall? I had a job, I always had jobs, I'm thirty years old and I should be able to take care of myself . . .

Selena believed, with every fiber of her being, that a person's worth was not defined by how hard they worked or how productive they managed to be. She also believed just as strongly that this did not apply to her.

There really ought to be some kind of card, Selena decided, something you could carry to prove that you weren't a freeloader. It could say something like, "Hard Worker, Temporarily Fallen on Bad Times." And on the reverse it would say, "Not in the Habit of Mooching."

All it took was one run of bad luck and it didn't matter how hard you'd worked your whole life, you were down in the gutter with the broken and the unlucky and the professionally helpless. And it hadn't even been bad luck, in Selena's case, just a sudden mad dash for freedom.

Maybe the Walter in her head was right and she'd done something foolish and needed someone to save her.

"Definitely a card," she muttered as she walked down the bleached road, dragging the suitcase. Then she stopped, because if you talked to yourself, you looked crazy—and even though she *was* crazy, she was still kind of hoping that nobody else would notice.

Jackrabbit Hole House. What a name.

As Selena walked through the middle of town, she could see that it wasn't the only named house. There were no numbers on any of the buildings, but they all had little plaques. Some of them were set too far back from the road to read, but most of them had big, bold letters, as if the house names were something people were proud of.

Pocket Gopher House. South Porch House. Tortoise on Its Shell House. House with Its Back to the Desert.

Some of them were self-explanatory—Under the Olive Tree House had a low wing tucked up under gnarled branches, and Three Saguaro House had three tall cactus growing in the front. Others didn't make any sense at all—the House with Its Back to the Desert was actually backed against the mechanic's, and It Fell Down House appeared to be in good repair.

No wonder Aunt Amelia's postcard was simply from Quartz Creek.

Selena passed the church. The plaque beside the door was brass instead of wood. House of Our Lady of the Palo Verdes.

That makes more sense. That's a church sort of name. You name churches. Houses get numbers, though, not names.

Apparently the people of Quartz Creek disagreed.

The house to the left of the church was Left-of-the-Church House, which made sense, but the house on the right was Bougainvillea House, so not even that was consistent. Selena sighed.

There were only two rings of houses on this side, although Selena could see a few straggling buildings off in either direction. Many of the houses had back gardens fenced with chicken wire, which did nothing to contain the roving chickens. A few were standing empty, with boards over the windows.

Can't keep people in 'em. You know how it is.

She wished she did.

The road curved along the base of the hill that she had seen from the train platform. There were more trees than she had expected, although she couldn't be sure if they were real trees or just more of the scrubby desert plants, grown unexpectedly tall in the shadow of the hillside. They rose up ten and twelve feet high, so that she and the dog walked together through a strange dry forest.

Brush, she thought. *Scrub. I have been using the words all my life and this is what they really meant and I had no idea.*

Copper meandered along the edge of the road, stopping occasionally to sniff. Selena watched her exploring all the little canine mysteries—why this twig was more interesting than those others, why this patch of ground needed to be peed on, why this rock was much more fascinating than all the other available rocks.

That last question was answered when the rock unfolded long legs and bounded away. Copper jumped back, startled, and the jackrabbit shot into the desert.

The dog gave half-hearted chase—her prey was running, and that's what you were supposed to do—but she stopped at the end of the leash.

Selena laughed. It wasn't much of a laugh, but it was there. She scrubbed at her cheeks with the heel of her hand. "Didn't expect that, did you?"

Copper looked vaguely offended. Rocks should not run away.

"You're a city dog, aren't you, girl?" She scratched behind the ears, in the good spot, and Copper thumped against her leg. "Not used to jackrabbits."

Not that I am either. Jackrabbit Hole House. Huh.

The humor didn't last long once she was out of sight of the town. The desert rose up around her like an alien landscape. The brush was full of noises that she didn't recognize: dry, skittery little noises. Something alive. More jackrabbits maybe, or lizards, or quail.

She hoped it was just quail.

A loud buzz broke out, mere inches away, and Selena jumped sideways, her mind suddenly full of rattlesnakes. *Oh god oh god what do I do do I grab Copper do I run—*

A moment later she recognized the rising buzz of a cicada. *You've got those back home. You know what they are.* She pressed the heel of her hand against her forehead. Copper, seeing that she had stopped, sat down and waited. After a minute Selena started walking again.

There are *rattlesnakes, though. They exist out here. What am I supposed to do if I see one? I work at a deli, for Christ's sake. I know deli things. I don't know about rattlesnakes.* While the customers could sometimes get very hostile, especially around the holidays, they weren't actually *venomous.* And Selena was pretty sure that you couldn't tell a rattlesnake, "I'm sorry, ma'am, I'm afraid that we just can't help you."

Well, you probably can, but I doubt the rattlesnake will listen. Not that the customers always did either.

She wished she could turn on her phone and search for *how to deal with rattlesnakes,* although there probably wasn't any signal out here anyway.

A house appeared on the left side of the road, around the curve of the hill. It looked old and there were cracks in the adobe. A low stone wall ran alongside the road, and trees crowded over it, dappling the dry earth with shadow.

There was a peacock on the wall.

Copper stopped and stared at it with deep mistrust. So did Selena.

It was definitely a peacock. There was nothing else it could be. He was bright blue and had a tail made for strutting and he was wildly out of place.

Peacocks don't live in the desert. Peacocks are, like . . . jungle birds, right?

The misplaced peacock turned his head and said, "Ai-yowp! Ai-yowp!"

The door of the old adobe banged open, and a woman came out.

She was a little taller than Selena, wearing a faded cotton skirt and an open leather vest. Silver and turquoise bangles clattered on bony wrists.

"Goddamn bird!" The woman charged at the peacock, arms waving. "Git! Go back home! Swear to the Lord, I'm gonna go down there and tell Jack to put you in a stew!"

"Ai-yowp!" shrieked the peacock, pacing down the wall toward Selena.

Selena took a deep breath. "Excuse me . . ."

"Sweet Jesus!" She reeled back, hand to heart. "Sorry, didn't see you there. I was yelling at the bird, not you."

"No, it's okay. I figured that." Selena glanced at the adobe, saw it had a blue door. "Um. I'm looking for . . . uh . . . Jackrabbit Hole House?"

"Sure, it's just a little bit up the way. Follow the road. You can almost see it, but there's trees in the way." The woman stuck out a hand. "I'm Grandma Billy."

"Selena." Selena shook. She had shaken a lot of hands today. "Grandma . . . ?" she asked tentatively.

"Grandma Billy," said Grandma Billy firmly. "Billy was my second husband and I'm too old to change it now."

Selena nodded.

The peacock, apparently annoyed that he wasn't the center of attention, shrieked next to Selena's ear. She jumped away, startled, and Copper let out a warning bark.

"Damn bird, you're causing nothing but trouble. Go on! Git!" Grandma flapped her skirt at the bird. He stuck his beak in the air and stalked away down the road, back toward town.

"That's Merv," said Grandma. "Samuel's oldest mail-ordered some chicks from the city, supposed to be some kind of new super-chicken. Half of 'em didn't hatch and the other half were peacocks, but he's never been able to admit he was had." She glared down the road after the retreating peacock. "Stupid bird comes around and my rooster loses his damn mind. I tell him he can't compete with a peacock, but he about kills himself trying."

"Well, they're very pretty," said Selena, carefully. *Was that a stupid thing to say? That was probably stupid.* Obviously *they're pretty. Damn.*

"Sure are," said Grandma. "Up on the mesas, they call 'em 'sun turkeys,' or so I'm told. Pretty sort of name. Shame about the personality. Can I get you something to drink?"

Fortunately Selena had lots of scripts for this sort of thing. "That would be lovely," she said, "if it's not too much trouble."

"No trouble," said Grandma. "You must be about parched. This lady too." She crouched down on her heels, skirt making a broad circle in the dust. Silver chimed as she held out a hand to Copper.

Copper, who knew that she was being approached correctly, perked her ears forward and gave Grandma's hand an emphatic lick, then thumped her broad skull into the waiting fingers. Grandma petted the Lab's ears gravely.

"She a chicken killer?"

Selena blinked. "I don't think Copper's ever met a chicken."

"We'll play it safe, then. Some good dogs out there that can't be around chickens. Stay out here on the front porch, I'll be right back."

She swept through the blue door. Selena wasn't sure if it was okay to sit down on the porch, even though there were rocking chairs with woven blankets thrown over them.

She leaned against one of the porch pillars instead. Copper, who had no such compunctions, flopped down on the boards.

There was a wooden plaque next to the door that said BLUE HORNED TOAD HOUSE, with a little drawing of a lizard under it, painted bright blue.

It was oddly quiet. The cicadas were buzzing, but you didn't notice the sound until they stopped. It didn't seem like noise as much as a manifestation of the heat, like the ripples coming off the road.

All she could hear was Copper panting and the sounds of Grandma banging around inside the house. A muffled *ai-yowp!* came from down the road and then the peacock was silent.

A bird skittered to the top of a nearby saguaro and looked around. It was brown and had a sharply downcurved beak. It looked annoyed about something.

Grandma shoved the door open with her shoulder and one foot hooked around the edge. She had two jars in one hand and a shallow clay dish of water in the other. Selena jumped to take the dish from her.

"There you go," said Grandma. "That's for Copper and this one's for you."

The jar was full of tea, something green tasting and faintly sweet. There was no ice. The glass sweated in the heat, and water rolled over Selena's fingers as she drank.

"Thank you," she said. She hadn't realized how thirsty she'd been. Copper slurped thirstily from the pottery bowl.

"No worries," said Grandma. "It's the desert. You get dried out before you know it."

An awkward silence fell, or perhaps Selena only thought it was awkward. She reached for a script that had served her well. "So what is it you do?"

Grandma snorted. "Do? Well, I get older, mostly. And dig around in the garden and keep chickens. And chase off peacocks." She fixed Selena with a bright eye over the rim of her jar. "And what do *you* do?"

"I'm a night manager at a deli."

The words came out and then stood there in the blazing desert light looking faintly ridiculous, as out of place as peacocks. Surely it was not possible that the world had both saguaros and all-night delis in it. No one would believe that.

"Was," said Selena, in an effort to shepherd the lost words away. "Was a manager. I'm not now, I mean." Her boss had said they'd hold the job for her if she needed it, but Selena didn't put much faith in that.

"Uh-huh. So what do you want with Jackrabbit Hole House? You looking for Amelia?" The corners of Grandma's mouth drew down slightly. "You one of her strays?"

Strays?

Selena took a large gulp of tea while she sorted through the words in her head. "Amelia's my aunt," she said carefully. "I know she passed away. The postmistress said to come look at it."

"Oh, *aunt*." Grandma's frown smoothed away. "I gotcha. She always picked up strays, you see—stray people, stray cats, baby birds fallen out of the nest, the lot. Keeping people from taking advantage was a full-time job, sometimes. But if Miss Jenny sent you, that's different. Your aunt was a friend of mine."

"I'm sorry," said Selena. *No, that was wrong. Crap.* "Not, I mean, sorry that she was your friend. Sorry she passed away. For your loss. Because she was your friend." She could hear herself starting to panic and shoved the rim of the jar into her mouth to stop the flow of words.

"I got the gist," said Grandma, looking faintly amused. "Didn't know she had a niece. Would have tried to get a letter out if I did, but Amelia didn't talk about her family much. Said she had a sister, but they didn't talk. That's all I knew."

"My mom," said Selena. Did she have to say anything more about her? Hopefully not. She didn't think she had the energy. Her mother had been troublesome while she was alive, and it was depressing, if not surprising, to discover that she continued to be troublesome after her death.

Grandma took a sip of tea.

"I hadn't seen Aunt Amelia in a long time. I didn't know she was sick. I would have come if I'd known. The last thing she sent me was a postcard—" The panic was bubbling up again. Selena dug out the postcard and held it out. Her hand was shaking a little.

Grandma took it, flipped it over. After a moment, she smiled. "Sounds like her, all right. She always wrote just like she talked." She handed the postcard back. "She wouldn't have told you she was sick. She didn't believe it herself. Said she was just tired, right up till she died."

"I should have come sooner," said Selena hopelessly. "A year sooner. I didn't know. I should have. I'm sorry."

Grandma's face softened, or maybe the hardness had been in Selena's imagination. "It's all right. Things show up when they're needed."

Not me, thought Selena. *I screwed that up too. I shouldn't have come out this way. I should have stayed at the post office. What good is looking at a dead woman's house going to do?*

What good was anything going to do? She'd staked everything on this ridiculous gamble, and of course she'd lost—there was no way she wasn't going to lose—and now she would have to go back to Walter and this whole thing would become the Story of the Time Selena Ran Away. Nothing she could say was going to hold up to the line between his eyebrows and the way he clucked his tongue when he was disappointed. There wasn't a script alive that could cope with that.

"Jackrabbit Hole House should be fine," said Grandma, interrupting her train of thought. "I made sure everything was cleaned out. Probably got mice in it, and I'd check under the stove for snakes, but the roof is good. Door's unlocked."

It had not occurred to Selena until that moment that she might actually go *inside* the house. *Of course you have to, did you think you were going to sleep on the porch?* She had finished her tea some time ago, but she gripped the jar until the words Ball Mason were imprinted on the pads of her fingers.

"You look like you've seen a ghost," said Grandma. "It ain't haunted. Amelia probably hung around her garden till everything died back for summer, then she went on her way. Nothing there now." She took a slug of tea. "Well, except the usual run of desert ghosts, I guess. But they're no bother."

Selena set the jar down and picked up Copper's leash. She had no scripts at all for this situation. You smiled politely when people told you about ghosts and said things like, "That must have been very unsettling," or even just, "My goodness!" None of that seemed to apply to the casual mention that the ghosts were gone or at least not bothersome.

"I'll just go look at the house," she said. "I . . . I suppose I'll probably stay overnight. Thank you for the tea."

"Hang on, then," said Grandma. "I've still got the sheets for the bed and a couple of Amelia's old things. No sense roughing it if you don't have to."

"Thank you," said Selena, who wanted nothing more than to bolt back to town. But the postmistress would still be there, and she was bound to ask what Selena had thought and she had to have something to say.

A minute later, her arms were full of bedding, with a pillow balanced precariously on top. She held it all awkwardly with one hand and dragged her suitcase with the other, while Copper's leash slid down her arm to her elbow, the way you were never ever supposed to hold leashes. But she couldn't very well turn down the bedding.

"If you decide you're staying, I'll bring over some of Amelia's old stuff. You'll need silverware and fry pans and whatnot."

"That's very kind," said Selena, because it was kind, even if it wasn't going to happen.

Grandma Billy saw her to the edge of the road and leaned on the stone wall. "When you turn the water on, it'll spit. Let it run for a few minutes. The pump's nearly new, but it ain't been on for a while."

Everyone thinks I'm staying. I'm not staying. Why are they talking as if I am? "Thank you for the tea," she said again.

"Glad to do it. You take care."

She followed the road around the curve of the hill, past the trees, until Grandma Billy was lost from sight.

She came around the corner, and there was the house, tucked up in scruffy green shrubs. An impressively multiarmed saguaro grew directly across the road, and an impressively dead one lay slumped beside it. Another low stone wall, like the one at Grandma Billy's, ran along the road here, then curved around both sides of the house, though this one was devoid of peacocks.

It was a small house. *Well, the postmistress said it would be.*

It might be two rooms, possibly three. Certainly no more than that. It was tea-colored adobe with two windows in the front, and a wraparound porch that sagged in the middle. Some aggressive vine had eaten two of the porch posts and was making threatening gestures toward a third. There was a rocking chair on the porch that had been cobwebbed into place and glazed in pale-white dust. Solar panels covered the roof, none of them new.

There was a dirt path up to the house. White stones like blocky skulls picked out the edges of . . . well, you couldn't call them flower beds. *Scrub* beds, maybe. Whatever the difference was between bare dirt and dirt with gray-green spiky things in it.

This is it. This is where Aunt Amelia lived, until a year ago.

A year ago. A year ago. A year too late.

She set that thought aside, for all the good it did her.

Once upon a time, Selena would have gone up to the house, walked around it, looking in the windows.

Once upon a time, she could talk without worrying about it, and didn't run every sentence through her head a dozen times first. Once upon a time had come and gone and there were no happily ever afters.

She let go of her suitcase, untangled Copper's leash, and put her hand on the stone wall.

It was hard under her fingers, the stones rough, the edges sharp. She closed her eyes. She could believe that the peacock and Grandma Billy were part of a dream, but the stone wall was too clearly a real thing. If the wall was real, then everything else was real. All right. Not a dream, then. It was all really happening and her aunt was really dead and she was really broke and stranded in a town called Quartz Creek and the dead woman's house was really in front of her.

It looked . . . friendly.

If the two windows were eyes, then the left one was half closed into a wink by the rioting vine. The porch sagged into a smile. The desert was enormous and the house was very small, but it looked brave and rather hopeful.

It reminded her of Copper when she was a puppy, deeply convinced that the world was full of kind giants who loved her, and if she only waited long enough, one would come and play.

I am losing my mind. I mean, I already lost it, I know, but now I am getting maudlin and reading things into a falling-down porch. It's probably heatstroke. I should sit down.

If I go up to the house, I could sit down on the porch. I could even open up the door and go inside. It might be cooler in there.

Selena stood by the wall and didn't move.

It was a nice house. She could see why her aunt might have lived there. But it wasn't hers.

If I go in, I might start to like it and if I do, somebody will take it away from me. You can't just walk up and lay claim to a house. That's not how it works.

She remembered the empty houses in the middle of town, with the boarded-up windows. *The postmistress told me—she said they can't keep people in them—but it can't be like that, not* really . . .

It was too easy, too unearned. You did not get things handed to you. It was a central tenet of Selena's mother's philosophy, that you did not just get things handed to you. Everything had to be earned.

And yet there was a nagging little grain of hope in Selena's heart. She was the next of kin, wasn't she? Her mother was dead, thank the merciful gods. If the house was abandoned and nobody wanted it . . .

It wouldn't be that way in the city, where everybody lived on top of each other, but maybe out here, in the margins . . .

Why would *anyone want to live out here? It's hot and weird and there's hardly anybody here and you can't go anywhere and the drones can't deliver packages and the train only comes once a day . . .*

Dear god, she was tired. The hard light was giving her a headache and she was holding an armful of blankets that were getting extremely hot where they pressed against her body.

She didn't have enough money to stay in Quartz Creek, but maybe if she spent the night here, she could deal with everything in the morning, when she didn't feel so utterly exhausted. Couldn't she?

Copper got up.

She gave the leash a practiced tug, pulling it out of Selena's lax fingers, and trotted up the walk to the sagging porch.

"Copper!"

The Lab ignored her. Three steps up, and she flopped down on the porch—*really* flopped, not her polite Sphinx pose while she waited for Selena to finish what she was doing. A full-body, over-on-her-side, legs-stretched-out flop, accompanied by a deep old-dog sigh of contentment.

Selena left the wall. Her feet dragged as she approached the porch. She had no energy left to argue, not even with the dog.

"Overnight," she said. "*Only* overnight. You got that?"

Copper rolled her eyes toward her person, but did not deign to lift her head.

Selena sighed.

She sat down on the porch steps and put her head in her hands, and that, more or less, was that.

Chapter 3

Eventually she had to get up. It would have been strangely comforting to sit on the steps until the sun went down, but Copper would get hungry. And thirsty. Thirsty was probably more important.

Now that she had to actually go inside, Selena eyed the door with suspicion. It might be cooler inside. There might also be snakes or scorpions or serial killers inside.

Well . . . probably not serial killers.

They'd get awfully bored out here, I imagine. Unless that's why they can't keep people around.

That seems unlikely.

There was a nail next to the door, with a little sign that read JACKRABBIT HOLE HOUSE. Selena put her hand on the door.

It didn't have a doorknob, just a handle: a piece of smooth, polished wood in a shallow arch. When she pushed, the door opened with a whisper of hinges.

The interior was very dark in comparison to the glaring sun.

She had to step over Copper to get inside. The Lab grumbled and rolled partway on her back.

"Some good you'll be, when the serial killer shows up."

Copper wagged her tail, perhaps indicating that the serial killer would be welcome as long as he knew how to pet a dog properly.

Selena felt for a light switch by the front door. Did the solars still work?

She found a switch. Something clicked inside it and the light came on. A moment later she heard the dull thud of machinery starting up, and smelled the burnt-dust scent of stale air in the vents.

The inside of the house was a deep yellow-orange shade, somewhere between terra-cotta and saffron. There was one large room, and a door in the left-hand wall, painted rich blue violet.

The walls had soft corners. Selena put out a hand to the nearest, puzzled. There was nothing hard there, a curve instead of an angle. The floor was terra-cotta tile, with a thick rug over it and an even thicker layer of dust over that.

She walked slowly into the main room, which seemed to serve as kitchen and dining room and just about everything else. There was a rickety card table set up in the center, also thick with dust, and an old couch with a print that had faded into obscurity. Bookcases lined the windows in the back wall, which framed another door, this one painted green.

Aunt Amelia didn't have any problem with bright colors, I see.

Walter would have hated it, but perhaps in this strange, bleaching desert light, colors had to be bright to keep from being scoured away.

There was a fireplace in the corner, although it looked more like a growth in the wall than the traditional brick-and-mantel arrangement. The only bricks ran in a line at the bottom, dusted with ash.

Well. First things first.

She went to the sink. The counter tiles were deep blue, the same color as the ones at the post office. She turned the faucet on.

For a long moment there was nothing, and then the faucet spat like an angry cat. (She heard Copper jerk upright out on the porch. Copper might not be familiar with jackrabbits, but she knew all about cats.)

The pipes made banging noises and the faucet shuddered as if it were going to take off into space. Selena cringed. Sometimes the pipes at the deli got air in them and they made awful noises, but they didn't usually *shake* so badly . . .

Another loud spitting noise. Copper let out a suspicious woof. Then a rumble and a drip of brown came out of the tap, accompanied by another round of banging.

She left it to run for a minute and studied the stove.

Most of the cupboards sat flush with the floor, but the stove was a little electric model, only two burners, that stood up about three inches off the floor. Brightly painted Talavera tiles formed a backsplash behind the range.

Check under the stove for snakes, Grandma Billy had said.

She looked around the room. No flashlight. There was a distinct lack of anything that might serve as snake-wrangling equipment . . . except . . .

The broom by the back door had seen better days. Bristles stuck out in all directions. But the handle was solid, and Selena wanted space between her and anything that might be living under the stove.

She knelt down and slid the broom into the dark.

If something hisses, I drop the broom and go tie Copper up. Um. Then . . . um . . .

I suppose I go back and ask Grandma Billy how to deal with snakes.

But nothing hissed, except for the air in the pipes. Selena dragged the broom back out, weak-kneed with relief.

The faucet gave an especially loud bang and water came out.

It was ugly and brownish and left gritty marks on the white porcelain sink, but it was water. Selena sagged against the counter. If she'd been less tired, she would have cheered.

She let it run for a minute, feeling guilty about wasting water in the desert. Eventually it ran clear and she filled Copper's bowl and drank from her own cupped hands.

Copper came inside the house for water. Selena fished out her last three granola bars. She ate one and fed two to the dog, who snuffled along her fingers to make sure that she wasn't holding out.

"That's it," Selena said. "We'll have to go to the church, I guess . . . or maybe there's a store in town to buy food . . ." Twenty-seven dollars wasn't much, but surely she could buy dog food with it.

The green door must lead to the back garden. She didn't have the energy to go back out in the heat and look. She looked at the fireplace instead, which still had half-burned logs in it and a dull gray film of ash.

There were two square recesses in the wall by the fireplace. They reminded Selena of the little niches that held statues of saints. One was empty, and the other held a rather ugly doll.

Is that a kachina doll? Selena had seen a museum exhibit with kachinas once. They had all been gorgeous, vital-looking pieces, as if the artist had caught the dancer in mid-turn. They had been carefully and lovingly painted, given tiny rattles or bits of fur to hold in their hands. This one was drab, with spiky hair, a chin that went down halfway to its belt, a wispy beard, and no apparent feet or legs. The museum kachinas had all been dancing.

Well, maybe there's a reason those were museum pieces. Or more likely, it's not a kachina at all, just some random art she picked up.

Selena opened the violet door and poked her head into the bedroom.

An old iron-frame bed cast thin shadows on the wall, which was covered in some kind of map. There was a mattress with faded navy stripes on it, but no sheets. Another open door led to the bathroom, which stopped Selena in her tracks.

The toilet was . . .

Well, it was . . .

She put both hands over her mouth and fought the urge to howl like a lunatic.

The toilet was painted in the Talavera style, same as the tiles behind the stove. It was deep blue, covered in swirls and sunflowers and daisies and abstract checks. The bowl had sky-blue peonies in it.

Oh dear, dear, dear . . . Oh Aunt Amelia, really?

Walter would have refused to use it. He would have insisted it be removed from the room, the house, and possibly the planet. He might even have taken a hammer to it.

Giggles leaked out between her fingers and she had to lean against the doorframe. Was she going to use it?

Well, it's that or the sink . . . or outside with the peacock . . .

The rest of the bathroom was rather more sedate. It was the smallest shower that Selena had ever seen, with sea-green tiles and no shower curtain. There was a slanted drain in the floor that appeared to lead directly through the wall into the backyard.

And that's where the snakes come in, I suppose . . .

She went back to the bedroom and sat down on the mattress. It was at least ten degrees cooler inside the house than it was outside.

Copper came into the bedroom, sniffed around, then heaved herself up on the mattress.

"I don't think this is big enough for two of us," said Selena. It wasn't a terribly small bed—you could fit two people on it—but Copper was a master of the canine art of oozing to fill in all available space.

Copper dug her shoulder into the mattress and gazed at the wall. If she didn't look at Selena, she did not have to acknowledge any get-down-now gestures that might be made.

Selena sighed. She pulled her backpack off. "We're not staying," she informed Copper. House or no house, this was still the story of How Selena Did Something Foolish.

Although if she could get home on her own, maybe this would be a different kind of story.

"Maybe I can wash dishes or something and make enough money for a train ticket home."

Home, where you have no place to live, no family, and probably no job. And the shelters won't take dogs. Home, where you'd have to go back to Walter.

Maybe you don't have to go home at all, whispered a little voice in her head, but that was ridiculous and Selena knew it.

Copper yawned and encroached on more of the bed.

Selena dragged the sheets onto the bed. She didn't have the energy to kick Copper off and certainly not to put a fitted sheet on, so she draped the top sheet over the dog's back and dropped the pillow onto the end of the bed. *I'll make the bed later,* she told herself.

And that was the last coherent thought she had until nightfall.

She woke up because somebody was yelling her name from the door.

"Selena? Hey, you in here? Snake didn't bite you, did it?"

Selena sat up and scrubbed at her mouth. For a minute, she could not think where she was or why the light was that strange color. Had she been sleeping in her clothes?

"Selena?"

Copper slid off the bed and trotted into the next room, tail wagging. Selena could hear her nails clicking on the tile floor.

"Hey, Copper," said whoever it was. "She dead? I don't wanna bother her if she's dead."

"I'm not dead . . ." croaked Selena. Her mouth was bone dry. She got up and blundered into the bathroom, where the sight of the toilet brought her crashing awake. "Oh, Jesus!"

"Ain't that toilet a peach?" called Grandma Billy. "Amelia won it at the church raffle. It was supposed to be a planter and Father Aguirre opened up the box and turned purple, but Amelia said she needed a new one anyway."

"It's very . . . dramatic," said Selena, backing away from the bathroom. There was not a script in the world for coming awake in a strange place and having to comment on a Talavera toilet. Her head was pounding.

"That's one way to put it. You decent?"

"Yes."

Grandma Billy came into the bedroom, carrying an armload of blankets. "Figured you'd want these. It gets cold at night." She paused, taking in Selena's condition. "Go drink some water, hon, it'll help a lot."

This seemed like excellent advice. Selena felt hungover, and she hadn't touched a drop for months. It was easier to remember her scripts when she didn't drink, even though Walter said that normal people could drink at parties without getting tongue-tied.

She staggered into the kitchen and turned on the faucet, slurping water out of her cupped hands.

"Cups," said Grandma Billy, slapping her forehead. "Knew I forgot something."

Selena braced herself on the edge of the sink. "How did you know I was staying?"

Grandma shrugged. "You didn't come back down the road, so you were either here or you'd wandered off into the desert to die. And I didn't figure you'd do that, on account of your dog." She scratched Copper behind the ears. Copper sat down and panted in approval.

"Oh."

"Besides, I didn't figure you for the dyin' kind. Close, maybe, but no cigar. Give me a hand with the wheelbarrow, will you?"

Wheelbarrow?

Selena followed Grandma onto the porch. Standing beside the bottom step was, indeed, a wheelbarrow. It had a couple of lumpy sacks in it and an old rag rug.

"Most of this stuff was Amelia's," said Grandma, handing Selena a sack. Selena staggered a little under the weight. "I was holding on to it till somebody in town needed it, but I'm glad it's you. Couple of these things might have been unhappy in some other house."

"Thank you," said Selena, a bit worried. Her sack was making clanking noises.

Grandma Billy hefted the other sack over her shoulder. "Cups. Bah. No cups. I remembered the silverware, at least. And a good pot and a frying pan."

She led the way back into the house. Selena was torn between mild horror—*she can't give me all this stuff, even if it's old, and anyway, I'm not staying that long*—and deep relief that someone else seemed to be in charge.

The sack proved to contain a coffee can full of *very* fresh eggs, fresh enough to still have bits of chicken crap sticking to them, a big square of cornbread, and a jar of olive oil.

"From Under the Olive Tree House," said Grandma. "You know how to use one of these?" She pulled out a coffee press that appeared to have been designed by the Spanish Inquisition. "You pour the hot water in and press down." She put a coffee can down beside it. "Don't get excited, it's crap coffee, but it'll do the job."

"I . . . thank you . . . but I don't have much money . . ."

"Pfff." Grandma waved a hand dismissively. "It's spring and all the chickens are laying like anything. *I* sure can't eat all the eggs. Just save the carton for me."

"Thank you," said Selena. "It's very kind of you." She didn't dare think about how kind it was, because she'd probably start crying. Now she could feed Copper for another day, at least until she sorted out what to do next.

Grandma sniffed. "Ain't nothing. I'd do it for anybody, let alone Amelia's kin." She picked up a handful of mismatched silverware and started to open one of the kitchen drawers. "Oh, hang on, you check for widows yet?"

"Widows," said Selena blankly. *Isn't Grandma Billy a widow? She said she had two husbands . . .*

"Black widow spiders."

Selena jumped. "That's a thing? You have those? I thought they were just—you know—" She waved a hand. *A made-up thing that might be real somewhere, but not here. Like quail. Oh dear.*

"Won't be a minute," said Grandma. She reached into a pocket of her skirt and pulled out a pair of leather garden gloves. "Stand behind me with the broom and if I yell, get ready to swat."

Selena picked up the broom. Copper eyed both humans with mild disgust and flopped down by the back door.

They went systematically through the cupboards. Selena clutched the broom and waited to whack something. Grandma kept up a running monologue the entire time.

"Clean . . . clean . . . oh dear, this one's sticking something fierce, needs a bit of oil on the hinge . . . clean . . . wait a minute, wait a minute . . . no, just a bitty little house spider, he won't do anything . . . clean . . ."

It wasn't until they checked the fireplace that anything turned up.

"Oh, there we go," said Grandma. "Scorpion."

"Scorpions?!"

"At least one of 'em." She grinned. "Don't worry. He ain't a bark scorpion—those like a little more water, if they can get it. These'll just itch if they sting you. We'll build a fire and clean it out."

Selena was torn between resistance to cooking anything alive and the fact that there were scorpions *in the house.*

It's only a few feet away! A real scorpion!

"Can I see it?" she asked.

"Sure, have a look." Grandma rolled one of the ancient charred logs aside, revealing a low brown body with a fat, puffy tail. Selena had envisioned a wicked stinger held aloft, but this one's tail was rolled to the side and looked a bit wilted.

"It's big," she said.

"The big ones are best. It's the little ones that pack a wallop. Here, pretty sure I left some wood on the back porch."

She opened the green door. Selena poked her head around the doorframe and exhaled in surprise.

The sun was setting over the desert. The sky had already gone deep blue overhead, but heavy bands of red and orange lingered in the east. On the left side of the property, the hill she had seen from the train platform rose up, stark black against the sky. A saguaro leaned out from the hillside, arms raised. It looked a bit like a boxer about to punch the sky, albeit one with three arms.

In the last red light, she could see that the stone wall ran back at least a hundred yards. The remains of garden beds were square shadows on the earth. The wall was topped up with chicken wire and broken by a ramshackle gate at the back.

A section of the back porch was screened with wire as well, and had a sizable stack of split wood piled up against the back wall. Grandma Billy sniffed.

"Now this likely *is* full of widows. And scorpions and anything else you want to name. Wear your gloves—I'll loan you a pair—and if you get bit, you come get me. Walk, don't run, though." She grabbed two likely-looking logs and banged them together.

"Where does the wood come from out here?" asked Selena.

"Red cedar," said Grandma. "Shit grows like a fiend and sucks up all the water it can. We go out and cut it down from around the creek every year, but seems like there's always more."

She brought the logs inside. Selena hovered, and finally steeled herself to ask, "Can we take the scorpion outside?"

Grandma Billy tilted a glance up at her. "You don't want to cook it?"

"It's not its fault that it's here," said Selena. *Am I being stupid? If she says that you have to kill scorpions, she's probably right, she knows the desert and I don't . . .*

"Fair enough," said Grandma. "See if I packed a spatula and bring me the frying pan." She addressed the scorpion in the fireplace. "You're getting your life by the grace of God, scorpion. Or the grace of Selena, anyhow. You be good and tell the others to stay out of her boots, you hear?"

"Does that work?"

"Probably not. Brains aren't big enough to shove gratitude into. Still, never hurts to try." She scooped the creature up with a spatula and shoved the frying pan handle into Selena's hand. The scorpion sat inside the pan, looking sullen (although Selena was willing to admit that she might be projecting a bit).

"Um . . ."

"Well, go on, take him out front. Mind you, don't step on any more of them while you're dropping him off, though."

Selena gulped.

The desert at night was very different. Things buzzed and chirped and rustled. Thin gray twigs caught the light like bones.

Copper wanted to help, and took "Stay! I mean it!" in poor grace. Selena inched out of the circle of light cast by the open door and held the frying pan as far away from her body as possible. "Um. Be a good scorpion. Just . . . err . . . go on your way . . ."

She flipped the frying pan over and bolted back for the house.

Grandma Billy had finished laying the fire. "Here," she said, holding out a match. "You light it. House needs to know you're moving in."

"I'm not staying forever," protested Selena. "Just a few days. I just . . ." *Don't talk about money. It's rude to talk about money. Telling people you're rich is crass and telling them you're broke makes them uncomfortable.* She trailed off.

"Sure," said Grandma easily. "Sure. That's fine. But it makes the house feel better."

Selena looked down at the match in her hands. She had to scrape it along the brick edge of the fireplace to light it. Thin white trails indicated that she wasn't the first person to do so.

The match flared up, and she dropped it into the fireplace. A strong, hard smell filled the house, powerful but not unpleasant.

Grandma straightened up and paused, her eye suddenly caught. "Oh," she said, in a rather different tone.

"What's wrong? More scorpions?" Selena grabbed for the broom.

"Just saw that thing." She pointed to the doll beside the fireplace. "Startled me, I'd forgot it was here."

"Is it a kachina doll?" asked Selena.

"Nah. That's Snake-Eater. Local sorta fellow." Grandma Billy frowned at the statue. "Never did like that piece much, though Amelia was pretty fond of it. Where'd you find it?"

"Find it?" Selena was puzzled. "It was here. Right there. I didn't touch anything. It's not my—"

She stopped. She had been about to say, "Not my house." *It's not, is it? I'm just borrowing it from Aunt Amelia. It doesn't belong to me.*

If it belongs to me, I have to worry about it, and I don't think I can stand to worry about something else right now.

Fortunately, Grandma didn't seem to have noticed. She scowled at the doll. "Could have sworn it wasn't here when I cleaned the place out. Must be going blind in my old age."

Selena picked it up. "Snake-Eater?"

"Roadrunner," said Grandma. "Except *that* name got all mixed up with cartoons and shit, and roadrunners ain't funny if you live with them. They kill rattlesnakes."

"But that's good, right?"

Grandma shrugged. "Depends on how you feel about rattlesnakes. Always thought they were polite fellows, givin' you lots of warning before things go bad. Could wish some people had that kind of courtesy."

Selena studied the doll more closely. The thing she'd thought was a chin . . . was that a beak? Suddenly the odd features snapped into clear relief. Yes, that was a beak, and the bit that looked like a straggly beard was actually the back end of a snake hanging out. The eyes were big and yellow, with a blaze of red on either side, and the spiky hair was a crest of sharp feathers.

"It's not very pretty," admitted Selena. "Still, I guess it was Amelia's."

"Yep," said Grandma. She frowned again, glancing at the doll, and opened her mouth as if to say something, then closed it again. "Well, harmless enough, I suppose."

"It's not going to come alive and stab me in my sleep or something, is it?" asked Selena.

Grandma aimed a swat in her general direction. "Don't be ridiculous. It's just a doll, not some bit of magic, even if it's tied up with people I don't much like."

"People?" Selena was getting more confused by the minute.

"A *kind* of people, anyhow. Amelia used to take in strays, like I said. Some of 'em . . . well." She clearly weighed out what to say next, then shrugged. "Amelia liked him well enough, and if you stay out of Snake-Eater's way, I imagine he'll stay out of yours. Most like."

Selena chalked this up with all the other cryptic pronouncements her neighbor had made, like Aunt Amelia's ghost hanging around the garden until summer.

"Anyway, that's enough to be going on with," said Grandma, dusting her hands off. "You'll be fine. There's dinner in the casserole dish. I'll come back by tomorrow and we'll figure the garden out. And I'll bring cups."

Outside, in the dark, the scorpion sat in the dust. Its mind was not, in fact, large enough to feel gratitude, but it understood death / not-death. It was not-dead. There had been large dark blurs and movement and at the end it was still not-dead.

Insomuch as a scorpion could find anything interesting, that would have been it.

Eventually, one leg at a time, it picked its way into the dark.

Chapter 4

Selena woke up in the morning and suffered a jarring sense of dislocation. She wasn't in her bed and Walter wasn't lying next to her. She wasn't on the couch in her mother's apartment, where she'd spent the last month of her mother's illness. She was somewhere with bright-white walls and light coming in through the window. Her mouth felt dry and her eyes were scratchy.

Apparently sensing that she was awake, the dog at the foot of the bed gave a jaw-cracking yawn and began to thump her tail against Selena's shins.

If Copper's here, it must be okay.

There was a large map pinned to the wall beside the bed. She squinted blearily at it. It was a topographic map of somewhere or other, with *US Geological Survey* printed in minuscule letters at the top. It wasn't until she saw *Quartz Creek* down in the corner, with a little star next to it, that the memories came crashing back down on her.

She was in a tiny town in the desert. She'd uprooted her whole life and run away, only to discover that her aunt was dead, and she had no money to get home.

Today she had to decide what to do next.

The thought made her want to pull the blanket over her head and hide, but Copper thumped down onto the floor and had the slight waddle of a dog who really needed to go outside, so Selena got up, pulled on her jeans, and went to the back door to let the dog out.

She leaned against the doorframe while Copper peed meditatively at the base of a bush. What now? She felt clearer headed for having slept, but her situation didn't look any better in the light of day.

Her phone was still in her jeans pocket. She pulled out the little glass brick and stared at it. Her face looked back at her in the darkened glass, at an extremely unflattering angle.

If she turned it on, Walter would know where she was and just how far away she'd gone. And then . . . well, then what? He'd call her, most likely. There were undoubtedly already messages waiting, probably all some variation on "What do you think you're doing? Call me."

She didn't want to call him. She'd sent him an email saying that she wasn't coming back and needed some time to herself to think things through. She'd agonized over that email for hours, as if, with just the right words, she could make everything come out right. But the real truth was that as soon as he started talking to her, she'd start second-guessing everything she was doing. The taste of freedom she'd had for that long, brutal month would turn to ashes. She would learn that she hadn't been competent and hadn't organized everything and hadn't managed just fine in a difficult situation. Walter would explain it all to her and she'd realize that everyone had been taking pity on her. Then he'd sigh and say, "What am I going to do with you?" and buy her a train ticket and everything would go back to the way it had been.

Copper came back up on the wooden porch and leaned against Selena's legs, looking up hopefully.

"Okay," said Selena, with a distinct feeling of reprieve. "Let's have breakfast and then I'll worry about it."

They shared scrambled eggs and cornbread, sitting on the back porch. Selena shuddered to think what it was going to do to the Lab's digestion, particularly since, if she couldn't buy dog food, it was going to be eggs for lunch and dinner as well.

And I get to share a bedroom with her. Yay.

The desert, in daylight, had reverted to hot white and drab green, and the sky was a hard, unbroken blue.

"The way I see it," she told the dog, "I've got two options. I call Walter and then . . . well, you know." She scowled. "Or I don't, and I stay here for another day or two, and see if I can scrounge up enough money to get home on my own. Ellen said she'd hold my job for me as long as she could."

Actually, what she'd said was "I swear to god, if you're leaving that man, I will do anything in my power to help you."

"I thought you liked him," Selena had said, astonished.

"I like *you*. I don't like who you turn into when he's in the room."

Selena's gratitude for that had felt almost like a panic attack, something that rolled over her and slapped her in the chest. Somebody else had seen it. It wasn't just Selena misjudging the situation again.

She'd told Ellen that she was leaving Walter and going to stay with her aunt. Telling her made it real, somehow. But even if Selena could just walk back into her old job, she didn't have anywhere to live while she worked, and she couldn't very well ask Ellen to loan her thousands of dollars for first and last month's rent. Walter owned the car, so she couldn't even live out of one while she scraped the money together.

It seemed unlikely that she could make enough money out here to cover that. But she did have a place to stay for a day or two, and maybe she could figure something else out.

And if she couldn't, there was always the phone call.

Selena took a deep breath, let it out, and nodded to herself. "Right, then." Copper polished Selena's plate with her tongue, determined to get the last remaining molecules of egg.

She had to go back into the little town. She needed dog food, and to see if there was someplace she could work. And she had to inform the postmistress that she was staying, didn't she? At least for a few days?

She changed her clothes, drank an extra glass of water, leashed Copper, and went out.

It was hot but not yet punishing. A bird hung in the sky overhead, though Selena didn't know a hawk from a vulture and didn't know if it was hunting or just waiting for something to die. She heard a shrill cry and thought for a second that it might be the hawk, but then realized it was Merv the peacock.

A group of quail—Selena thought the word might be *covey*, but she couldn't remember—hurried across the road in front of them, all in a line. They looked concerned about the woman and the dog approaching, but not concerned enough to do anything so crass as break formation. Copper went on high alert but was too well mannered to try to break off the leash.

Quartz Creek looked different today. Perhaps it was the angle she was approaching from. She could see more back gardens, caged in chicken wire, with a low green haze against the ground. Was it spring? She couldn't quite remember. The final month dealing with her mother's illness and death seemed cut apart from the rest of time. Had it still been winter outside?

If I sat down and thought about it, could I go, "It started here, in this month, and it was in this month I left"? Maybe. But it's just easier to accept that it's the beginning of March.

But how strange that the rest of the world had gone on existing, seasons rolling one after another, without her notice.

Selena's lips twisted up. *It's almost like I'm not the center of the universe or something.*

Copper, who did believe that Selena was the center of the universe, paused by the entry to the church and anointed a shrub. Selena sighed.

A man in a Roman collar came out of the church, and the sigh turned into a cringe.

A priest. Oh god, it's a priest, and my dog is peeing on his church. Well, his shrubs. Oh god, no.

"Good morning!" called the priest.

"I'm sorry!" blurted Selena.

The priest looked down at Copper, who had the expression of intense concentration worn by dogs doing important business. He laughed. He had brown skin and very white teeth, and there were large pores across his nose.

"I'm Father Aguirre," he said. "It's nice to meet you both."

Selena had no real scripts for meeting Catholic priests. Walter was devoutly nonreligious and Selena's mother had held that Catholics were, if not going to *hell*, at least going to a much less nice heaven than Protestants. Selena's entire experience with Catholics consisted of a boyfriend in college who had crossed himself before exams.

Saying "You're the one who gave my aunt the wildly tasteless toilet!" was *right out.*

"I'm really sorry," said Selena again. "Um. I'm Selena. This is Copper." *Do I call him Father? I'm not a Catholic. But Mr. Aguirre is probably rude. Being a priest is like being a doctor, right? Even if it's not your doctor, you still call them Dr. So-and-So, I think.*

But if you're not actually the right religion—no, you call vets Dr. So-and-So, even if you're not a dog, so that *means—*

"It's nice to meet you, Father Aguirre."

This seemed to be correct. Selena breathed an internal sigh of relief.

Copper, having finished, indicated that she wished to make a new friend by banging her skull into the priest's hand. He obliged by scratching behind her ears, which in Copper's mind resolved all issues of religious tolerance forever.

"Are you new in town?"

"Just yesterday. Um. I was here to see my aunt Amelia, but I learned she . . . well . . ."

This is stupid. He obviously knows she's dead. You're not sparing his feelings.

Father Aguirre's smile faded. "Oh, of course. I'm so sorry you had to come all this way to find that out."

Selena stared at her feet. "Um. I was going to the post office—"

"Here, I'll come with you. The mail carrier came in yesterday, but I haven't gotten there yet."

He was wearing a black button-down shirt and crisp jeans and seemed immune to the heat. Selena was suddenly very glad of the fact that she had dragged her suitcase all the way to Jackrabbit Hole House so that she wasn't meeting him in a T-shirt that had spent several days on a train.

She was sneakingly glad to see that white road dust was beginning to powder the bottoms of his jeans.

Father Aguirre cleared his throat.

Oh god. Is he going to talk to me about my soul? Selena had scripts to deflect the persistently religious, but they had mostly been evangelical friends of her mother's. Catholic priests who liked dogs were another matter.

But he did not talk about her soul. Instead, he pointed out dangerous chickens. "That one," he said. "The big red one with the comb that looks like it's been split in half. That chicken is a devil, and I say this as a professional." He grinned at her, apparently inviting her to share the joke.

"He is?"

"He'll go for the back of your legs every time. The big white-and-black one over there acts tough, but he's all show. Watch your feet when you walk by the mechanic's place, there's a hen that will try to herd you. She was raised by a border collie and thinks she's a dog. It's very confusing for her. She's excellent with other chickens, though."

"This is a *very* strange town," said Selena, and then cursed herself, because obviously it was his town and that might have been considered an insult.

Father Aguirre laughed. "It has its peculiarities. But also its charms." He sobered. "Your aunt was one of them, and we were all very sorry to lose her. Would you like me to take you to her resting place?"

Selena blinked.

It had not sunk in, not entirely, that her aunt was dead. Not *really* dead, with a body and everything. She was more just . . . *not here*. Selena had come looking for her and not found her. Surely Aunt Amelia was just . . . somewhere else.

She had to lick her lips a few times to get the words out. "Resting place?"

Father Aguirre nodded. "She was not Catholic, though she was a good friend, so she is not in the churchyard. We buried her on the hillside. She had proper last rites—or as proper as I could make them—"

Selena, highly sensitive to awkwardness in herself, could recognize it in others. *Is he scared I'll accuse him of not treating my aunt right? I wasn't here, I don't get to do that.*

It seemed very strange. Selena was thirty years old and Father Aguirre was certainly in his forties, if not older. And he was a priest. You didn't have to reassure priests, did you?

"Thank you," she said. *Thank you* always seemed to work, if you couldn't think of anything else. People liked to be thanked. "I'm sorry I wasn't here. We lost communication for a while."

He nodded.

She was relieved to reach the post office. Father Aguirre went ahead of her while she tied Copper to the porch, and Selena could hear the hum of conversation through the open door.

Copper settled down and put her head on her paws, and then Selena could not put it off any longer and slipped through the doorway.

"Selena!" said Jenny. "Good to see you again. Found the house all right?"

Selena nodded.

"Good, good. I was a bit worried, since it's a long walk in the heat, but I figured Grandma Billy'd take care of you."

"She did. She's very kind."

"She's good people," said Jenny.

"Salt of the earth," said Father Aguirre, a bit dryly. "Certainly the most interesting Virgin Mary we've ever had at the nativity play . . ."

Jenny grinned. "We've got a shortage of young women in these parts, if you hadn't noticed, Father. Maybe Selena here will agree for the next one."

"I'm not staying that long," said Selena hurriedly. "Just a few days—just—I need to save up for a train ticket. Only till then."

"Sure," said Jenny agreeably.

Why does everybody say it like that?

"I'll put down that you're in residence right now, okay?" asked Jenny. "No time limit on it."

"Sure," said Selena, and then kicked herself mentally, hoping that didn't sound like mockery. Father Aguirre chuckled.

"Is there a place in town that sells dog food?" asked Selena, hoping to change the subject.

"Absolutely," said Jenny. "Go around the circle, third place on your left is the store. Connor ought to be in by now."

Just before they parted ways on the porch, Selena said, "Um, Father Aguirre?"

He looked up. His expression was oddly hopeful. *What's he hoping for?*

"I've got to take the dog food back to the house, and it'll probably be too hot, but in a day or two, if you could show me where my aunt is, I'd appreciate that."

He nodded. "I'd be glad to. Will you come by the church for the evening meal tonight? We do a community meal in the evenings on Wednesday and Saturday, it's easier for those of us living alone."

"Thank you," said Selena. An evening meal might be a good time to ask about places to find work too.

She found the store easily enough. The battered pickup from yesterday was parked along the side, and when she walked in, the old Latino man who had given her the ride was behind the counter.

Connor. His name is Connor, but I shouldn't call him that because we haven't been introduced. Selena hated it when people used her name too much in conversation, it made them sound like salesmen. *Selena, hello, Selena, so nice to meet you, Selena, what can I sell you today, Selena, we have a lovely selection here today, Selena.*

Connor smiled at her. "We meet again," he said. "What can I do for you?"

I would like to buy dog food, please. No, wait. Do you have any dog food? By chance?

"Do you have any dog food, by chance?"

"Sure," said Connor. "Only the one kind, though, twenty bucks a bag. If your dog's got some weird allergy, it's cheaper to feed 'em chicken and oatmeal than it is to import the expensive stuff. It's made outta unicorns, for the price they charge."

"No allergies, thankfully," said Selena, smiling. She knew this conversation—every pet store in the world had some variation of it. Twenty dollars was more than she'd wanted to spend and would leave her even more broke, but Copper had to eat. She pulled the wad of cash out of her pocket. "Can I buy a bag?"

"Nope," said Connor.

Selena's smile faltered.

What? Did I say something wrong?

She could feel her smile turning bewildered, and Connor took pity on her.

"You can't buy a bag, because your aunt already paid for it." He patted a binder on the counter. "Shipped off a load right before she passed away. Credit's been sitting on the books for a year."

"Oh," said Selena faintly, not sure how to feel. Apparently news traveled very fast in Quartz Creek. "Is that . . . are you sure?"

"She's got no other kin to use it," said Connor. "I'd give it to Grandma Billy, but she wouldn't take it, said it belonged to Jackrabbit Hole House. You're living there now, and you're her kin, so it's yours."

He flipped open the book. "Looks like five hundred and twenty-eight dollars. I'll take the dog food off it for you, and have Samuel drop it off in the truck later."

"Oh . . ." said Selena again, and before she quite knew it, she was standing on the front porch of the general store, with Copper thumping her tail amiably against her shin.

It occurred to her, as she walked down the dusty path to Jackrabbit Hole House, that she could have asked to take the credit in cash so she could buy a ticket and leave Quartz Creek.

No! She felt a strong internal revulsion at the thought, as if her mind had suggested something indecent.

No. That would be like asking someone to take a gift back and give you the money instead.

She would treat the credit as an unexpected windfall, as a gift, not as something she had a right to. And if she was stuck here for more than a day or two, as seemed likely, at least she'd have dog food.

It made it easier if she thought of it as being for Copper. Nothing was too good for Copper.

The dog in question was panting, her tongue out a mile. Selena patted her and felt how hot the black fur was.

"Poor girl, you're dressed wrong for the desert, aren't you?"

Copper grinned hugely and lolled her tongue out even farther.

It was hot enough to give anyone pause. Selena could feel a headache starting over her left eye. The glare off the white dust was achingly bright. Maybe she should have used some of that credit to buy a pair of sunglasses.

When she glanced up and saw the wall around Jackrabbit Hole House, she sagged with relief. To be inside, where it would be cooler, and have a drink of water . . .

She dragged herself up onto the porch. Copper flopped down and panted rapidly.

The faucet only spat a few times when she turned it on, before settling down. Presumably the well was getting used to being used. Selena took a bowl out to Copper, who gulped noisily.

She drank out of her cupped hands, feeling ridiculous with water running down her chin, and had to blot her face on her arm. She should have bought a mug at the store—

"Who are you?" asked a man's voice, practically in her ear. "Why are you here?"

Selena jerked upright, splashing water everywhere. Even though Jenny and Grandma Billy had assured her that she could stay in Amelia's house, she was immediately sure that the real owner had come back and she was trespassing and she was already starting to apologize as she turned around to face . . .

No one.

The kitchen was empty. But she'd heard the voice, she was sure of it, it had been *right there*. Was she losing her mind? What little was left to lose?

"Yoohoo!" called Grandma Billy from the door.

Selena's breath went out in a whoosh. *Of course. She said something to Copper and it echoed strangely, that's all.*

"Brought you cups." Grandma Billy waved one from the doorway.

Selena laughed, even though it caught a bit at the bottom like tears. She propped herself up against the sink. "I was just thinking about that."

"'Course you were." Her neighbor came inside with a swirl of brightly printed skirts. "Perfectly normal thing to need in the desert." She paused, frowning. "Jeez, you don't look so good. You drinking enough water?"

"Thanks," said Selena. "I'm just . . . I . . ." She was too tired to construct a polite fiction. "Too many people today. I'm not good at . . ." She grimaced. "I'm . . . shy."

She hated the word *shy* with a passion. It took problems big enough to blot out the horizon and crammed them down into a cute little word, as if she were a five-year-old hiding behind her mother. *No, no, it's not that she has to memorize all the normal parts of human interaction by rote, like some kind of alien. She's just* shy.

She used to wonder whether she would have been shy if she'd been born to a different mother, whether she'd have learned a different set of reflexes that weren't always wrong. Whether she'd have known what to say to people by instinct, instead of drilling scripts into herself, over and over.

Eventually she stopped wondering, because it didn't do any good. Her mother had raised her, and there was no going back and snatching her infant self away, and that was just all there was to it.

Walter had called it *socially awkward*, which had been remarkably freeing at first, and then became its own kind of hell. But at least socially awkward didn't sound twee.

"Shy?" said Grandma Billy. "Can't-meet-new-people shy or wish-all-these-people-would-go-away shy?" She paused. "Or just I'm-too-damn-tired-to-deal-with-your-shit-right-now-Grandma shy? That's a pretty common one, don't worry."

Selena rubbed her hand over her face. "The first two," she said. "Sort of. Meeting new people. I'm bad at that."

"You've met plenty in the last few days," said Grandma. "You met Connor, didn't you? And Jenny. And me, obviously. That's three."

"Four," said Selena. "I met Father Aguirre too."

"Sure. Nice fellow. That's four. And I'd wear anybody out." She grinned. "Plus you had to walk around in the heat. Go take a nap, hon. I'll come back this afternoon and we'll go get dinner at the church."

"I'm sorry," said Selena. The thought of a nap was glorious. "I don't want to be rude. I really, really appreciate your help."

"Pffff!" Grandma Billy waved a hand. "It ain't rude to ask for what you need. And I'd be a pretty poor neighbor keeping you standing here talking when you're ready to drop."

She moved toward the door.

Is she offended? I hope she's not offended. Oh god . . .

"It's not you," said Selena desperately.

"'Course it ain't," said Grandma. She grinned again and Selena felt vaguely soothed despite herself. "Amelia used to say, 'Look, Grandma, not feelin' social today,' and I'd say, 'Right, come on by if you change your mind!' and there were never no hurt feelings on either side. It's easier to get sick of people when there ain't many around. Don't ask me how that works. I'll come by 'bout three, that sound good?"

"Three would be perfect." Selena gripped the doorframe. "I'm looking forward to it."

She was surprised to find, when she woke up, that she had been telling the exact truth.

Chapter 5

The meal at the church was easier than she had expected. Selena had had too much time to think about it and had been bracing herself. A new social group full of unwritten rules that she might accidentally break was her worst nightmare. She could usually get by on scripts, and having Walter to help her, but Walter wasn't here, and what if she did something horribly egregious and didn't realize it?

When the worst didn't happen, she felt unsettled, as if she'd been leaning against a wind that suddenly stopped blowing.

It was Grandma Billy who made it work, of course. She swept into the rectory with Selena and Copper in tow, carrying a coffee can full of hard-boiled eggs and some early greens. Selena was lugging a bag of potatoes that Grandma had handed to her. She felt a little embarrassed to be bringing someone else's food to the potluck, but it felt good not to come with empty hands.

There were half a dozen people in the kitchen. Selena recognized Jenny and waved tentatively to the mayor, postmaster, and chief of police. *Is she the fire department too? I think she said she is.*

Jenny waved back. "Selena!" she shouted over the noise of the kitchen. "How's Jackrabbit Hole House treating you?"

"It's very nice," said Selena, which was an acceptable thing to say, even if it didn't come anywhere near describing the relief and the strangeness in equal measures.

"Come sit here," said Jenny. "We'll wrap those potatoes up in foil and let 'em bake for a while. The solars still working? Well didn't go dry?"

"They're working fine," said Selena. She sat obediently next to Jenny. Nobody seemed to care that Copper lay down under her chair, which was a relief.

The mayor scrubbed each potato and handed it over for wrapping. The tinfoil looked as if it had been used several times, but still crinkled in her hands.

"No trouble with spiders?" Jenny asked as she scrubbed.

"Grandma Billy helped me look for them." She seemed genuinely interested, so Selena added, "There was a scorpion, though."

"Oh yeah, those'll come right in. Big or little?"

"Big."

Jenny nodded. "Easy to see, then. No worse than a beesting if it gets you, though it isn't much fun. You or your dog get stung by a little one, though, come back into town and we'll have Rosa patch you up."

"Rosa?"

"Sure, Lupé's sister. She mostly takes care of sheep and goats, but she's good with people in a pinch. Good enough for the little stuff, and we'll call in the doctor for the big stuff."

Selena cringed at the thought of having to call in a doctor for anything. God only knew how much that would cost, and they probably wouldn't take credit from the general store. Still, if Copper got hurt, that was another matter.

She dropped her hand down, and under her chair, the dog thumped her tail in acknowledgment.

She concentrated on wrapping foil over potatoes, and the small talk went on over and around her, without making any demands. She smiled at obvious jokes, and Jenny asked her only easy questions about the house, not hard ones about why she'd left the city or what she was going to do next.

And she was good at being in kitchens. Selena understood kitchens. The deli had mostly made cold salads and hot soups out of bags, but it was still a familiar space. Maybe all kitchens were the same, when you got down to it, little fragments of some ur-kitchen, where the first grandmothers had cooked on flat rocks and turned mammoth bones into soup.

She was introduced to everybody, but some of the names went by in a blur, too fast for Selena to catch—the small, round-faced Latina woman in cotton skirts was Lupé, and the tall, stooped man with wispy hair was Gordon, but there were four other people at the table, and all Selena could do was smile and nod and hope that there wouldn't be a quiz.

When the meal was ready, Grandma Billy sat down by the head of the table and hooked her foot around a chair, pulling it out for Selena. Selena settled and Copper oozed under the table, watching hopefully for tidbits.

Father Aguirre sat at the head of the table. When he asked everyone to bow their heads while he said grace, Selena did, feeling vaguely uncomfortable. Then Grandma Billy elbowed her and she had to fight back a grin, feeling like a teenager again.

". . . Amen," said the priest. "Dig in, all. Grandma Billy, if you don't quit fidgeting, I'll make you say grace next time."

"No, you won't," said Grandma, digging her spoon into a casserole dish. "Unless you want 'rub-a-dub-dub, thanks for the grub.'"

Father Aguirre sighed. "You are a positive heathen."

"Damn straight. Always positive, that's me." She passed the serving spoon over to Selena. "Get some of those beans before they're gone. They're good, even if the father does make them himself."

Selena met Father Aguirre's eyes over Grandma Billy's head. The priest smiled and shook his head ruefully, and Selena smiled back.

It was easy. It was easier than anything had been since her mother's funeral, and that had been hedged about with rituals and scripts to make it as easy as possible on everyone.

When it was all over, she helped wash up. It was never terribly fun, to put your hands in scalding water and rub your fingers over the slimy forks, but Selena was glad to be able to do something that meant that she was contributing, not merely showing up at someone else's table.

But no one had treated her like a poor relation. There was even a bottle of wine passed around, and Father Aguirre poured her a little bit before it occurred to her to put her hand over the glass and demur.

"That's fine," she said instead, and he stopped pouring.

"You sure?"

"I'm not in the habit anymore," she said, "and with the heat, I'll probably fall asleep if I have any more." Which was a script, but a well-worn one. She could plug anything in instead of *heat*.

"It'll knock you right out," said Jenny, from down the table. "The heat, I mean. When it gets about August, nobody does anything until sunset."

"Ah, but you'll be used to it by then," said Lupé, next to her. "It doesn't take as long as people think."

Selena thought about protesting that she was certainly not going to be here in August, but then that would make the conversation about her and perhaps people would try to convince her otherwise. She took a swallow of wine instead.

Now she washed the wineglasses, and remembered the taste.

Copper had been given the job of precleaning the plates, which probably meant that Selena would be sleeping in a room with a very gassy dog. Still, she hated for the food to go to waste, and she'd been rationing their food out so carefully that Copper was thrilled with the feast. And everyone just put their plates down on the floor as if it was normal to have a black Lab helping in the kitchen, so she couldn't very well complain.

"You've been eating eggs and sandwiches for two days," she told Copper, picking up another cleaned plate. "Chicken and rice must be better for you." Copper lolled her tongue, pleased.

After the meal, there was more wine passed around. Gordon and Grandma Billy told stories and laughed at each other's jokes. Father Aguirre sang a hymn in a very good baritone, and everyone joined in, even Selena, although she didn't know the words and could only do the chorus.

She felt awkward singing in public—always had—but everyone else was, and it would be more awkward not to do it. It sounded enthusiastic more than beautiful. Walter would have cringed.

When the song stopped, though, everyone laughed and cheered as if they'd accomplished something. Lupé sat on the floor and scratched Copper's belly. Copper, who had no dignity at all, lay on her back and moaned cheerfully, one hind leg kicking now and again.

Before everyone could gather their things to leave, Selena had tried, delicately, to broach the topic of employment. It proved the night's only disappointment.

"Not that I wouldn't hire you to wash dishes over at the cafe," said Lupé, "but there's barely enough work to do right now as it is. In a couple months, maybe, when the tourists show up."

Selena's heart sank. A couple months seemed like an eternity. Though she could probably get by with the credit that Aunt Amelia had left her . . . but then, how long would it take her to earn the money for the train ticket?

"Do you know anything about sheep?" asked Gordon. Selena was forced to admit her ignorance of sheepkind. "Ah, well. I ask 'cause people can always use help with the shearing. But I'll keep my ear to the ground for you, yeah?" She thanked him, because what else could she do?

There were tons of leftovers, including most of a large tray of tamales that Lupé had brought. Selena tried not to eye them with lust in her heart. *This is what I'm reduced to. Coveting my neighbor's tamales.*

"Somebody take those," said Lupé. "They need eating up and I'm changing the special tomorrow." She scraped them out of the pan into several plastic containers, then tucked her tray under her arm and waved. Gordon took a small container and followed, and everyone else trickled away in ones and twos.

Grandma Billy and Selena were the last ones to leave. "Good to see you again," said Father Aguirre, shaking her hand. "I hope you come out again. It's good to have a new face at dinner."

"Particularly one who will wash dishes!" said Grandma.

Selena ducked her head, embarrassed. She was about to ask if she could claim some of the leftover tamales, when Grandma Billy made the matter moot by picking up the remainder and piling them into Selena's arms.

"Oh—I—err—" She looked at Father Aguirre helplessly. "Is it okay if I . . . ?"

"Please do," the priest said. "Lupé believes firmly that she is all that stands between any of us and starvation. My refrigerator is already groaning with past daily specials."

Selena wasn't entirely sure if she believed him, but if he was being charitable, he was doing it gracefully. She followed Copper and Grandma Billy out into the desert night.

It was much cooler than she'd expected. The desert had released its heat quickly, and the breeze was almost cold. It was also much louder. The cicadas had stopped their sound-numbing buzz and things chirped and yipped and skittered. She tightened her grip on Copper's leash.

Grandma Billy didn't seem concerned by the noises. "That was fun," she said. "Sorry nobody's got anywhere to work right yet, though."

"All those years as night manager of a deli," said Selena wryly, "when I should have been learning about sheepshearing."

Grandma snickered. "When I was young, they told us to learn typing. Said you'd always have something to fall back on. Might be true in a city, but out here, I can't say there's much of a secretarial pool." She spread her arms wide. "Still, I wouldn't want to live anywhere else. Look at those stars!"

Selena looked up. The stars blazed fiercely overhead, brighter than any sky she'd ever seen in the city. Not that you could see the stars very well through the haze of light pollution.

"When I was little," she said out loud, not stopping to think about it, "and my dad took me camping, the stars looked like that." She thought that she could make out the thick band of the Milky Way. Was that even a thing you could see with the naked eye? She knew roughly as much about astronomy as she did about sheep.

"What about in the city?" Grandma Billy asked.

Selena shook her head. The city sky was dull orange at night. Even with all the scrubber systems in place, there was nothing to be done about the light pollution. She hadn't seen the stars in a long time.

"Right," said Grandma Billy, as they reached her house. "I'll come 'round tomorrow and we'll see about getting your garden put in." She bent down and petted Copper. "It won't take hardly any time at all, you'll see."

Selena put away the stacks of tamales. The sight of the refrigerator actually half full made something in her relax. She might still starve, but not today.

She checked the clock on her aunt's bookcase and saw that it was only nine thirty. She sat down and perused the rows of books. There were a few nonfiction volumes, mostly guides to plants and animals of the Southwest. The bottom shelf held dozens of slim books with unlabeled spines. She pulled one out, opened it up, and saw a postcard of the Eiffel Tower pasted to the page, along with a doodle of a baguette wearing a beret. "Got into Paris last night," read the handwritten text. "The traffic at Charles de Gaulle is the worst. Sally's so jet-lagged that she nearly cried when the hotel said our rooms weren't ready. Pretty knackered myself. Went and ate at a little café. That feels like a cliché."

"These must be Aunt Amelia's travel journals," Selena told Copper, who wagged politely. She turned the pages, seeing more doodles, ticket stubs, and occasional photos pasted in. Her aunt's handwriting was neat and surprisingly readable. She put the journal down and picked up another one, which showed something she recognized as the Seattle Space Needle. A third yielded photos of a temple festooned with prayer flags and a drawing of an unimpressed-looking yak.

An enormous yawn caught Selena by surprise before she could start reading more closely. "Tomorrow, maybe," she said, and got to her feet to let Copper out back.

She leaned against the doorframe, watching the stars visible beyond the overhanging porch. They really were breathtaking. *You could get used to a view like that.*

Copper had just returned, tail held high, when a scream ripped through the darkness.

Copper let out a yelp. So did Selena. She clutched the doorframe, dog jammed against her legs in clear alarm. It was a high, inhuman scream, throbbing with anguish and loss, the sound of something dying in pain.

Was that a person? Is someone hurt? Oh god, is it Grandma Billy? Should I go check on her?

Another scream followed the first, and Selena noted that it was coming from the deep desert, not from the direction of the town. And it didn't sound like it was coming from a human throat at all.

"Oh Jesus," Selena said, releasing her death grip on the doorframe. "I think it's an animal." God only knew what kind of animal made such a horrible sound, but she'd heard peacocks at the zoo before, and they had sounded like someone being murdered, so it was hardly a surprise that there was something with an equally awful voice out here in the desert.

Hell, maybe it *was* Merv the peacock. Maybe he wandered around and screamed at night. What did Selena know about peacock behavior?

She maneuvered Copper back inside, which was a trifle difficult as the Lab wanted to stay attached to her shins, and shut the door against the night.

Lying in bed a few minutes later, Selena found herself listening, tensed for another scream. It didn't come. Instead, she became aware of the strange silence that underlay everything. There were no passing cars, no distant voices. The sounds of insects and night creatures seemed like a thin skin over a much deeper quiet. For someone who had lived in the city for her entire life, it was unsettling.

She got up and went to the living room. She thought she'd seen a radio on the bookcase, and sure enough, there it was, a small black AM/FM number that probably dated to the Obama administration.

Selena took it to the bedroom and plugged it in. The familiar strains of "Good Day Sunshine," filled the room, which wasn't what she would have chosen, but was better than silence. She looked for another station, but it was mostly static up and down the dial. On one channel, they seemed to be having an intense political discussion, but since they were speaking in Spanish, Selena couldn't understand more than one word in twenty. The only other channel that came in clearly was in a language that she thought might be Navajo. Embarrassed by her monolingualism, she went back to the Beatles.

"And that," said the DJ, in a smooth, androgynous voice, "is the culmination of my ninety-seven-song thesis that songs about being happy are inherently worse than songs about being horny or miserable."

Ninety-seven-song thesis? Selena thought. *Did they nail them to the station door or what?*

"You're listening to KQDZ, the Voice of the Desert, serving Quartz Creek, Salt Lick, and Masonville. I am, as always, your host, DJ Raven. Now, let's listen to something wildly different, shall we?"

Theremin music rose from the speakers. Copper lifted her head, clearly puzzled. "'How the Camel Got His Hump,'" a man read, "by Rudyard Kipling. 'In the beginning of years . . .'"

It was a weirdly delightful reading, even with the theremins, and it drowned out the alien quiet outside her window. Selena lay back down. Kipling was followed by Led Zeppelin, Taylor Swift, and a mariachi cover of "Bye Bye Bye." She fell asleep to the strains of Vivaldi's *Four Seasons* and slept without dreams.

Chapter 6

"Why am I planting a garden, if I'm just staying for a few days?"

Grandma Billy straightened up from where she'd been bent over the garden beds. "Insurance," she said, after a moment.

"Insurance?" Selena gazed over the neat rows of Aunt Amelia's garden. Everything was laid out in narrow rectangles, easy to lean in and harvest. The dirt was rich brown, overlaid with white dust. It was good dirt. Amelia had put a lot of love and a lot of chicken manure into it over the years.

"Probably you'll be gone in a few weeks," said Grandma. "Maybe get a couple of lettuce leaves out of it, not much else. Maybe beet greens. So it's a couple seeds now and a salad later, right?"

"Right."

"But say you decide to stay—and I'm not saying you will, mind—you get beans and squash and corn out of it. And if you don't stay, maybe I'll nip over and harvest a few things myself when you're gone."

"Well, as long as you'll get some use out of it."

Truth was, Selena didn't mind working in the garden. She had spent a few seasons with a community garden plot in the city, though she hadn't been much good at it. Walter had refused to eat the gnarled carrots she brought home, saying they looked like weird orange dog turds.

They sort of did, honestly. Carrots are hard.

This was thinner, sandier soil than the heavy clay she'd had back in the city. Maybe the carrots would be happier here.

Mostly, though, they were planting beans and peppers and hills of squash. There were wooden tripods all along the rock wall, and Grandma Billy had her placing a bean at the base of every leg.

"Can I pay you for the seeds?"

"Lord, hon, seeds are cheap. I been saving. Amelia gave me so many seeds out of this garden over the years, least I can do is put them back."

"But you started these squash already . . . they've got leaves on them . . ."

Grandma Billy waved her hand. "There's always too many. You start a couple extra in case some of them die, and then they all grow like gangbusters."

Selena sighed. "I'm not sure how I'd pay you anyhow," she confessed. "I was hoping there'd be a restaurant or something in town I could wash dishes at . . . clean at a motel . . . something. But I didn't see anything like that in town."

"Oh, well," said Grandma. "When tourist season starts up, Lupé lets rooms over the café, and she can use a cleaner then. Or out at Rivendell, they've got guest cabins and they always need extra hands. Stick around till then, maybe. It's not long."

"What kind of tourists do you get out here?" Selena asked. She was finding the desert interesting, even in some lights oddly beautiful, but they were a long way from the big tourist hubs like Sedona and Jerome. There weren't any big red-rock mesas looming over Quartz Creek.

"Mostly rich white folks who don't want to live like this, but like to know that somebody is. They come out, do a little tour of Sally's ranch with the sheep, go to Rivendell, eat a couple fancy local meals, then go away again. They can be a pain in the ass, but they're the reason historic zones exist and aren't all snapped up by developers." She thought for a minute. "Bird-watchers too. Gordon does tours for 'em. And sometimes you get a couple half dozen college students who want to talk to you about dry farming."

Selena pushed the last of the beans into place. "I suppose dry farming's the only kind you can do here."

"Pretty much. Most of us get by on it, though. There's stuff you can't grow in the city. Remind me, we'll plant you some corn for smut."

"Smut," said Selena blankly. *Err . . . is this some kind of vegetable pornography?*

"Corn smut!" said Grandma. "Not as fun as it sounds." She winked. "It's a mold thing, grows on corn. Looks like hell, and you can't grow it on that fancy corn they grow in Iowa. And corn breeds by the wind, so you don't get it within ten miles of those cornfields."

"Why do you *want* to grow mold?"

Grandma grinned like an elderly shark. "'Cause there's fancy restaurants in the city that'll pay a goddamn fortune for the stuff. Most of us grow it out here and take it in to Connor. He's got a flash freezer and ships it back to the city, and we get paid. Couple other things too—there's a market for young prickly pear pads in another month, and Jenny grows some wicked-ass peppers that fetch a good price. I'll bring you some seeds for those if you like. And you've got some fine chiltepin bushes alongside the house, and those are good money too. But corn smut's the biggest bang for your buck."

"The town runs on gourmet corn fungus?" said Selena.

"Pretty much, pretty much. Oh, the weaver sells her rugs, brings in cash, and she buys plenty of veggies from us, since her land ain't good for nothing but sheep, and people make carvings or sell beaded necklaces or whatnot. I'll show you how to make genuine heritage wild-crafted sachets if you want. Ain't nothin' to it. But mostly it's little fancy things you can't grow in the city. We sell 'em and then people feel virtuous 'cause it comes with a story about how it's all grown by little homestead farmers in a tiny historic town, all organic, farm-to-table stuff. Real nice boy with a cute ass comes out twice a year or so, represents some kind of fair-trade deal, makes sure the doctor's comin' through regular, makes sure we don't feel exploited." Grandma Billy managed to look wistful and dirty at the same time. "I'd exploit *him* if I was twenty years younger."

In a desperate attempt to change the subject, Selena asked, "Grandma Billy? Are there any animals around here that scream at night?"

"Sure," Grandma said. "You hear one?" Selena nodded. "Did it sound like somebody bein' murdered or the torments of the damned?"

"Err . . ." This was not something she'd ever had to quantify before. "More like someone being murdered, I think?"

"Probably a fox." Grandma nodded sagely. "They start going at it, sounds like babies in a blender."

Selena contemplated this distressingly vivid image and said, weakly, "I think I need a drink." She cleared her throat. "Ah, will you have some? I found some tea in a cupboard."

"Believe I will," said Grandma. "And if we check in my bag, I might have a drop of something to go with it."

When Grandma Billy left that evening, Selena found herself tired but not sleepy. She made another cup of tea—which admittedly was more like brown water, given how many times the tea bag had been used, but tea still felt like an extravagance—and flopped down on the couch to read some of Aunt Amelia's travel journals. The one about traveling in Tibet was interesting, although the first ten pages were mostly complaints about the airport in Beijing and white-knuckle driving in various Chinese cities. There were photos of the Great Wall with half a dozen people in front of it, four women and two men, all of them dressed like tourists and grinning like fools. Selena picked out her aunt and was struck by how young she looked. Middle-aged, definitely, but her hair was salt and pepper instead of white. The writing was just how she remembered her aunt, though, the same snappy wit and bright-eyed interest in everything from yaks to hot pot.

Selena had just finished a lengthy but hilarious diatribe about altitude sickness, accompanied by a stick figure begging for oxygen, when she became aware of the feeling that she was being watched.

She looked up, thinking that maybe Copper was doing her patented Stare Hard Enough and the Human Will Give Me a Treat trick. But Copper had had a long day chasing after lizards and lay on her side, sleeping the sleep of the just.

Just my imagination, Selena thought, and went back to the journal.

The feeling didn't go away. It persisted through Tibetan Buddhist temples and ancient ruins and military checkpoints.

Selena got up and checked the doors to make sure they were locked. They were. The windows looked out into darkness and she glanced at them quickly, then away. She'd never liked windows at night. She always had the feeling that if she looked up too quickly, she'd see a face pressed against them. She'd made the mistake of telling Walter that once, and he'd pointed out that they were on the second floor and anything that looked into the windows would have to climb up to do it, which made it even worse, because then Selena pictured things climbing up the side of the building, things with long, soft toes like geckos', flesh pressing into the cracks in the brick, pushing themselves upward . . .

She hadn't told Walter that bit. He wouldn't have understood at all. At any rate, there was nothing at the windows and the doors were locked and anyway, Copper might be white muzzled and snoring, but if someone was sneaking around the house, she'd be on her feet and barking hysterically before you could say, "Good dog."

Selena sat back down, but even though she was turning pages, she was only half reading. Where was the feeling coming from? She might be crazy—*heh, might*—but she didn't run to paranoia about anything but social interactions. This was strange.

She finished the Tibet journal and looked up, scanning what part of the house was visible. Bookcase, chair, couch, rug, fireplace . . .

Statue in the niche beside the fireplace . . .

Selena got to her feet. Was that it? Its eyes were crude yellow circles set in pointed white ovals, with black circles of pupil, the sort of eyes children draw when they have moved beyond black dots, but only just. But she could see the eyes from where she sat and that meant it could see her.

It's a statue. It can't see anything, said the voice in her head that sounded like Walter.

She took a few steps forward. *Snake-Eater,* Grandma Billy had called it.

Either it wasn't a very good statue or Snake-Eater was ugly. The wood had been chopped away and never smoothed, and the paint was thick and blobby. Even Selena, who suffered pangs for every imperfect stuffed animal and teddy bear missing a button, couldn't find much to appreciate.

Maybe it was its expression. A beak shouldn't have an expression and certainly those eyes shouldn't, but the overall impression was of judgment. Snake-Eater looked back at the viewer and found her lacking.

No, it's not just that. It looks . . . sly. As if it found that lack amusing.

Selena felt a strong urge to take it down and put it in a cupboard somewhere, where it couldn't look at her.

But if she did that, she would be acting as if this was her house, and it wasn't. She knew it wasn't. It belonged to Aunt Amelia, and even if Amelia was dead, that didn't give Selena the right to go in and start changing things.

Still . . .

She stood up on her toes and turned the doll so that it faced the wall instead of looking out into the room.

"There," she said out loud. Copper looked up, clearly wondering if the word had anything to do with her, and whether it might lead to a trip Outside or, better yet, a Treat. When Selena sat back down in the chair, the dog heaved a sigh of despair at the lot of poor starved hounds and dropped her muzzle back to the floor.

Selena picked up a second journal. Her aunt had gone to Paris, which had always sounded gorgeous and exotic. Amelia had a different opinion. "Paris is a beautiful city and a very ugly one, living on top of each other." Also it was apparently not a good place to visit if you didn't like mustard.

The doll was still watching her. Not nearly as strongly as before, but she could still feel it like a prickle against her skin.

She turned a page, which had several photos of the Loire Valley pasted to it. The chateaus were magnificent, but she couldn't focus on them while the damned doll was staring at her. Finally, she got up again, got the radio from the bedroom, and turned it on.

"This is your host, DJ Raven. If you've got any complaints about the programming, please tell my uncle. He owns the station. While you're talking to him, tell him that my last vacation was three years ago and that my aunt wants to know if he's ever going to fix the hall light. Now let's get down with some Nick Cave and the Bad Seeds . . ."

The DJ's voice drove away some of the feeling of being watched, but not all of it. Selena got through two songs and a reading from Sandburg's *Rootabaga Stories* before her skin started to prickle again.

She got up and stalked toward the doll, and realized that she hadn't turned it far enough around in its niche. It could still see the room out of the corner of one yellow eye.

You're being ridiculous, Walter said inside her head.

"Yes, I am," she said out loud. "And there's no one else here to be bothered by it." She turned it the rest of the way toward the wall.

She sat down and went back to reading Aunt Amelia's travel journals. DJ Raven played the theme songs to children's cartoons, interspersed with Dolly Parton's greatest hits. The sense of being watched was gone, and it stayed gone all evening, until Selena went to bed.

It was early morning on the fifth day when she woke up in someone's arms.

She was still mostly asleep and he was warm and comfortable, even if his arm was heavy where it lay across her waist. Selena burrowed into the pillow, trying not to wake him up, since she wasn't ready to get up yet herself. *I could go back to sleep for an hour or two still.*

Realization came slowly, creeping across her skin like gooseflesh. Her eyes snapped open. She stared at the wall opposite, feeling the weight of the stranger's arm across her, his chest solid against her back. His breath stirred the fine hairs on the back of her neck.

Did I get drunk last night and bring someone home? She'd never done that in her life. And she hadn't even gone out last night. She'd had to split firewood for the first time, and she'd been tired and sore and a little nervous that she would hit herself in the shins with the axe and chop her own feet off. She'd had a hot shower and then she'd gone to bed early.

Fear sang along her nerves. A thousand questions flooded her mind—*how had he gotten in without waking her, why hadn't Copper barked, why was he here, who was he*—but the only one that mattered was *how am I going to get away?*

The arm holding her felt like a bar of iron. Selena tilted her head down, very slowly. She caught a glimpse of mottled gray, as if the man was wearing a tweed suit, and then, with an inarticulate screech, he shoved her, hard.

She hit the floor with one shoulder, legs still tangled in the sheets, and let out a yelp. Copper bolted upright at the foot of the bed, woofing in panic. Selena tried to roll, got one elbow under her, and faced . . .

Empty sheets.

There was no one in the bed, unless you counted Copper. The dog came off the bed and began snuffling Selena's face with deep concern. Selena pushed her muzzle away and sat up, staring at the bed.

There was no one there. Morning light streamed through the window, across the pillows. She stared at the one against the wall, trying to see if there was an impression from someone else's head. *That could be one? Maybe?*

Yes, and where exactly did he go then? Flew over your head? Turned invisible?

"I dreamed it," she said aloud, and laughed with sudden relief. *It must have been one of the ones where you're almost asleep or awake, something quick and super vivid, then you jerk violently and wake up. Instead of falling, I just thought someone was in bed with me.*

It had felt incredibly real, but dreams always did when you were having them, didn't they?

Copper was still looking around to see what the problem was. Had Selena spotted a jackrabbit in the bedroom? Copper would deal with it if she had, no questions asked.

Selena reached out and ruffled the Lab's ears. "It's okay," she said. Her voice didn't sound quite certain of that, so she said it again, with a little more conviction this time. "It's okay. I just had a weird dream, that's all."

Copper considered this for a bit, then apparently decided that if her person was awake, that meant her person could take her outside to pee on something, and Selena resigned herself to not getting that extra hour of sleep after all.

Chapter 7

She made coffee, such as it was, and fried a few eggs, then took her breakfast out onto the back porch. It was still cool enough to be bearable, though the sky was already turning into a hard turquoise bowl. She sat down, letting the coffee chase away the last dregs of the dream, and that was when she saw the man in green at the far end of the garden.

Selena blinked a few times, but he didn't go away. He was wearing skintight green clothing, or perhaps body paint. There was some strange hat or mask on his head, all green stripes, and he wore a golden collar around his neck.

He had been crouching down over the seedlings, but now he stood up. He was short and compact, and there was something strange about his forearms, as if something green grew on them. The mask turned toward Selena.

She glanced quickly down at Copper. The dog was stretched out on her side, a picture of unconcern. She noticed Selena looking at her and thudded her tail against the boards.

When she looked up again, the man was gone.

He would have had to move quickly to get out of the garden and into the brush. The gate was still closed.

Don't be silly. Nobody could open the gate without the hinges screaming bloody murder.

It occurred to Selena that she might be hallucinating. *First the dream, now this?*

It had been five days since she took possession of the house. She had been living largely on eggs, cornbread, and leftover tamales, in various combinations. It did not seem likely that cornbread and eggs could make you hallucinate, but perhaps there was something in the water.

Is it a mirage? Do mirages look like that?

She looked down at her chicory coffee, then back up again, hoping to catch the green man in the act of reappearing.

He still wasn't there. The air over the garden was sharp and clear, with no trace of heat haze. Even the cicadas hadn't started up yet.

A cold prickly chill settled over her.

Selena knew that she was crazy. Walter had made that abundantly clear. He was a jerk, but that didn't make him *wrong*.

It was the simple kind of crazy, though, the can't-cope-anymore crazy, the kind that has you bursting into tears at small setbacks and contemplating your own mortality with sneaking relief. You could fake your way through life with that kind of crazy.

The kind of crazy where you saw people who weren't there, where you hallucinated green men at the bottom of the garden—that was the major leagues. If she was going really truly *insane* . . .

I can't be expected to deal with being insane. Nobody should be required to put up with that.

The notion that this was really too much for anyone to deal with was strangely appealing. She wasn't doing it wrong. She was just insane, that was all. No wonder she had such a hard time making conversation right.

Dear Walter . . . it turns out that it wasn't my fault that I kept saying the wrong thing all the time . . .

She finished off her coffee and had just turned back toward the house when Grandma Billy banged through the front door. "Yoohoo! Anybody home?"

"Come on in," said Selena, a bit dryly.

"Thanks, I have." Grandma grinned at her, perfectly aware of what she was doing. "How are you this morning?"

"I think I'm hallucinating," said Selena, surprised into honesty.

"Nice weather for it," said Grandma. She dropped two heavy sacks on the table. "Cornmeal for you. Samuel's oldest had some bags left over from last year, but he mixed the blue corn with the yellow, so the meal turned gray. Tastes fine, but looks like hell."

"Can I pay him for it?"

"No," said Grandma, "he doesn't deserve money for this stuff. You're helping him hide a sin against culinary decency. He ought to be paying you."

Selena recognized charity when it was happening to her, but she also recognized Grandma Billy—and presumably the absent Samuel—were giving her a way to save face. She wasn't sure how to feel about that.

"So, what're you hallucinating?" asked Grandma, helping herself to the last of the coffee.

Was it more humiliating to go insane or to take someone's gray cornmeal? Selena did not feel that she was cut out for this kind of social arithmetic. Clearly they were far beyond scripts, so she stuck to the bare facts. "There was a man wearing green stripes in the garden. He had something on his head, and then he vanished when I looked away."

"Green stripes? Squash god," said Grandma, nodding. "Probably glad somebody's planting in the old earth again."

Selena stared at her blankly.

"There's one like him what belongs to them up on the mesas up north, or they belong to him, however it works with gods. Hopi, or maybe Zuni, not sure which. This all used to be Native land, after all. Either this is the same one and he just wanders around a bit, or he's a different one and they all look like that." Her lips puckered in a frown. "Kinda got the impression theirs was bigger, but what do I know about it? Take care of those plants, though, and he'll likely come back."

"I'm not sure I want strange men in my garden," said Selena, focusing on the one sentence that she understood.

"He's a god," said Grandma reasonably. "Or nearly one, anyway, I've never been clear on the difference. Maybe a spirit instead, though I call him a god to be polite."

"You're saying . . . there's a god . . . in my garden." She hoped the words did not sound as mad out loud as they did in her head.

"Nothing to worry about. It's not like he's gonna be peeping at you in the shower. And if he likes you, you'll get a better crop than you might otherwise." The bangles on her wrists clattered as she tapped a finger against her lips.

"But gods aren't *real*," Selena blurted, then realized that might be terribly offensive and put her hand over her mouth in horror.

"Sure," said Grandma, clearly not offended. "Okay." She considered. "So, let's say you got *spirits* in your garden then . . ."

Selena said, "I need more coffee."

She wrestled with the old press in silence. Grandma stayed out back, petting Copper.

By the time she'd coaxed another cup (albeit a weak one) from the remaining grounds, her mind was a bit clearer. Grandma Billy knew what Selena had been talking about. She'd filled in details. Therefore *something* was there, and Selena wasn't any more insane than she thought she was.

That was a trifle disappointing from one direction, but an enormous relief from the other one.

That there might be actual gods wandering around in her garden was . . . well, too absurd a thought to get her mind around, frankly.

"So this squash person . . ." she said, coming out onto the back porch.

"Pretty benign for a god," said Grandma. "Not going to drag you into anything. He just likes plants." She tucked her thumbs into the waistband of her skirt. "There always was a thin spot at the end of this garden. That's probably why you can see him."

"A thin spot," Selena said, wondering if she was doomed to just keep repeating Grandma Billy all morning, like a skeptical parrot.

"Yeah. Amelia had all kinds of friends. Not all of 'em were, y'know, human."

Copper came and sat down with a thump. Selena put her hand down, feeling sun-warmed black fur, which was good and real and solid and made sense, unlike the words that Grandma Billy was saying.

On the one hand, she'd seen *something* in the garden. On the other hand . . . Selena's mother had believed in spirits and demons and spiritual warfare and all sorts of things that made her incredibly tiring to be around. Whenever Selena had argued with her, her mother would yell, "Satan, get out of my daughter!"

Often very loudly. In public.

Selena really didn't want to step back into that world, not even for Grandma Billy.

She sipped her coffee. The chicory wasn't as soothing as real coffee would be, but it was better than nothing. The sky blazed blue. A raven made its rattlebone call from somewhere on the hillside, and another one answered.

"You're saying it's a god," said Selena finally.

"Yep."

"Like, a *god*-god."

"Dunno. Is that different than the usual run of gods?"

"You're saying gods are real," said Selena.

Grandma shrugged. "Sounds like a question for Father Aguirre. There're things out here in the desert, that's all I know. People, but not human people. And I don't mean people like Copper here, or my rooster."

"Are we talking about magic?"

"Sure, why not?"

"Because magic isn't real!"

Grandma Billy cackled, a really good cackle, the sort you could only manage if you were over sixty or had a well-trained smoker's cough. "Sure," she said. She leaned back in the chair so that the front legs left the ground. "Sure, if you say so."

Selena considered this. She considered various scripts, none of which seemed to apply to anything, and eventually settled on honesty. "This is a completely batshit conversation to be having."

"Sure," said Grandma Billy cheerfully. "Have to be a bit touched to live out here, I imagine. I mean, I am, and Amelia sure was." She paused. Her eyes were old but raven-sharp. "I'm a bit surprised *you* saw him, even with the thin spot. Two old desert women, eh, that's one thing. Young girl like you, something must've banged you pretty hard to knock you half out of the world like that."

"I'm thirty," said Selena testily. "I'm not *that* young."

"I'm seventy-eight. I'm not *that* old. Still."

Selena recognized a losing proposition and switched tactics. "*Why* do you think there are gods wandering around in my garden?"

"Well, there's only the one just yet," said Grandma judiciously. "And he's pretty harmless. Word of warning, though, there's others who aren't so nice. If anybody shows up with coyote eyes and tries to get into your pants, slam the door. Some people don't take 'Oh, *hell* no!' for an answer."

Selena almost mentioned her dream from early that morning, then just stared into the sky until her eyes started to hurt.

"Anyway, I wouldn't suggest inviting just anybody in, but if you want to make friends, most spirits around here like a bit of cornmeal."

"Cornmeal," Selena said.

"Just not that gray crap I brought you." Grandma snorted. "Wouldn't give *that* to a god. Tobacco also works."

"Why tobacco?"

Grandma shrugged. "Dunno, it just does. Do I look like a priest?"

Selena cocked an eye at her. With her vest and skirt and craggy brown face, and enough jewelry to jangle when she walked, Grandma Billy looked like the more bohemian sort of shaman.

"We might do better if more priests looked like you," she said, and then could have bit her tongue for embarrassment. *What kind of thing is that to say out loud? I'm doing it again, oh damn, saying stupid things, I'm so frazzled with this god business . . .*

Grandma laughed, delighted. "Be a damn sight more interesting services. But don't let Father Aguirre hear you say that. He's a good sort, for a priest." She stretched. "*Anyway*, just wanted to tell you that I was going into town, if you wanted to come along."

Selena didn't actually want to go see other people very much, but it occurred to her that belief in little green gods might be a sign of dementia, and maybe she should talk to someone about it. "Sure," she said. "I'll get Copper's leash."

◆ ◆ ◆

She left Grandma Billy shooting the breeze with Connor and went over to the post office. Postmistress Jenny was sorting envelopes and waved as she came in. "Hey, Selena. What's up?"

"I . . . err . . ." Selena rubbed the back of her neck. Now that she came to talk about it with someone, it sounded mean-spirited. She took a deep breath. "Um, I don't know how to ask this, but is Grandma Billy . . . err . . . okay?"

"Far as I know." Jenny straightened up and came over to the counter. "Why? Something happen?"

"Well, no, not exactly." She couldn't bring herself to say that she'd seen a green man in her garden. "It's just . . . um . . . she was talking a lot about seeing gods. Or spirits."

"Oh, that." Jenny shrugged. "Lots of people out here believe in spirits and whatnot. It's religious, more or less. Folk Catholicism gets mixed up with bits of Native spirituality, along with stories somebody's abuela told them."

Selena winced internally. "Ah . . . I don't think it was religious, exactly. She seemed to be saying she actually saw them."

"Eh, she's not the only one around here. Between heat mirages and legal weed, there are people who'll swear that they met Jesus, Elvis, and little green men all hanging out together. I wouldn't worry about it. Just smile and nod, that's what I do." Jenny paused, her eyes sharpening. "But that said, she's nearly eighty. Your aunt used to keep an eye on her. I'd be obliged if you did the same."

"Of course," Selena said automatically.

She was halfway back to the store, and Grandma Billy was waving at her, before it occurred to her that she hadn't said she wasn't going to be staying.

The dinner at the church Saturday night, which had started to feel comfortable, was suddenly fraught again. Selena kept opening her mouth to ask if anyone else had seen the squash god, then closing it again. How did you even start that conversation?

Do I say, "By the way, Grandma Billy says there's a strange god in my garden and I saw something and I don't know what it was?" No, of course I don't. They'd lock me up.

They hadn't locked Grandma Billy up, but that probably didn't signify. You would need something more than walls to hold Grandma Billy. Barbed wire and a moat, at the very least.

She realized that Father Aguirre had been talking to her, and jumped, startled. "Sorry!"

"It's fine," the priest said, even though she'd flung bits of soapsuds everywhere. He blotted one off his shirt with his palm. "I was just asking if you wanted to visit your aunt's resting place tomorrow."

Selena blinked a few times. She'd almost forgotten that he'd offered. "Yes," she said. "Yes, I'd . . . really like that. Thank you."

"No problem." He smiled. "I'll come by in the evening, once it starts to cool off."

"Oh," said Grandma Billy, as they prepared to leave with their arms full of leftovers. "You got any good cornmeal lying around, Father?"

"I expect I could put hands on some," said the priest. "Why?"

"Selena's got a god in her garden," said Grandma, as if a god were of no more interest than a coyote or a raccoon. (Did they have raccoons in the desert? Selena hadn't seen one.)

She cringed, expecting—well, she wasn't sure *what* she was expecting. You certainly didn't tell a Catholic priest that there was a god in your garden, that was for sure.

Her mother would have screamed about demons. She was pretty sure she could weather that, but she was half afraid that Father Aguirre would start trying to cast the devil out of Grandma Billy and she didn't know if she could handle it.

"Oh, I see," said Father Aguirre instead. "Well, then. Let me find some."

Grandma winked at her. The priest climbed up onto a chair and dug around in the back of one of the kitchen cabinets, pulling down a white paper sack.

"It's not that fresh," he said apologetically. "I don't bake much. But it's the thought that counts, they tell me."

He handed her the bag.

Selena stared at him. "You believe me?"

Father Aguirre smiled. "Tell me what this god looked like."

"I . . . well . . ." Put on the spot, Selena found herself saying, "I don't know what it was, but I thought I saw something green . . ."

He listened to her halting description, said, "One moment," and vanished deeper into the rectory. She caught a glimpse through the door of an office with papers strewn across the desk. Then he returned, holding a wooden carving in his hand.

"Is this like what you saw?"

Selena's mouth fell open. He was holding a statue, about a foot high, of a dancing figure with the same striped green skin as her visitor.

"Yes!" she said. Then, a moment later, "But . . . not the same, actually. Mine was shorter and dressed differently, and looked less . . . less . . ." She tried to come up with the right word. The dancing figure looked powerful, not timid, and carried rattles in its hands. "Less everything," she said finally.

"Not surprising," Father Aguirre said. "This is a carving of the Squash Kachina, and what you saw wasn't a kachina, just a little local spirit. Although, this is one of the ones they make for tourists, so even that may not be entirely accurate."

Selena's expression of profound bafflement clearly spoke to him. He coughed. "It's not my place to explain how the kachinas and the Pueblo people fit together, and I doubt anyone would appreciate a Catholic priest sticking their nose in. But I can say that the Pueblo people were and are often very skilled observers. The kachina looks this way because that is how a spirit of squash would look, the same way that the hawk or owl kachinas look the way they do because that's how their spirits would look." He set the carving carefully down on the table. "So it's no surprise your little spirit looks similar, but is *less everything*, as you say. Quartz Creek is very small, and all our gods are small too."

Grandma sniffed haughtily, possibly considering defending the honor of the local gods, but apparently thought better of it.

"You believe this?" Selena said faintly. "About there being gods? I mean, other than . . . ?" She gestured vaguely in the direction of the church.

Father Aguirre smiled. "The first commandment is 'Thou shalt have no other gods *before Me*,'" he said gently. "It doesn't say that there aren't any others, or that you shouldn't be polite when you meet them. I'd probably try to talk you out of worshipping one, but . . . well . . . we all make our own peace with the desert. Call them spirits if it sits easier with you. And if you're worried for your immortal soul, come talk to me."

He saw them both out, patted Copper, and closed the rectory door behind them.

"Does . . . does *he* believe in them?" asked Selena. She felt as if she were treading very near the edge of a cliff.

"He'd better," said Grandma Billy. "His mother was one. Nice woman, but I wouldn't cross her for all the money in your city. Come on, let's get home. You ought to take the chicken and the potatoes, but I'll take some of Lupé's slaw for myself, if you don't mind."

After they'd walked home and Grandma had gone into Blue Horned Toad House, Selena found herself wandering around the house as if stray gods might be lurking in the corners. *I don't believe in that,* she told herself. *I don't.*

I just . . . don't believe a little less than yesterday. Everyone was so matter-of-fact about it.

She was almost relieved to find a scorpion in the bathroom sink. At least something else in the house was as confused as she was. She put a cup over it and slid a piece of paper underneath, then escorted it outside.

As she came back in and passed the fireplace, she saw the statue of Snake-Eater looking at her. "Now how did you get turned back around?" she asked it. Grandma Billy must have done it, though she was generally very polite about not touching other people's things without asking. Selena turned it back, shook her head, and turned on the radio.

KQDZ, the Voice of the Desert, played a prerecorded weather forecast, then a zydeco cover of "Fly Like An Eagle." DJ Raven came on and said, "Do you ever really think about linear time?"

"I try to avoid it," Selena muttered.

"It's like . . . it's like horses, okay?" the DJ continued. "Now, we all know that horses didn't show up until the Spanish conquistadors came through, right? But once they were here, it was like the horse spirit, old Caballo, had *always been here*. Like it was retroactive that way. How does that work?"

"Oh god," Selena said, "not you too." She reached for the knob.

"I'm just saying that linear time is a headfu—"

Click.

Selena rubbed her forehead. "I'm going to bed," she told Copper.

Once in bed, though, she didn't sleep. She lay under the blankets and gazed at the map on the wall. There were tiny notations on it in blue ink, presumably from Amelia. She could only read a few of them in the light from the bedside lamp. Many of them seemed to be draws: *Dogtail Draw. Chuckwalla Draw. East Havoc Draw.* Presumably a *draw* was some kind of desert feature. There was also a place called Johnny's Hole, which sounded vaguely obscene but presumably also involved geography.

Annnd I'm thinking about this because I don't want to think about gods or spirits or why everyone seems so calm about them.

She was utterly incapable of dealing with the notion of gods. Probably everyone was having a collective hallucination—or Grandma Billy was sliding gently into dementia and everyone was humoring her. That Selena was actually thinking about getting up tomorrow and putting cornmeal out for a god was probably a sign that she was cracking up gently herself.

Is this whole town in a cult? Is it like when my mother joined that one church—the really weird one, where they thought Satanists were everywhere, and that people praying over meals were praying to Satan unless you heard them say "Jesus" at the beginning? Everybody's going along?

They didn't seem very cultlike. Jenny clearly didn't believe in spirits. Father Aguirre believed in them but didn't seem to see any conflict between that and being a Catholic priest. Grandma Billy didn't seem like a good candidate for a cult, unless she was running it, and then it probably would be more about mojitos than squash.

For that matter, if I was going to hallucinate spirits, would it really be of vegetables*? There are so many other things that seem like they'd have spirits. Why squash, of all things?*

Hell, if I was going to hallucinate vegetable gods, you'd at least think I'd pick a brassica. Then you could have a dozen different gods for the price of one.

She snorted at her own joke, then wondered if spirits of cabbage and cauliflower would be vengeful.

Selena sighed. There were other, more pressing concerns than gods. She ran the conversations of the day through her mind—had she said anything horrible? Was everyone offended, but too polite to say so?

It was hard to imagine Grandma being too polite to say anything. Maybe she'd gotten lucky.

I did okay. I think I did okay. Father Aguirre agreed to take me to Aunt Amelia's grave tomorrow.

Copper groaned and stretched out against her legs. Selena grimaced. She knew that she was going to spend tomorrow trying to think of every possible thing that he could say, and what the proper response was to it.

He's a priest. Priests have to forgive you if you apologize, don't they?

Oh, probably. But it would be better not to say anything horrible in the first place . . .

She adjusted her feet, much to Copper's dismay. What did you say at your aunt's grave?

Why was she even going?

Because it's normal to go to your aunt's grave. It would be strange not to go.

She had handled her mother's funeral arrangements just a few weeks ago. It had been strangely easy. Nobody knew what to say and everybody was following a script, so Selena didn't feel strange. They said, "I'm so sorry," and you said, "Thank you. I know she would have appreciated everyone coming." And it all played out like that, with only a few variations, and you just had to say the same thing over and over again *and it was okay.*

She missed that.

Walter would say that it was totally unnatural to miss making your own mother's funeral arrangements and that it just proved how broken she was.

He's wrong about some things, but probably not about that.

She sighed. If visiting her aunt's grave was like attending her mother's funeral, it would be easy.

How different can it be? I'll just say, "It's pretty" and "I'm sure she would have liked it here." And "Thank you so much, it's good to know she was taken care of." Treat Father Aguirre like the man who ran the funeral home.

"It's pretty," she said, under her breath, trying to commit the words to muscle memory. "I'm sure she would have liked it here."

Copper, who was used to her human muttering to herself, sighed in her sleep.

Chapter 8

It *was* pretty, as it turned out—a hard, rocky beauty, on the hillside, with a great saguaro rising a few yards away. There was no gravestone, only a wooden cross lashed together with wire.

"We'd have put her under the saguaro, but you have to be careful of the roots," said Father Aguirre. The sun was starting to set over the hillside and the hard blue of the sky had softened. "The saguaros are tough as nails in some ways, and very fragile in others."

"It's beautiful," said Selena. "I'm sure she would have liked it here."

Father Aguirre nodded. "She chose it specifically. This was one of her favorite places to come. She'd sit on the rock there."

It had been a long walk from the church, but they were only about ten minutes from Jackrabbit Hole House. There was a path of sorts, although it was hard to tell what was a path and what wasn't, the way so many of the scrubby bushes grew without quite touching each other. You could get lost strangely easily for a place with no trees.

Selena sat down on the rock. It seemed like the proper thing to do. The stone surface was a few degrees cooler than she'd expected it to be.

It was hard to place the Aunt Amelia she remembered in this strange, stony place . . . but perhaps not so hard to place the owner of Jackrabbit Hole House.

"She named the saguaro," said Father Aguirre, sitting down next to her. "She told me that."

"What was its name?"

"Now *that* she never told me. Only that it had a name." He leaned back, studying the saguaro's many arms. "Names are important. I suppose she didn't want to invoke one lightly."

Selena had no prepared script for this, so she ran the words through her head a few times, hoping that the silence was not too awkward. "Speaking of names—" *Yes, that's a good opener, and we were speaking of it, it's not weird.* "—can you tell me why all the houses here have names? Like Jackrabbit Hole House and Blue Horned Toad House?"

Father Aguirre smiled, but not as if she'd said something stupid. "It's a good question. I could answer, but I'm not sure the answer will make much sense to someone who—ah—hasn't lived here for a while."

Selena kept her eyes on the saguaro. It was harder when there was only one other person. She was never sure if she was making enough eye contact or not enough.

That was one thing she'd *always* had trouble with, ever since she was a child. Part of being "shy."

"If you name a thing," said Father Aguirre, sounding as if he were picking his words out carefully, "you have a handle to hold it by. You can put Blue Horned Toad House under your . . . ah . . . *protection.* It's harder to do that with 145-A South Lane, or 'the second adobe on the left.' The one is a set of coordinates, but *Blue Horned Toad House* is an entity in its own right. Does that make any sense?"

It did, in an odd fashion. Except . . .

"Protection?"

Father Aguirre pulled his ankle up onto his knee and fussed with one of his socks. He had surprisingly small feet. "Everything needs to be protected sometimes. And people change a house's name occasionally, when they feel it no longer describes the house properly. Or the occupants properly, I suppose." He tapped a nail against the sole of his shoe. "Jackrabbit Hole House used to be called Sunflower House. Your aunt changed it about five years ago. The funny thing is that jackrabbits don't live in holes."

"They don't?"

"No, they live in little scrapes. I always wondered why she chose that name."

Selena had no idea how to respond to that. She studied the saguaro again, wondering how you learned a cactus's name. Did it tell you? Was it written along the length, in a braille made of spines?

If it was written there, she couldn't read it. The only writing was on the wooden cross. She hadn't noticed before, perhaps because of the angle. She rose and went to it, touching the letters. They had been carved in the crosspiece, in short sharp strokes, like runes.

WHERE IS SHE?

"What does this mean?" she asked.

"Hmm?" Father Aguirre joined her. "What does . . . oh. Hmm." She could hear the frown in his voice, though she was looking at the cross. "Now that's odd. I didn't write that. Someone else must have come up here and carved it."

"It seems like an odd thing to write."

"Well." The priest made a small sound that was somewhat less than a laugh. "Sometimes people write odd things on tombstones. Or perhaps they meant something else, and ran out of space."

"A friend of my aunt?"

He shrugged helplessly. "I fear that I have no idea. Though Amelia had many friends."

Selena nodded. Grandma Billy had said something similar about strays. Perhaps one of those strays had carved the words.

Grandma Billy had also said that not all Amelia's friends were human, and that Father Aguirre's mother was a god. Selena could think of absolutely no way to bring that up organically in conversation.

"I wanted to thank you," Father Aguirre said, startling her. "My mind's been easier since you've been here."

"What? Why?" Selena blinked at him. "All I've done is eat your food and let my dog pee on your bushes."

The priest laughed. "I'd forgotten about that. No, it's Grandma Billy. She's pretty old, even though she doesn't believe it." His smile faded. "I've been worried about her, out there on the edge of the desert. What if she fell down? I'd sort of resigned myself to going out to visit someday and finding her gone, and then wondering if I could have done something if I'd gotten there sooner." The smile that returned was rueful, and he didn't meet Selena's eyes. "So it's entirely selfish of me, but I'm relieved she has a neighbor again."

It was much like what Jenny had said, and again, telling him *I'm not going to stay long* didn't feel right at all. Selena studied the tall saguaro instead. Two of its arms were still small round blobs sticking out from the trunk. "Grandma Billy seems so alive," she said finally. "It's hard to think of her as old."

"I know. I've always hoped that when it happens, it's very fast. She'd hate a long decline."

That led to a question she hadn't felt right asking before. "My aunt . . . how did she . . . ?"

Father Aguirre sighed. "That was, unfortunately, a rather long decline. She was always a very vital woman, always hiking and traveling into the desert. But she slowed down, and at first it just seemed like she was feeling her age, and then it was obviously something more. The doctor said chronic fatigue syndrome, but he admitted that was just a label for 'you're tired but we don't know why.' It was as if her energy was being drained away by—by something. She went to the hospital, and for a little while, we thought she might be making a recovery. But then she came home, and . . . well." He gazed at the saguaro but didn't seem to see it. "It seems she only came home to die."

Selena stared at her hands. "If I'd just arrived sooner . . ."

Father Aguirre reached over and took her hand. His palms were warm and dry. "She could have written you, if she wanted you to come. She chose not to. Amelia would not want anyone to remember her as a weary old woman."

"But maybe I could have . . . I don't know . . ." She trailed off helplessly.

"When I was in seminary," Father Aguirre said, after a moment, "I would beat myself up constantly. If anything bad happened to anyone I knew, I would ask why I hadn't been there to stop it. If I'd paid attention, or been present, or even just prayed harder, surely I could have done something. Finally one of my teachers took me aside and said, 'Manuel, you are not God. You aren't omnipotent. Wanting to help is good, but this belief that you, personally, have so much power to affect the universe is starting to border on personal idolatry.'" He snorted. "He wasn't wrong."

"Did that help?" Selena asked.

"Not really, but at least then I felt guilty about feeling guilty, which is *very* Catholic." His laugh was infectious and Selena joined in.

They sat together in silence for a little while after that, but it didn't feel awkward. Perhaps priests understood silence better than most people.

"We should be getting back," said Father Aguirre finally. "Or I should be, at any rate." He stood up, dusting off his trousers. "If you're not familiar with the desert, I'd suggest going back soon. It's easy to lose your way in the dark and accidentally run into a cholla."

"Cholla?"

He pointed through the growing dusk to a plant that looked like an odd, misshapen lollipop, covered in a thick fuzz of spines. "Cholla. You'll swear you haven't come anywhere near it, and then you'll have a ball of it attached to your leg, and you'll be pulling bits out for hours. If Copper hasn't run afoul of some yet, she probably will—most dogs have to learn that one the hard way."

"Oh *no*," said Selena. Copper had been left with Grandma Billy and was probably being alternately plied with treats and abused by the peacock.

"'Fraid so. Bring her down to the rectory if she does, I've got pliers and a lot of experience pulling out spines." He smiled.

They parted ways at the road. He tipped a little wave to her, almost a salute, and then made his way back toward the town. He was a tall, dark figure on the pale-white road.

She walked up the steps to Jackrabbit Hole House. *Protection. Hmm.*

It was only a few minutes before there was a knock on the door. Selena opened it, and Copper strolled through, looking as pleased as a dog full of treats can look.

"Hey," said Grandma, holding up a pitcher. "Figured you could use a drink. I made desert mojitos."

"Desert mojitos?"

"You use sage instead of mint. We got lime and honey too." She rattled the pitcher and ice clicked against the sides.

"What about the rum?"

"Best not inquire."

"Right, then," said Selena. She opened the back door and they settled down into rocking chairs. Copper stretched out between them. The sky was a blaze of orange and red, shading to violet at the top.

"Saw the grave, then," said Grandma, pouring. "Everything shipshape?"

"It's a good spot," said Selena. She couldn't help but think of her mother's grave, a flat slab with angels stamped on it, in the middle of a flat field of hundreds of other slabs. She didn't know if any part of your spirit hung around after you were buried, but if they did, at least Aunt Amelia would get to watch quail and lizards.

"She liked that place," said Grandma. "We did a little ceremony up there for her and everything. Father Aguirre would have bent the rules and buried her in the churchyard if I'd leaned on him, but I figured she'd like it better up there."

Selena nodded. "Mom's in a church cemetery," she said. "Never any question about that."

"Ah, yeah. Amelia said her sister was a Holy Roller, but that was as far as she ever got."

"Right," said Selena with a sigh. "That's my mom." Did she want to talk about it? Maybe she did. These days, her past seemed less like a tragedy and more like an unpleasant chore to be got through as quickly as possible. Maybe it was time to get through the chore. "See, my mother was really into Jesus."

Grandma Billy snorted.

"Like *really*. And Jesus, um, agreed with all her opinions. So if you did what she wanted, you were Mama's little angel, and if you didn't, there was a demon in you. That went for everything. I don't mean just big things." Selena stared into her drink. "Like if I didn't want her to use the curling iron on my hair before church, it was the devil talking. Or if I wanted to wear sneakers instead of saddle shoes. Jesus was not okay with that."

"Didn't figure Jesus went in for the small stuff," said Grandma Billy. Merv the peacock yelled somewhere nearby, which made Copper lift her head briefly, then drop it back to her paws.

Selena slugged back more mojito. "Apparently he has a real hard-on for saddle shoes. I never figured it out."

Grandma Billy cackled appreciatively.

"Anyway, I knew it was nuts. I mean, you couldn't *not* know. It wasn't like anybody else I knew believed that stuff. And Aunt Amelia—the couple times she visited—she was super nice, but she'd tell Mom, 'Don't pull that demon shit with me.' I thought she was *so cool* for saying that."

Grandma raised her glass in a toast to the absent Amelia.

"Once I went to college I didn't go back much. Mom was okay with me going to a good Christian school out of state, and I didn't apply to any local ones, just in case. I wanted to get as far away as I could. I didn't go back much, and I sure wouldn't bring any of my boyfriends home. I mean, I didn't say *no* when she asked me to visit—that'd be demons—I'd just, um, get busy. With school, or my job. She eventually decided that Satan must set my work schedule, if I couldn't get the time off, but I told her I didn't have the money to travel and she understood that."

"I smell a *but* coming on here," said Grandma.

"Yeah. Sooner or later, I had a real boyfriend . . . well, I mean, he was my partner, that was Walter . . . and I had to bring him home, and . . . yeah. I kept hoping that she'd have gotten better, but she didn't. We were going to go to the movies and she did a full-on Satan's-got-my-sweet-girl meltdown at me, right in front of him . . . god, I could have *died*."

It had been over a decade now, and the humiliation was well scabbed over. Which was, ironically, partly Walter's doing. Selena shook her head. "And you know, we went to leave, finally, and he turned to me in the car and said—I can still remember the exact words—'What your mom was saying is *really* messed up. I'm amazed you came out as well as you did.'"

"Well, sure," said Grandma.

"Yeah, but nobody'd ever *said* it before. I mean, he saw what was happening and how awful it was and he *said* it was awful and he still loved me anyway and—just—*wow*. I would have followed him to hell on my hands and knees. I swore I'd never leave him." She shook her head ruefully at her younger self.

"Well," said Grandma. "Well. Good for him, then, I suppose."

"Mom called me up a few days later," said Selena glumly. "Said she couldn't support such a godless union and it was the devil on me. Or in me. Around me. Something." For some reason, remembering the exact preposition seemed important, even though she knew it wasn't.

It's not like it matters anymore. Let it go.

She sighed. *Let it go* was such wonderful advice, as if she were clinging to the past with both hands and could set it down whenever she liked. *God, if only.*

Grandma reached out and touched Selena's arm. Her hands were hard and bony and had calluses along the palms. But they were also much warmer than Selena's own, and they squeezed once, kindly, and then let her go.

The warmth gave her enough strength to get the last bit out—not that it really *was* the last bit, but enough of it for one night. "Anyway. She said that she loved me and I couldn't come home as long as I was with him." Selena shook her head. "God, I was so relieved. Well, at first, anyway. Going home was the last thing I ever wanted to do. And after that—"

After that, she'd learned that just because someone would tell you that your mother's behavior wasn't okay, it didn't follow that their behavior was any better.

After that, she'd learned a lot of things, most of them much too late.

She could feel tears just under the surface. "Gah," she muttered. "That's enough. I can't talk about this any more right now."

"No reason to," said Grandma. "You don't owe anybody your story. Have another mojito."

"There's only ice left."

"Have some ice."

Selena barked a laugh and poured the last of the ice into her glass.

"Never went in much for Jesus myself," said Grandma. "He didn't seem like a bad sort, mind you, just a little bland. I'm from down by Juárez originally, and his mother got all the attention there. And the saints, of course. Couldn't move in my folks' house for saint candles."

"But you still believe in gods," said Selena.

"All I know is what's in front of me." She pointed a finger.

At the end of the garden, what looked like heat haze swam in the air, and then a little green figure stood there, crouching over a seedling. Selena watched, holding her breath. He shuffled slowly, on his knees, from one plant to the next. Thin green tendrils curled up his wrists and around his shins, giving them a shaggy look. His head was bowed over each plant, like a benediction. A less threatening figure would be hard to imagine.

"Well, there you go then," said Grandma. "If it looks like a god and quacks like a god . . ."

"I'm gonna go talk to him." Selena sat down her empty glass and stepped down from the porch.

She made three steps into the garden, and the green figure looked up. There were no eyeholes in the mask—was it a mask?—and then the heat shimmered again and he was gone.

Selena took another step and stopped. There was no one there, and no place that the figure could have gone. If he'd jumped over the wall, his silhouette would have been stark against the blazing sky, but he hadn't. He'd just . . . vanished.

This is impossible, said the voice in her head that sounded like Walter.

"You scared him off," said Grandma Billy mildly.

"I didn't mean to," said Selena, feeling suddenly guilty. She'd never had someone run away just because she walked toward them before. Not just run, but vanish completely out of existence. "I didn't . . . why would a *god* run away?"

Grandma Billy shrugged. "Like I said, maybe *god*'s the wrong word. I don't know. Maybe *spirit*'s a better one. Maybe he's just a not-a-human person who likes squash plants." She considered. "Seems right fond of cucumbers too. Don't know his feelings on zucchini. Anyway, he's shy."

Selena's shoulders sagged.

She did not understand gods, but she understood shyness.

She walked around the edge of the garden bed. There were no footprints on the hard ground, not hers, not a person who might be a god's.

Of the dozen squash seedlings, five stood up tall and had an extra set of leaves.

"The ones he was paying attention to are bigger," she said, trudging up the path to the porch. She picked up her drink. The ice had melted into cold water with a faint flavor of alcohol at the bottom.

"No surprise there. Plants like him right back."

Grandma Billy leaned back in the rocking chair. Selena had the feeling that the old woman was waiting to see what she would do next.

Maybe it was because the voice in her head sounded so much like Walter. He would never have believed in gods. He'd have claimed that the drink was laced with something or that she'd been brainwashed or that she'd had another nervous breakdown.

Maybe "because my ex wouldn't" wasn't a good enough reason to believe in something, but Selena thought she'd rather be in a cult with Grandma Billy and Father Aguirre than home with Walter any day.

Also it would have made her mother completely batshit.

"Huh," she said. "So that was a spirit."

"Just a little one," said Grandma Billy. She swirled the last of her drink. "The little ones are better. The bigger ones start to get ideas."

"Ideas?"

Grandma Billy shrugged. "You know. Anyway, probably time for me to be getting back h—"

A cry went up from the shadowy desert, anguished and mournful, a soul so tormented with loneliness that it had no choice but to cry out. Grandma Billy came out of her chair as if it were an ejector seat. Selena didn't, but only because she'd heard it before. Copper jumped up, a growl forming in her throat.

"What the *hell* is that?" Grandma said.

"Er, you said it was a fox?"

"If that's a fox, I'm a virgin."

"But you said that horrible screams are—"

The cry went up again, despair given voice, then tapered off so slowly that Selena wasn't sure what was real and what was memory. "—usually foxes," she finished, her voice very small against the stillness.

"Yeah, well, foxes sound like a baby in a blender, not like somebody's so miserable they're gonna puke." She scanned the horizon, even though it was too dark to make out anything more than the shapes of trees. "No idea," she muttered after a moment. "Maybe some kind of owl."

"Owls sound like that?"

"Owls sound like all kinds of things." She sniffed. "I don't trust 'em."

I will be sure not to lend one money, Selena thought. Then, *No, if I say that out loud, it'll probably turn out that she has lent an owl money somehow and everyone here does it and they'll say, "Yes, of course, First Bank of Owls," and I'll go away wondering which one of us is losing our mind.*

Later on, after Grandma Billy had left, Selena went to the back of the garden and poured cornmeal into her palm.

She didn't know how much she was supposed to use, or where to put it. Did you make a pile? Scatter the bits around?

"Well, I wouldn't want to have to pick up bits of it out of the dirt," she said aloud. "So I guess . . ."

She crouched down and placed the cornmeal on one of the stones edging the raised bed. It didn't look like much. A handful of yellow grains, nothing special. But Grandma Billy had said that's what spirits liked, and if you accepted that there were spirits at all, there was no reason they wouldn't like cornmeal.

When you were rude, you apologized and tried to make it right. That was the most basic script, the one down at the bottom of the others. It didn't matter about magic or gods or anything else.

She straightened up. "Um," she said. "I . . . uh . . . want to apologize. I didn't mean to startle you. It's very nice that you're interested in my plants. I hope this is okay. I know I'm not from here, and I'm probably doing this wrong."

As prayers go, it could have been a lot better. Selena grimaced. Hopefully the squash god wouldn't judge her too harshly.

"And . . . uh . . . thank you," she said. *People like to be thanked. Spirits too, probably.* "It's kind of you to look after the plants."

She went back inside. Copper sniffed briefly at the cornmeal, wrinkled her nose, and followed.

In the morning it was gone, which might have meant something, or nothing at all.

Chapter 9

Days piled on top of days, and still she didn't call Walter to be rescued. Some days she ate eggs for all three meals, and some days she brought home most of a pan of Lupé's cooking. Selena wasn't sure how the woman's café operated, since surely there weren't enough customers in Quartz Creek to keep it profitable.

"Oh, it's not," Grandma Billy said, when she asked. "She makes all her money during the two, three months of tourist season. The rest of the time she runs it like a cross between a soup kitchen and a personal vendetta."

Selena felt bad taking so much charity, but no one else even seemed to notice. And Grandma Billy did teach her how to make a "genuine heritage wild-crafted sachet," which was basically a handful of twigs and some scented leaves from various shrubs in the desert, wrapped up with twine.

"How can you tell them apart?" Selena asked. "They all look the same to me."

Grandma Billy considered this, her gnarled hands still tying off knots in the twine. "Dunno," she said finally. "It's like telling apart people, I guess. You might not recognize someone after the first time, but the third or fourth or tenth time, you know who they are. It's the same with plants. You just have to get good at looking at them."

Selena suspected that she wouldn't be around long enough to get good at looking, but she had stopped saying it. Connor paid five dollars each for the genuine wild-crafted bundles, and that was enough to buy beans and rice and another bag of dog food without dipping into the credit, and that was another week that she didn't have to call Walter.

And then there was a day when Grandma Billy was feeling under the weather and called Jackrabbit Hole House—on the landline! an actual landline!—to ask Selena if she'd come water the chickens. Selena had come out and Grandma Billy had assured her that it was nothing, just a headache, and no, she didn't need to call anyone. Selena watered the chickens—the bantam rooster eyed her with deep suspicion, and Merv the peacock strutted along the wall, sounding his barbaric yawp over the landscape—then went back home, called the operator, and managed to navigate a phone tree to get the number for Our Lady of the Palo Verdes.

"Should I worry?" she asked Father Aguirre.

"Probably not yet," he said. "If she's not up and around tomorrow, call me and I'll make a pastoral visit." He paused, and even through the crackle of the line, she could hear the warmth. "Thank you. This is exactly what I meant when I asked you to keep an eye on her."

Grandma Billy was her old self the next day, and allowed as how the glare made her headaches a lot worse, but the thought that she was being useful warmed Selena for a good deal longer.

The garden grew surprisingly quickly. Once or twice, Selena caught a glimpse of something shy and green at the end of the garden, and a shimmer of heat haze. Whether it was a spirit or a hallucination, the hard facts were that the plants grew much faster down at that end. *Which is more proof than my mother ever had from her god.*

Indeed, the only discordant note came at night. Selena found herself dreaming of dark rooms lit by fire, and someone whose face she couldn't see shouting at her, demanding answers she didn't have. Copper was the only witness to how often she woke, tangled in the sheets, crying, "I'm sorry! I'm sorry! *I don't know!*"

It wasn't restful, but at least it only happened once a night. "And it's not as if I have to look very hard for the symbolism there, do I?" Selena told Copper. "My therapist would have a field day." Copper thumped her tail twice and then immediately began to snore.

Selena's third week in the desert was just starting, the day the roadrunner came to the house.

She had stepped out onto the front porch after breakfast when she saw a blur of motion along the wall. Her first thought was that one of Grandma Billy's chickens had gotten out.

Her second was that whatever that bird was, it wasn't a chicken.

All Selena knew about roadrunners came from cartoons, and if she'd ever thought about them at all, it was that they looked sort of like ostriches and made meeping noises.

This did not look like a cartoon. It looked like a small dinosaur, one of the agile ones that hunted in packs. The long, snake-killing beak was as pointed as a javelin, and it had golden-brown eyes that glittered in the sunlight. There was a patch of brilliant blue streaked behind its eyes, like paint.

Snake-Eater, she thought, and swallowed hard.

The roadrunner *moved* all of a sudden, blindingly fast, scurrying a few feet up the path, then froze again, more like a lizard than a bird. That was what the roadrunner made her think of, something reptilian.

It moved again. It was probably only ten feet away now.

It's not that big, she told herself. It probably didn't even come up to her knee. It was skinny, not bulky. It couldn't possibly be dangerous to a human.

Selena told herself that three or four times, very firmly, and tried not to imagine it jumping for her face, that powerful beak going for her eyes.

The roadrunner stomped one foot and raised its crest, feathers spiking like the fur on Copper's back when she was angry.

Speaking of Copper—

The Lab's head shoved against her leg. Selena hadn't heard her move. She grabbed for the dog's collar. Copper leaned forward, not growling yet, but intent.

"Let's just go back inside," she said, in the too-calm voice you used when something was going horribly wrong. She hauled back on Copper's collar. Copper did not wish to be moved. She made a low, breathy *hwuff*, her claws scraping on the tiles as Selena put some muscle into it, and then the roadrunner was up on the porch and Selena slammed the door in its face.

"Right," she said, letting Copper go. "That was certainly . . . a bird. Yes." She tried to laugh at herself for being so silly as to be frightened of a bird. Then she thought about how she'd feel about a snake or a lizard that came up to her knee, and didn't feel quite so silly.

She shut Copper in the bedroom and went back to the front door, cracking it open to look through the gap.

The roadrunner was still there. It looked up and turned its head slightly to look at her. Its eyes seemed to be set farther forward than a chicken's. Selena had read somewhere that predators had their eyes in front. There was a white ring around its pupils, which should have made it look cartoonish and didn't.

They watched each other for a long moment. She could see the mottled brown-and-white feathers, and a pulsing at its throat.

Even knowing how fast it could move, its lunge startled her. The sharp beak was suddenly *right there*, driving into the crack in the door. Selena yelped and slammed the door involuntarily, feeling a moment of resistance—*oh Jesus let me not have caught its beak*—then it was gone and she worked the bolt with fumbling fingers, flimsy little metal hook and eye that it was, but surely that would be enough, it was only a bird, only a stupid lizard-dinosaur-bird that killed rattlesnakes and was trying to get into her house.

She leaned against the door. Something scraped against it, several times. What was *wrong* with the miserable thing? Selena had never seen the old movie *The Birds*, only knew about it from the cultural gestalt, but she'd never heard that there were roadrunners in it.

She backed away, let Copper out of the bedroom, turned on the radio, and moved the chair so that she could watch the door.

Surely it won't just stay *there. There's no* reason *for it to stay there.* Of course, there was no reason that a wild bird would be trying to get into the house either.

She dug her fingers into the loose skin on the back of Copper's neck. The dog leaned into it, growing heavier and heavier, until she finally slid down to the floor with a grunt.

"It's Tuesday," the radio said, "and that means it's time for community announcements on KQDZ, the Voice of the Desert. If you've got something to say, give me a call. Meanwhile . . . let's see . . . Fire Marshal Jenny reminds everyone that our fire risk is extremely high, and if you burn down the desert, everyone's going to be pissed. Watch where you throw those cigarette butts, people. And Father Aguirre reminds everyone that there is a potluck on Wednesday and Saturday evening at Our Lady of the Palo Verdes in Quartz Creek. It's free and open to people of all faiths or lack thereof. If you can't bring a meal, that's fine, just bring yourself."

Despite the tension of the roadrunner outside, Selena smiled to herself at the mention of the potlucks.

"Right. Let's see if there's anything in the want ads that you all should know. Hmm . . . Larry out at the Masonville General Store has a litter of beagle puppies for sale. I'm sure they're adorable, but don't forget they grow up into beagles. Fifty dollars or best offer. And—oh hot damn, we've got a caller! What's your name, caller?"

"Galadriel," said a firm female voice.

Galadriel? Really?

The DJ did not seem surprised by this, but maybe if you called yourself Raven, you were more open-minded about other people's peculiar names. "Sure, out at Rivendell. What's up, Galadriel?"

"Damned if I know," Galadriel said, sounding somewhat annoyed. "Some kind of weird energy brewing to the northeast. *Something's* going down over there."

"Weird energy, huh? Anything more specific you can tell our listeners?"

"I can tell 'em I don't like it. It's all angry and jittery and . . . look, it's *weird*. That's all I know."

Selena started to roll her eyes at the concept of "weird energy," then remembered that she'd seen a god in her garden. Something, anyway. She still wasn't quite sure if she believed in gods, but there had been *something* there.

"Northeast," DJ Raven said musingly. "Does seem like something's going on, doesn't it? Some spirit's in a mood."

"Feels like more spirits are out and about these days in general," Galadriel grumbled.

"Stands to reason," said DJ Raven, as if they were still talking about the weather. "The more human-people go off to the cities and the arcologies and right off the world altogether, with that moon colony up there, the more space there is for the spirits to stretch out. Spirits always do like a good bit of elbow room."

"God knows the historic zones are bleeding people," Galadriel added. "Which reminds me, if anybody knows which end of a sheep is which, I'm down a hand this year."

"Yeah, your youngest is off to college, isn't he?"

"And-we're-all-very-proud-of-him," Galadriel said. Selena could recognize a well-worn script, even in somebody else's mouth.

"You heard it here, listeners," DJ Raven said. "Rivendell needs your sheep expertise. And keep an eye out for anything weird, particularly to the northeast."

"Do roadrunners count?" Selena asked the radio.

"Thanks, Galadriel. Now let's see, we've got an ad here for a high-end fishing rod, gently used . . ."

Selena leaned her forehead against the cool plaster of the wall. She still didn't know how to feel about gods or spirits or anything like that. For every staunch disbeliever like Postmistress Jenny, Quartz Creek seemed to have multiple believers. She wondered how her aunt had felt about spirits. Amelia had never mentioned them, but then again,

Selena's mother had usually been present, and that would have been like waving an entire matador in front of a bull.

She had certainly never mentioned roadrunners.

"Right," said Selena. "It must have gotten bored by now." She went to the door and opened it a crack again.

The roadrunner was gone. Selena poked her head out, scanning the porch, and saw nothing. She gathered up her courage to step outside, still scanning, and then Copper trotted past her, off the porch, and squatted next to the path with a meditative expression.

Selena let out a shaky laugh. "Right. Just a weird damn thing that happened, then."

She turned back to the door and saw scrape marks in the blue paint, at chest level. *Claws,* she thought, *two and two.* The roadrunner *could* jump, it seemed.

A quick shudder ran through her skin, only briefly felt before it was dispersed by the desert sun.

At the potluck dinner a day later, she told the story about the roadrunner trying to get into the house, to general laughter and shaking of heads. "They're weird birds," Lupé said, gesturing with her wineglass. "You ever seen 'em hunt a rattlesnake? It's something. They do it in pairs sometimes, one playing decoy and the other stabbing it in the back of the head."

"They mate for life," white-haired Gordon said. "The pairs you see doing that are mates."

"You're the bird-watcher," Lupé said. She shook her head. "Friend of my brother's worked wildlife rescue and they had a roadrunner come in with a broken wing. Said it was the worst bird he ever worked with. It was always trying to stab his feet, and once it figured out that didn't work, it laid in wait for him to come into the run, jumped off a ledge behind him, and got him in the back of the head."

"Good god," said Selena. "Was he okay?"

"Yeah, but it took off a chunk of his scalp. He wore a motorcycle helmet into the run after that. Said he was never so glad to release a bird in his life."

Selena shook her head. "I guess I was right to be nervous."

"That was a very unusual situation," Gordon said. "Yours was probably just curious. Roadrunners generally aren't afraid of people, but I've never heard of one attacking a human outside of captivity. The biggest problem is that they'll get territorial and go after a dog or a cat."

"Maybe it saw Copper," offered one of the other women at the table, who Selena was *almost* sure was named Elizabeth.

"I guess that's possible." Selena mulled this over. "That makes more sense than that it was trying to get in the house."

"They *are* very curious," Gordon said. "I wouldn't put it past one to poke its beak somewhere, wanting to see what was going on."

"We had a wren get into the café last week . . ." Lupé said, and began spinning out a story of a panicked bird and attempts to wrangle it. Selena let the tide of conversation wash over her. It was only later that it occurred to her that neither Grandma Billy nor Father Aguirre had said anything at all.

Chapter 10

It was just after sunset and Copper wanted to go out.

Selena was feeling like an early night in. They'd been planting again today, in the heat, something called succession planting, and then she'd gone around and watered every little mound of dirt to wake the sleeping seeds.

Then she'd been pulling weeds. There were fewer weeds in the desert than there had been in the city, but they all seemed very angry and covered in spikes.

It hadn't seemed like much work at the time, but she'd found herself ready to drop by midafternoon. Even a nap hadn't revived her much.

"Desert air," said Grandma Billy. "You'll get used to it."

"I'm only staying a few weeks," muttered Selena, as if she had not been here for three weeks already, as if she had not just planted an entire garden's worth of seeds.

"Sure," said Grandma. "Sure."

Had it really been three weeks? She tried to do the math in her head, and that's what it looked like.

It had been . . . easy. She woke up and ate and she worked in the garden with Grandma Billy, and she had lunch. Three or four times a week, they walked into town and had the evening meal with Father Aguirre. She wasn't expected to talk, and if she did, nobody acted as if she'd said anything unusual.

And Grandma doesn't tell me, when we're walking home, that I've offended everybody and they're too polite to say so. Father Aguirre even told me last time that he was glad I'd been coming, that it was nice to have a new face at the table, and he said it like a person, not like a priest.

Grandma had, in fact, promised to take Selena out foraging for young prickly pear pads to sell to Connor at the store. It was beginning to seem like the only way she was going to make money was the same way the locals did.

It'll be a couple months to the corn smut season. I guess I could stay that long. Grandma says that's the good money.

Would it really be so bad, staying here for a few months?

In a few months, Walter will have given up trying to find me. I mean, I told him not to—I sent the email—but it's not like he would have paid attention to that. She rolled her eyes. At least there was no chance he'd find her out here. The notion that someone might leave the city to come to the ends of the earth, surrounded by cactus, would be so alien to his way of thinking that he would be incapable of imagining her doing it either.

Copper wouldn't mind. Copper had chased a jackrabbit yesterday, and even though she hadn't caught it, she was still feeling insufferably proud of herself.

Jackrabbit Hole House was starting to feel like—oh, not *home*, maybe, but what was home, anyway? Had there ever been a place that was really home, as opposed to just a familiar place where she kept her clothes?

Maybe my room, growing up. Or my first apartment.

The house felt familiar, anyway, and friendly. Even the ridiculous toilet made her smile in the morning. And unlike her room growing up, or a succession of apartments shared with roommates, this space was *hers*, and if she shut the door, it stayed shut.

And Grandma Billy had tact enough to tell when she was tired, and to take herself off and save Selena the awkwardness of asking her for a break.

She's a good neighbor. The best. And I'd probably have starved without her.

Granted, it wasn't easy work, gardening. She'd been amazed that she'd ever thought it was. She lugged water from the rain barrel and pulled weeds and sweated and grumbled. She'd carted a dozen wheelbarrow loads of manure from the pile Connor had delivered to Grandma Billy's yard, which her neighbor had shared freely. But it wasn't any worse than being on her feet all day at the deli, and it wasn't backbreaking, and there were pods forming on the beans now and little green balls in the white hearts of the pepper flowers.

A yawn started somewhere in the base of Selena's throat and came out wide enough to strain her jaws.

I'll take Copper out, she thought, yawning again, *and then I'll just have some leftover cornbread and go to bed. I don't think I'm up for cooking dinner tonight . . .*

She pushed the front door open—and Copper growled.

Selena's head jerked up. In the dim light, it took a moment for her to pick out a shape silhouetted against the dark brush. Then it snapped into focus and she was astonished she hadn't seen it immediately.

Someone was watching her across the road. Someone or something. Not an animal. It was taller than she was, draped in cloth. It had no apparent shoulders or waist, its body a straight line, and it watched her, unblinking. It had huge eyes and its face was very wrong.

Grandma Billy saying, *People, but not human people,* came back to Selena suddenly, the words ringing in her ears like a heartbeat.

Copper's fur spiked up along her back and Selena could feel the dog's growl through her legs.

It's a person, it has to be, it's someone from the town, they're wearing a mask, they're trying to scare me that's all—

Oh, yes. Because people from town wearing masks and staring at me is much *less terrifying.*

She couldn't move. The thing didn't move. It had no apparent nose or mouth, only the eyes, but those were definitely watching her. They stared at each other across twenty feet of desert. Did it even have arms? She couldn't tell. They might be lost in the hanging lines of cloth.

There was a sudden rattle, a series of hollow clacking sounds like bamboo lengths being banged together. Had the thing made it? She couldn't tell. It wasn't moving, but where else would the sounds have come from?

The clacking stopped. The desert was silent.

Whether she saw it move or it simply faded into existence, she couldn't tell, but a second thing appeared next to the first one.

Two of them. Oh Christ, oh Christ, it's not just some weirdo there's two *of them—oh god, I think the clacking noise* called *the other one—*

The clacking started again. Copper's growl modulated into a snarl.

It broke the spell. She took two steps back, hauling Copper by the collar, and slammed the door. She threw the bolt, and turned toward the back door to lock it as well.

There was another one on the back porch.

It was standing *right there*, on the other side of the screen.

Selena's back hit the door behind her, but she didn't scream. If she screamed, it would break the horrible trance and maybe the things would be able to move and chase her down. But not screaming took all her resolve and she made a hoarse, choking sound instead and Copper snarled beside her.

What are *they? Who is doing this to me?*

She grabbed for the door handle and stopped. If she unbolted the door and threw it open, would the first thing be standing right there? She could run down the road to Grandma Billy's, but would they chase her?

The house, which had felt like a sanctuary a moment ago, suddenly felt like a trap.

The one on the back porch blinked.

She saw the eyelids slide down over the enormous dark eyes and, oh god, it wasn't a mask.

That's its face. Its real *face.*

It's really *standing there and in a minute it's going to reach down and grab the door handle and come inside—*

It didn't move. It was staring at her, but it didn't move. Her heart hammered in her chest.

She moved sideways, along the wall, to the kitchen, and slid the silverware drawer open blind. She was not going to take her eyes off the thing at the door.

It blinked again.

Had she put the big kitchen knife on the right side or the left? She groped for it, found a familiar handle, and pulled it out. It looked stupidly small in front of her. She needed an axe or a gun or a sword *or to not be here in this house with horrible things standing at the door—*

She took a deep, shuddering breath. *I have to bolt the back door. I can't leave it. I have to bolt it. Otherwise it can just open the door and walk in.*

In order to bolt the door, she would have to walk toward the thing. She would be only a few feet away, with only a thin layer of mesh between them.

Even if I close the door, if it breaks the window, it can still come in.

If it breaks the window, it'll have to reach through broken glass to get me. I'll have a few seconds. If it comes through the door, though, it'll be in here with me.

The clacking started again, muffled by the thick adobe walls—*clok-ock? clok-ock?*

Oh shit, what if they're calling more of them oh shit oh shit this can't *be happening—*

Copper snarled again, and again it broke the spell. For her dog's sake, she could go toward the thing. It wasn't courage, but that didn't matter. Love and terror could stand in for courage if need be.

She threw herself across the room to the screen door, with Copper hard beside her, and the thing watched her and the light caught its eyes and made them flare flat reflective green and it clacked like a wind chime made of bones and another one answered from the front porch and if she turned her head, there was going to be one at the front window but she did not turn her head because she was slamming the back door in this one's face and throwing the bolt and then she was running for the bedroom and shoving the chair under the door and there was a shadow cast on the wall from the one standing in front of the window there.

Clok-ock?

She shoved Copper into the bathroom and went in after. The door lock was a flimsy little thing, she could probably have kicked the door off the frame herself and who knew how strong those things were?

They weren't human. They weren't natural. She'd spent so long dithering over whether gods or spirits could be real, and here she should have been worrying about whether *monsters* were real.

This is what I get, she thought reflexively. *I left Walter and the city and came out here where I don't belong so of course—*

She grabbed hold of that thought as if it were wearing a dog collar. *Of course* nothing. *You don't get monsters clacking at you just because you broke up with your partner! That is not how life works!*

She set her back to the shower tiles and held the knife in front of her. Copper stared at the door and growled as if she would never stop.

Outside, the clacking noises continued.

"Selena? Selena, hon, you there?"

There was daylight under the bathroom door. Selena jerked awake. Had she fallen asleep? It seemed incredible—or no, she'd had a dream, it must have been a nightmare—

She was in the bathroom with the big kitchen knife beside her, and Copper wedged into the little space between the toilet and the sink.

"Selena?"

Copper recognized a person she approved of and barked.

"Selena, your door's locked . . ."

It wasn't a dream. It hadn't been. She'd locked the door and grabbed the knife.

I wasn't hallucinating. If I was hallucinating, Copper wouldn't have seen it too, but she did and that means they were there.

Unless I hallucinated Copper seeing it, or she was reacting to me hallucinating, or . . .

This was too much to deal with before coffee. She crawled to her feet and fumbled with the bathroom door lock.

Her first panicked glance toward the bedroom window revealed only daylight. No strange clicking thing stood there, watching her.

It wasn't a dream. I didn't make it up. Oh god . . .

She staggered to the front door and pulled back the bolt.

What if it isn't her, what if I open it and one of them is standing there and—

She opened the door the smallest crack and saw a faded sundress. She threw it wide and Grandma Billy stared at her over a coffee can full of eggs. "Shit," the old woman said. "You look terrible."

Selena burst into tears.

She had to tell the whole story twice over to get it to come out sensibly. Grandma Billy sat her down at the table and went into the kitchen to make coffee.

"So then they . . . one was at the back door . . . it was watching me and there was this clacking noise—oh, this sounds crazy!"

"No, it doesn't," said Grandma Billy. "Or yes it does, but that's 'cause it's a story about crazy things, not a crazy person telling it. Go on."

"So I ran to bolt the back door and it *blinked* at me. Grandma, it actually blinked! If it was a mask, it was—I don't know, some kind of amazing one, animatronic or something, it looked so real—"

"Wasn't a mask."

Selena exhaled. She'd *known* that it wasn't, but it was still a relief to hear from someone else. Someone competent. "Then it was real? There were real monsters outside my windows?"

"Yep."

"And . . . you're frying eggs. There were monsters outside my window and *you're frying eggs.*"

Grandma Billy cracked an egg into the frying pan with a practiced flick. "Scrambling. You'll feel better if you eat something."

"Eat something?!" Selena could hear her voice rising hysterically. "We have to get out of here! There are *monsters*!"

Grandma threw in another egg. "Well," she said. "Yes and no. You did exactly the right thing, locking the doors. They wouldn't have hurt you, mind, but it would've been an awkward night if they got in and all crowded into your bedroom."

She set coffee down on the table. Selena gulped hers, not caring if the roof of her mouth burned. She had too many questions and couldn't think of what to ask first. "Do you know what they *were*?"

"I got a pretty good notion." Grandma shuffled the eggs around in the pan. "Somebody's trying to throw a scare into you, that's all."

"Well, it worked!" Selena clung to her coffee cup, the only anchor in a mad world.

"Yeah, but if they'd wanted you hurt or dead, there'd be none of this foolishness with things standing around and staring at you. So that's good."

"Good?" Selena's teeth were chattering. She was freezing, even though the desert was getting hot and she had scalding coffee in front of her. "Why is someone trying to scare me? *Me?* What did I do to them? I didn't do anything!"

"Nope," said Grandma. "You've been nothing but polite, which means whoever's doing this is a right bastard."

"But why are there monsters? *Monsters aren't real!*"

"Says who?" asked Grandma.

"Says—uh—I—" Selena had to stop and think. She wanted to say something about science that would make the awful masked things retreat from reality, but they'd been *right there* and science usually said that if a thing was right in front of you, you didn't say that it didn't exist, you started trying to figure out what it was.

The only other thing she could think of was her mother saying, "There's no monsters under your bed, Selena, go to sleep."

Her mother, who believed in angels dutifully and demons enthusiastically.

Selena entertained the notion that the things outside the house had been demons, then rejected it after approximately three seconds, mostly because she couldn't bear a world where her mother had been right.

"Lotta monsters out there," said Grandma. "Most of 'em human, but some of 'em ain't. It's a complicated old world." She shoveled eggs onto Selena's plate, and scraped the rest into Copper's food dish. "Now eat something. I gotta think."

Selena would have been willing to swear that she could never eat again, right up until she smelled the eggs.

There was general silence until she had finished. Grandma dropped the pan in the sink and wandered around the room with her lips pressed together. By the time Selena finished her breakfast, the old woman was leaning against the back door with her arms folded, glaring at the doll by the fireplace.

"What is it?" asked Selena.

"Nothing," muttered Grandma. "I ain't got any proof, and he gets bent out of shape awful easy. Gonna have to catch one of the damn things."

"Catch one?" Selena stood up so fast that the chair nearly went over backward. Copper let out a startled half woof at the motion. "We're not catching one! We have to leave! I can't stay here! There's *things* out there!"

Grandma grabbed the end of her gray braid and tugged on it. "Selena, hon, if you want to leave, you can come stay with me. Or we'll go to Father Aguirre and you can cry sanctuary, and he'll put you up at the church. If that's what you want to do, we'll do it."

Selena took a deep breath. When somebody said that, it usually meant that there was something else they thought you should be doing. If it had been anyone but Grandma Billy, she might have screamed.

Instead she picked up her coffee mug and took another drink, forcing herself to sip this time. "You're not going to tell me that if I leave, whatever . . . whoever . . . *wins*, are you?"

Grandma snorted. "Ain't about *winning*. Winning's stupid. Mostly it's about figuring out what's goin' on. But I won't lie—it's Amelia's house and it chafes me to think of Amelia's kin being driven out of it. And you're a good neighbor to a nosy old woman and I'd hate to see you go."

Selena took another sip of coffee.

"Look," said Grandma, "you did wonderful. You did exactly what you should do, okay? Don't worry about that. If you want to do this my way—and you sure don't have to—I'll stay here with you tonight and we'll see if we can't put a stop to this."

I am mad. I have fallen down the rabbit hole. The Jackrabbit Hole, in this case. This is insane. I should be running away.

You ran away once already . . . said a small voice inside her head.

Yes, and it worked wonderfully! These last few weeks have been so much better—so much—not waking up and wondering how I'm going to get through the day—there's no comparison! Running away was the best thing I ever did!

She let out a long breath. It had been the best thing she ever did, because it brought her here.

If she left here, where would she run to?

There was no answer to that, not even inside her head.

"All right," she said out loud, and surprised herself. She sounded much calmer than she thought she was. "One night, if you stay here with me. *Just* one."

"It'll do," said Grandma, nodding.

"Are you going to do some kind of magic?" asked Selena. Even hearing herself say it was insane—but apparently it was the world that was insane, not her.

And that was an improvement.

"Maybe, if it comes to that," said Grandma, and grinned. "First, though, I'm gonna try a shotgun."

"Right," said Grandma Billy. "First things first. We're going to go up to the church and tell Father Aguirre what's going on—"

"What? No!" said Selena, shocked.

Grandma raised an eyebrow and waited.

"I—but—"

She floundered. She wasn't sure why her first instinct was toward secrecy, a desperate feeling that nobody could know what had just happened, or they would . . . they would . . .

What, exactly?

I'm afraid he'll think I'm crazy. Except Grandma doesn't. But she could be crazy too—but it really happened, I know it did, but—

"Look," said Grandma kindly, "I dunno what all happened to you, and you sure don't gotta tell me. Thinkin' your ex had something to do with it, probably, and I'm guessin' you got in the habit of hiding when something bad happened."

Selena gulped.

Grandma nodded. "Right. And maybe that works sometimes, 'cause a lot of people do it. But we don't have time for all that today, 'cause there's a lot of work to do before the sun goes down, okay?"

Selena took a deep, shaky breath. "You're right," she said. "Of course. I'm being stupid."

"No, you're being human, and that's not always an easy thing to be. Now come on."

Selena followed her onto the porch. It took an effort of will to get to the stairs, even with Copper trotting unconcerned in front of her.

"You're fine," said Grandma. "There's none of 'em out here. That sort of thing don't like daylight, usually."

Selena scanned the road. No cowled figures waited for her. The cicadas were buzzing. A hawk drifted overhead.

Copper wandered over to the place where the things had stood, sniffed the ground, and then squatted over it.

She had to snort at that. She shut the door behind her.

The walk felt very long. The space between her shoulder blades itched. If Grandma had not been stumping along beside her, she would have turned and run back to the house.

She was very glad when they reached Grandma's house.

Her relief lasted almost ten seconds, and then a tiny monster exploded from the back garden and went for Selena's ankles.

"Ah! Ah! Get it off! Ah!"

Copper barked and made a brief, confused charge. Selena shook her leg wildly, and her assailant rolled off and into the dirt.

"Oh, don't mind him," said Grandma. "Sorry. He gets ideas."

"He . . . ?"

The creature glared up at her. It had an extraordinary topknot of feathers, like a fright wig, over black plumage and thin, scaly legs.

"That's not a *rooster*, is it?" asked Selena. It was the smallest chicken she had ever seen, but it had a sweeping tail like a rooster and a red flap of skin under its bill.

It made another run at her foot. She dodged out of the way. The peck had been more surprising than painful, but she didn't want to give it another chance.

"Of course he's a rooster! He's a bantam. What else would he be?" Grandma scooped the creature up under one arm. It glared at Selena from the safety of her elbow.

"It looks like a rat with feathers," said Selena, too tired to be tactful.

"Don't listen," Grandma told the rooster. "You're a handsome beast. And a good guard rooster."

Selena dragged a hand through her hair. Copper barked again, in case the bird got ideas.

"Right," said Grandma. "Let me go put him back in the pen, and I'll get my gun."

She vanished into the house. Selena looked at Copper. "Is this really happening?"

Copper chewed meditatively at her flank.

We've gone from horror to farce. Or perhaps I'm hysterical. Yes. I think I deserve to be hysterical for a bit.

Grandma reemerged from the house, carrying a shotgun.

"Holy crap!" Selena had very little experience with guns. This one appeared to be made of wood and metal and unpleasantness. It had a well-cared-for look.

It did not help that Grandma was cradling it in much the same way she'd been carrying the chicken. Selena looked for something to hide behind.

"Relax," said Grandma. "It ain't loaded. Yet." She patted her pocket.

"You're going to walk into a church with that thing?"

"Gotta, if I want it blessed."

They walked down the road, while Selena tried to think of something to say and drew a blank.

Am I insane? Have I gone insane and dreamed monsters and pulled Grandma Billy along with me?

Maybe it was good that they were going to see Father Aguirre. *If this is crazy, he'll stop us, right? Catholic priests don't let little old ladies run around with shotguns fighting monsters . . . unless the monsters are really there. Right? Right?*

She had no answer for herself. Grandma Billy whistled tunelessly as she walked. The white road was hard, the blue sky was hard, and neither one seemed like it could contain monsters.

"Grandma Billy?"

"Yeah?"

"How do you know about this stuff?" *Please don't let her tell me that everybody in the desert knows about monsters and I just haven't found out yet. I don't think I can handle that.*

"Oh, *that.*" Grandma actually looked a little embarrassed. "Ain't some mystic wisewoman shit, if that's what you're thinking. It was my husband, Billy."

"Wait, your *husband* was named Billy?"

"Indeed he was."

"Is it your last name?"

"No. Look, he was Billy and I was Billy Jean, and when we hooked up, everybody called us the Billys, and it stuck for about fifty years." She shifted her grip on the shotgun. "Now, Billy was the kindest man you ever laid eyes on, but his mother was a prize piece of work. Called herself a *bruja*, which is a word with a good bit of weight in Billy's hometown, or maybe I mean baggage. And she was dead set on having grandkids and wasn't too keen on Billy stepping out with me, since grandkids ain't really on the table. And one day after he walks me home, I turn on the light and there's a dead rat in the middle of the kitchen with its guts wrapped 'round a nail in the floor, and the little bastard gets up and goes for my ankles. And trust me, it was *dead*-dead."

Selena put her hand to her mouth. "What did you *do*?"

"Put a saucepan over it and pulled the nail out. It stopped moving then. Had myself a fine freak-out, then called Billy. He knew right away who was behind it, but we didn't let on we knew, because his mother would've denied it and I didn't want to give her the satisfaction." Grandma's upper lip curled. "She did another rat or two, and a squirrel—that thing got into the cabinets and it took three gallons of bleach to clean up the mess—but finally gave up on that. Next thing she tried was something like your critters, only made outta a couple of cockroaches sewed together. That's how I know bullets generally work, at least if I'm right about what these are."

"Good god," said Selena, because it seemed like she ought to say something.

"The cockroaches were a mistake, because I got one of the skins—or shells, I guess—and took it to a friend of my daddy's. He knew twice the tricks Billy's mother did, but he never called himself anything. He was just the fella you went to if you had a certain sort of problem. Anyway, he looked over what was left and knew right off who done it. So he put a line of salt over the doors and windows and waited inside, the next time Billy and I had a date. If they couldn't get past the salt, see, she'd have to come herself, the way she'd done for the first rat. And she did and he caught her red-handed and let her know he knew what was going on."

"Did that stop her?"

"Pretty much. He put out the word that if anything happened to me, he'd be lookin' into it, along with some friends of his who were in the business of breaking bones." Grandma grinned at Selena's expression. "Like I said, he was the fella you went to if you had a certain sort of problem. Sometimes that problem was uncanny, but sometimes it was somebody comin' round that needed a reminder to mind their manners, if you get my drift."

She's talking about a mobster witch. Oh god. The real world seemed to be sliding further and further from Selena's grasp.

"Anyhow, we moved up here to Quartz Creek pretty quick, in case she decided to try something anyhow," Grandma Billy said. "Even knowin' she'd pay for it wouldn't do me much good if I was dead. And Billy, rest his soul, knew a few things he'd picked up growin' up in her house, and I picked them up myself." She shrugged. "No different than knowin' trigonometry or something like that. Comes up now and again, that's all."

Selena was fairly sure that trigonometry emergencies did not often involve zombie squirrels with their guts on a nail, but was still trying to think of a way to phrase that when they reached the outskirts of town.

If Selena expected someone to comment on an old woman carrying a gun down the road, she was disappointed. One of the mechanics was sitting in front of the garage. He nodded to Grandma and didn't utter a word.

Our Lady of the Palo Verdes shone white in the noonday sun. Grandma pushed the door open and yelled, "Hey, Father! You in?"

It was cool and dim inside. The narrow stained glass windows threw violet shadows over the pews.

Selena was so distracted that she forgot to tie up Copper. The clack of nails on the floor reminded her. She caught for the dog's collar and turned back toward the door.

Father Aguirre filled the doorway. He looked from Selena to Copper to Grandma Billy.

"Staging a religious coup?" he asked mildly.

"Not today," said Grandma. "Got troubles. Need you to bless my gun."

Father Aguirre sighed. "Let me get the oil . . ."

They followed him into the dining room. He went to a sideboard and began rummaging through it.

"What sort of troubles?" he asked. "Or can you not tell me?"

Grandma leaned against the doorframe. "Fetches, I think. Not sure, though. Poor Selena here had some damn things staring at her half the night, anyway, and I expect they'll be back tonight."

This is it, now he'll say we're insane, now he'll tell me I'm taking advantage of an old woman with a questionable grip on reality . . .

Father Aguirre frowned. "Why does somebody want to bother Selena?" He glanced at her. "Forgive me for saying so, but you don't seem to be of a particularly mystic bent. And I can't imagine how else you'd attract something's attention."

Selena spread her hands, not sure how to answer that.

"Might have been one of Amelia's old friends," said Grandma Billy. "Could be they're not best pleased to have somebody else in the house. Or might think she had a debt owing, and now she's dead, they're coming to collect from her kin. That's all I can come up with, anyhow."

"What?" said Selena. "You didn't tell me that!"

"Nope," said Grandma. "Didn't want to say it out where things might be listening. They won't come into town, though, or at least not up to the church."

Selena rubbed the back of her neck. Copper leaned against her shins. "Are you telling me that monsters don't like churches?"

"Monsters don't like *this* church," said Grandma. "Mind you, I think that's got less to do with the pope and more to do with Father Aguirre, here."

The priest sketched a small, ironic bow. "I think you're giving me too much credit, ma'am, but we'll agree to disagree. Give me your gun."

She passed it over. Selena watched with a growing sense of unreality as the priest sketched the sign of the cross and dabbed oil on the barrel of the shotgun.

This is not really happening. There is no way that this is really happening.

She had to say something. "You believe there are monsters?" she asked. "Like—*really*?"

"Of course," said Father Aguirre. "There have always been monsters. The ones in the desert are a bit more straightforward than the ones in men, that's all."

"And fewer people complain if you shoot them," said Grandma Billy.

Chapter 11

"I have mentioned that this is crazy, right?" said Selena.

"Couple times now," said Grandma Billy cheerfully. "It's all right. Everybody copes in their own way. Once I've shot one of the things, though, I'd appreciate if we could sorta move the conversation along."

"What if it's really a person in there, and you shoot it?" asked Selena.

"Then some bastard's hanging around staring in your windows and they damn well deserve both barrels in the chest."

Selena wrung her hands. She had never actually known what wringing your hands entailed, but she seemed to be doing it. She watched her fingers tug at each other as if they belonged to someone else.

Copper shoved the food dish with her nose and looked hopeful.

It was coming on evening. They had spent longer with Father Aguirre than Selena realized at the time, and then Grandma had insisted on feeding the chickens and making dinner. The tiny rooster had gone for her ankles again, and Copper had refused to protect her, apparently believing that to maul such a small enemy would be considered bad form.

Now they were both sitting in Jackrabbit Hole House. And waiting.

Selena slid her eyes along the counter, where the shotgun lay. It was probably her imagination that it was exuding menace.

Shadows crept along the windows and the light went red. On the hillside, the boxer saguaro punched at the sky.

"Not too long now," said Grandma kindly. "Why don't you make some tea?"

"Is this busywork?"

"Absolutely. But we could still use the tea."

Selena put a pot of hot water on.

"Should get you a proper kettle," said Grandma. "It's barbaric, not having a kettle."

Selena nodded, glanced up—and shrieked.

One of the things stared in the kitchen window.

"Grandma!"

"Hot damn!" said Grandma. "Hold Copper!"

"Wha—I—"

She grabbed for Copper's collar. Grandma flipped the latch on the front door open, hooked her foot around the edge, and yanked the door inward.

A pale-faced, dark-eyed thing, taller than she was, stood in the doorway.

"Three seconds," said Grandma cheerfully. "This is your only warning. One—two—"

Selena knew what was coming and threw her arms around Copper's neck.

The sound of the shotgun going off was shatteringly loud in the small house. The mugs bounced on the counter and the pot clanged on the stove. Copper yelped.

And then . . . silence.

And swearing.

"Damnit," muttered Grandma, rubbing her shoulder. "Swear that thing kicks harder every time."

Selena lifted her head.

The thing was gone. There was no body, just a pile of cloth. Grandma calmly shut the door, leaned against it, and fished in the pocket of her skirt for shells.

"Is that it?" whispered Selena. (Or perhaps she only thought she was whispering. Her ears were ringing.)

"Nope," said Grandma. She lifted the shotgun and pulled the door open again.

A second thing was standing there.

She didn't bother with the warning this time. The gun went off again. Copper yelped again. Selena thought she was probably shrieking every time. The thing dropped.

"They ain't smart," said Grandma. She reloaded and opened the door.

There was nothing there but the increasingly large pile of cloth. The one at the window had vanished.

"Back door," she said calmly, bolting the front. "Still sticks, don't it? You'll need to open this one for me, then."

Selena dragged Copper into the bedroom and shut the door, then moved to the back. She could hear the dog's claws scrabbling at the wood.

"Stay low," said Grandma. She held the gun pointed off to the side. "And move fast. I don't think it's anything but more of the same, but you never know."

Selena grabbed the handle, took a deep breath—and flung herself to the side, pulling with all her strength.

The door stuck for a minute, then scraped open.

Selena caught a glimpse of a white face, white . . . feathers? . . . and then the gun went off and she actually felt a puff of hot air across her face.

The cloth crumpled to the ground, as if it had been hollow.

"Right," said Grandma. "Shut it."

She reloaded again. Selena knew that her hands were shaking and yet she felt remarkably calm about the whole thing. Grandma knew what she was doing. There were clearly no people inside the robes.

They really were monsters. I'm not crazy. It's reality that ought to apologize.

"Open," said Grandma.

It only stuck for a moment this time. Grandma swung the gun up, then paused. "Nothin'. Okay. May be the last of them, but we'll go look. Bring Copper, but keep hold of her."

Selena let Copper out. Copper lunged for the back door, gave the cloth a good sniff, then looked around. There was a growl in her throat, slowly dying away.

"Around the side of the house," said Grandma. "If you see one, point and get behind me, got it?"

Selena nodded.

The three of them—old woman, young woman, dog—went around the house. They didn't move fast, but they didn't move slowly either. Grandma's head turned ceaselessly, and she even looked up to the roof a few times.

When they had circled the house twice, she lowered the gun and relaxed. "Think we got 'em," she said. "Come on, let's go have a look."

She set the gun down on the porch and pulled on her garden gloves. Selena opened the door to shed a little more light.

"Empty robes," said Grandma. "And . . . let's see . . ." She held something up to the light. It shed small white feathers down her arms.

"Fetch," said Grandma Billy, sounding disgusted. "Thought so. Some bastard got himself a pile of owl skins."

"Owl skins?" said Selena blankly.

"Yep. That's what was looking in at you. Barn owls." She held up the owl skin and the empty face. It had hollow eye sockets and a familiar shape, with a dark triangle at the bottom.

"But—they were a lot bigger! You saw them! And they had real eyes!"

Grandma nodded. "They stretch a lot. There's not a lot of smarts in a skin, but it's got a little bit of memory to it. Enough to give it eyes and walk it around and follow some simple orders." She sighed. "We better take these to Father Aguirre. I want 'em burned, but I'd rather do it there. The smoke might call things."

"He won't mind?" asked Selena weakly.

"Hell, no, he'll love it. He ain't had a baptism or a marriage to worry about for ages. Even priests get bored eventually."

Selena would have balked at making the long walk to the church again, particularly in the dark where there might be more of the monsters, but she didn't get much chance. Grandma loaded the skins and the cloth into her wheelbarrow. "Gonna have to ask you to push. I need to keep my hands free."

"For the gun," said Selena. "Um. Yeah." She rubbed her palms along her jeans to scrape off the sweat. "It's a very big gun."

Grandma grinned. "Ain't the size that matters, as I used to tell my second husband. Mind you, wasn't being exactly truthful with him." She patted the stock.

They walked down the road. Selena's hands, despite wiping them, were slick on the handles of the wheelbarrow. The wheel was well oiled but still made a soft *squeeka-squeeka-squeeka* that grated on her nerves.

Copper paced alongside, looking only mildly interested in what was going on. Copper was taking this rather better than her owner was.

Well, she's a Lab, they're gundogs, she's probably got some kind of gene for standing next to people who are shooting things . . .

The moon was very bright and the pale road shone in it. It was easier to pick her way than she expected. The desert was full of odd, sharp noises that made Selena jump.

"Toad," said Grandma, as she flinched. "Spring's their calling season. We get a good rain, you won't be able to hear for the singing."

Something only barely seen skittered across the road. Both Copper's head and Grandma's gun jerked up.

Whatever it was, it moved too fast to see. Grandma made a snorting sound through her nose and lowered the gun again.

"I hate this," said Selena quietly.

Grandma bumped a shoulder into her, kindly. "Yeah, but you're not saying it's crazy anymore, and I do appreciate that."

They kept going. Selena was pretty sure she was going to get blisters. She needed to get a really good pair of gardening gloves, not the ones from Grandma Billy that were a size too large. If she were wearing gloves, it would help.

I'm thinking about gloves while I'm pushing a load of possessed owl skins to the church. Of course I am.

It occurred to her that she had not been worrying about scripts or saying the right thing for most of the evening. She mulled this thought over for a minute.

There are no scripts for this. My instincts are usually wrong, but—well—they're what I've got.

It came to her, as she pushed the wheelbarrow over a hump, that Walter would not be doing any better. In fact, he would be doing much worse. He would be yelling and demanding that someone tell him that this wasn't happening. Or he would simply be yelling that it wasn't happening, when it obviously *was*.

"You're doing fine," said Grandma, as if in echo of her thoughts. "Just want you to know that. No more than the usual amount of 'this can't be happening' and a lot less than some people."

Praise was rare enough in Selena's world that it warmed her to the heart, even as her skin crawled and the bushes rattled and sang with god-knew-what creatures or monsters.

I am doing the right thing. Grandma knows what's going on. I am not yelling or screaming or saying that there are no owl monsters in the dark.

I am behaving correctly.

Something snorted in the bushes. Something *big*. Copper made a querulous noise somewhere between a growl and a yip, a "what is going on?" noise.

Grandma tensed, turning toward the scrub oaks. Another snort rang out, and she relaxed.

"Ha! All right. Keep going, girl, we're likely fine now."

"But there's something there!" Selena couldn't quite hear it breathing, but she could feel it on her skin, the presence of some large thing in the desert.

"Yeah, but it's on our side. Keep on going. Won't say something won't try for us, but we've got backup if it does."

"What *is* it?" demanded Selena.

"Friendly," said Grandma firmly.

Selena took a deep breath. Copper wasn't acting alarmed. After the first yip, her ears had come up. She wagged her tail briskly as they walked, a dog going somewhere familiar. Selena kept walking, hearing the occasional snap of twigs, the scrape of dried leaves against a body larger than Selena's own.

"Is it Merv?" she asked weakly.

"What?"

"The peacock." Selena hunched her shoulders. "Doesn't he wander around at night?"

"Shit, no. A coyote'd think it was his lucky day. Merv's tucked up on my roof under a solar panel, where he thinks I can't see him."

"Oh."

They reached the circle of the town, and whatever it was stopped following them. Selena looked over her shoulder and had a brief impression of bulk and shadows and small piggy eyes. Then it faded into the dark, and when she looked back, they were in the middle of town, walking past the mechanic. A sleeping chicken roosted inside one of the trucks on blocks.

The door of the rectory was ajar. Light spilled out over the steps.

"Take the wheelbarrow right up there," said Grandma. "Won't be the worst thing that's been in there."

Selena nodded and shoved the wheelbarrow up the steps, wincing with every bump. The metal legs scraped against the steps. The skins weren't heavy, but the whole thing was unwieldy and barely fit through the door.

Father Aguirre was nowhere to be seen.

"Give it a minute," said Grandma cheerfully. "He'll turn up." She set the shotgun down on the table and went into the kitchen.

Copper, recognizing a place where she frequently received table scraps, flopped down under the table and made chewing noises.

Selena stared at the wheelbarrow. It seemed desperately out of place in the rectory's main room. She'd sat at the table and eaten coleslaw and potato salad and chicken enchiladas, and now she was standing here with a wheelbarrow full of barn owl skins.

The door creaked. Selena jumped.

"It's only me," said Father Aguirre. His Roman collar was slightly askew and he had white dust on his cuffs.

"'Bout time you got here," said Grandma Billy. She set a jar full of water down on the table in front of Selena. "Drink that. Panic makes you dehydrated."

"It does?" said Selena faintly.

"Yeah, sure. Especially if you piss yourself." She took a slug from her own jar, which, judging by the smell, had something stronger than water in it. "You got something to put down on the table, Father?"

He vanished into the back and returned with a pair of black plastic trash bags. It occurred to Selena that those were the first trash bags she had seen in weeks—everybody composted everything and there was hardly any packaging to throw away.

He spread them out over the table and nodded to the wheelbarrow. "What have you got?"

"Fetch, like I thought," said Grandma Billy. She pulled on her heavy gardening gloves and picked up one of the skins. Cloth had been sewn to skin and feather with pale-white thread.

"Hmm." Father Aguirre took out gloves of his own and laid the hide out over the table. "Well. Look at that."

"What *is* it?" asked Selena.

"Oh, it's definitely a fetch," he said. "Which is—ah—a thing you make out of magic and hide and send out after someone. They're usually harmless. They're only air inside. A sharp knife would have done it."

He held one up. The shotgun blast had left an enormous hole in the back of the hide, even though it had contracted somewhat, like a deflated balloon. "The shotgun was probably overkill," he said.

"Ain't no kill like overkill," said Grandma Billy. "Anyhow, I wasn't sure. Could have been something worse." She flipped a chair around and straddled it. "Didn't want to put Selena on the line in case I was wrong."

"This isn't a Native thing, is it?" asked Father Aguirre. "Because my friends and I have a professional agreement about that. I don't try to exorcise anybody's god and the nice fellows up on the mesas don't come after me with yucca whips. It's worked well so far."

"No," said Grandma. "Huh, like I'd come to a Catholic priest about *that*."

"You might," said Father Aguirre mildly. "If you needed some of my other talents."

"Well, maybe," Grandma allowed. "But it'd be a bad precedent and I'd go ask around on the rez first. No, pretty sure this was all caused by a well-meaning white woman, and you know how much trouble we are."

Father Aguirre gazed at the ceiling with an expression indicating that courtesy forbade him from saying anything.

"Err . . . do you mean me?" asked Selena.

"What? No. I was talking about your aunt."

"At any rate . . ." Father Aguirre picked up the next skin and laid it out. The shotgun had taken the head off, but the body was mostly intact. The cloth was ancient and crumbling.

"Yucca thread here," said the priest. "Pretty crude, and the cloth's old." He set it aside and picked up the third. "Ah, here we go. That's newer."

Grandma craned her neck. "That's rayon or something, ain't it?"

He nodded. "Pretty well weathered, but you know how those fabrics are."

The idea that something magical had attacked her was surreal enough, but that the attack had involved rayon was entirely too much.

You could have a world of magic or a world with synthetic fabric, not both. Selena leaned against the wall, slid down, and put her head in her hands.

"You okay?" said Grandma.

No, I am not okay, I am not remotely okay, I am the farthest thing from okay.

But she couldn't say that. If somebody asked if you were okay, you said you were fine. That was the script. That was always the script. If she had been in a car accident and they'd cut her arm off with the Jaws of Life, she still would have said, "I'm fine."

She didn't have a script for what to say when you *weren't* okay.

Copper decided that her human should not be sitting on the floor without a dog and heaved herself up. She shoved her nose into Selena's face and licked her worriedly.

"Good girl," said Selena, which meant that she didn't have to answer the question of how she was. She pushed Copper's face away to avoid being licked to death. "Where did the rayon come from?"

"Could be from an old tent. Could've picked it up off a body, if a hiker went missing. Could have just snatched something off a line too. Might have been years ago." Selena lifted her head in time to see Father Aguirre shrug. "Everything lasts forever in the desert. I can ask around, but I doubt anyone in town is missing anything."

"It . . . it wasn't someone in town who did this, was it?" A new weight sank in Selena's stomach. She knew a few people in town now, and she didn't think she'd done anything to deserve this, surely she couldn't have offended anyone *that* badly, even if she'd said something very stupid, surely not . . .

"Well, not in the usual manner of speaking," said Father Aguirre. "A local, but not a human local, I'd say."

She looked at him blankly.

"Spirit trouble," said Grandma Billy. "There's things out in the desert meaner than your little squash god."

Selena pinched the bridge of her nose. If she accepted that someone could send animated owl skins after her, it shouldn't be hard to accept that that someone might not be human. *People, but not human people.*

She shuddered hard, once, like Copper shaking herself after getting wet. "Why?"

"Hard to say," said Father Aguirre. "Spirit logic isn't like the rest of ours. But I've got to say I'm surprised anything would fasten on you . . ." He frowned down at the skins.

Selena shrank. "I'm sorry," she said.

"No, no." He looked up. The light winked off his glasses. "That's just it. You're polite to a fault. I can't imagine you offending anyone badly enough." He smiled at her.

"Some things are attracted to sadness," said Grandma. "And you came in here a nervous wreck, Selena."

"Thanks," said Selena. She thought she'd hidden it better than that.

Grandma grinned at her. "Hey, you got better. That's the important thing, huh? What would you have done that first day if a bunch of fetches showed up on your doorstep?"

Selena tried to picture it and drew a blank. "Curled up in a ball," she said finally. "Just . . . stopped. I don't think I could have done anything."

"See? And here we are now. You pushed the wheelbarrow and everything."

"Grandma," said Father Aguirre, giving Selena an apologetic glance. "Not everybody enjoys having their psychology aired out in public."

"Eh, you're a priest. Put the seal of the confessional on this."

"It doesn't work that way. You'd have to be a priest too."

"I could be."

"You could *not.*"

"I'd be a great priest."

"You aren't ordained."

"Can't be that hard."

"You didn't go to seminary."

"School of hard knocks. *Seminary* of hard knocks. Whatever."

"Vow of celibacy."

". . . damn."

Selena put her face in Copper's side and laughed weakly, because she couldn't think of what else to do.

"Barn owls," said Father Aguirre musingly. "Why barn owls, though?"

"Had to use owls at night," said Grandma. "I'm not saying whoever did this is a daylight creature, but I've got my suspicions."

The light flickered off the priest's glasses as he peered over the skin. "I'm not finding anything," he said finally. "Whoever did this must have left a bit of themselves in the skin, but don't ask me where. A little bit of fur or a drop of blood could hide in all this fluff, and I'd never find it."

"Or a pinfeather," said Grandma grimly.

"From a different kind of bird? Maybe. I'm a priest, not an ornithologist."

Grandma Billy scowled. "Don't you have a book about it? You got all those field guides and stuff back in your office . . ."

Aguirre looked frankly skeptical. "I don't think there's a field guide on earth that could identify a feather that size. Assuming there's even one here."

Selena kicked herself internally, as if she were an engine that was too slow to start. "Are you saying a *bird* might be angry with me?"

"Bird spirit, anyway," said Grandma Billy.

"I *suppose* it could technically be a feathered serpent," said Father Aguirre, "but it would be a long way out of its home territory. And from what little I have read of those, I do not think it would be sending owls to stare at you. No, this is probably a local spirit. Have you walked anywhere in the desert recently?"

Selena shook her head. "I went down the road maybe twenty minutes," she said. "And back to town, and up the hill with you. I'm not really . . . it doesn't feel safe." She waved her hand in the direction of the desert.

In truth, she was afraid that Copper would find a rattlesnake and get bitten before she could do anything, but if she tried to explain that, someone was undoubtedly going to tell her that rattlesnakes were fine as long as you were careful, and then she'd have to pretend to be convinced and she didn't have the energy.

"You know perfectly well who it probably is, Father," said Grandma Billy.

"I'm sure I don't—"

"Oh, don't give me that crap."

The priest took off his glasses and cleaned them. "As I was saying, I'm sure I don't *wish to speculate*. Out loud. Where someone might be listening."

This shut Grandma up for almost a minute.

"Wait," said Selena, processing this. "Are you saying that you two *know* who's doing this?"

"*Know* is a pretty strong word," said Grandma. "I got an idea. I've been wrong before, on occasion."

"Father?"

He sighed. "Your aunt had some friends," he said. Grandma Billy snorted explosively, but Father Aguirre stared her down. "Sometimes friends get . . . jealous."

Selena tried to picture her aunt making friends with bird spirits. There was the green squash god in her garden, of course, but . . . "But she's dead!"

"People get jealous of the dead too," said Father Aguirre.

"But—" Selena rubbed her forehead. "But these aren't *people*!"

"Yes, they are," said Grandma Billy. "Wipe that thought right out of your head. These are people. Dangerous people, some of 'em. Good people, most of 'em. But people, same as you and me. Just wild and not real prone to talking."

Selena flinched at the reproach.

A normal person would have known better—

Bullshit, said a smaller, fiercer voice somewhere in the back of her head. *A normal person would be just as lost as I am. Normal people are only good at normal life.*

"You have to tell me who it is, if you know!" said Selena, riding on that fierceness. "So I can fix it!"

Father Aguirre sighed. "That's fair," he said. "I don't know that you can fix this, but you have the right to know who might be angry with you. But don't forget that we don't have any proof." He looked at Grandma Billy.

"Fine," said Grandma. "I'm old. I ain't afraid to say it. Snake-Eater took a shine to your aunt a while ago."

"Snake-Eater?" said Selena. For a moment she couldn't place it, then remembered the strange little statue in the alcove, and Grandma saying something about it. "You mean the *roadrunner*?"

"Another one of her strays. I didn't much like him, and I let her know it," said Grandma stiffly. "And I don't have any proof it's him, except that one tried to get into your house the other day." She glared at a spot somewhere near the ceiling. "You hear that, Snake-Eater? I ain't saying you're responsible, if you're listening. I am telling her that you and Amelia were friends. And that's true, and you can't hang a person for speaking truth."

Father Aguirre snorted. "I doubt that's going to appease him, if he isn't responsible. Some spirits don't like to have their names in other people's mouths."

"He's prickly," admitted Grandma. "But I'm prickly too, come to that. Anyhow, Selena, I suppose it's possible he's a little miffed at you moving into Amelia's old place. Some people don't deal well with change. Or—"

Apparently she thought better of what she had been about to say, because she trailed off and closed her lips firmly over her teeth.

Selena shook her head. "You're saying my aunt was friends with a roadrunner—"

"Roadrunner *spirit*."

"—and now it's mad at me for—something—just being there? But . . . how—"

She stopped. She rubbed her forehead. This conversation was utterly ridiculous and clearly Grandma Billy was utterly mad and . . .

. . . and you saw owl-faced monsters staring in your windows and they turned into rags of cloth when she shot them.

"Perhaps something a little stronger than the communion wine's in order, Father," said Grandma. "You know, for medicinal purposes."

"Under the circumstances, I think I can do that," said Father Aguirre. He went into the back room.

"Look," said Grandma Billy in an undertone, "people do things, all right? And Amelia wanted to save everyone. She was my friend and I loved her, but she had some bad relationships with men before, and she came out here and maybe had a bit of a bad relationship with a spirit, all right?"

Selena stared at her in utter disbelief.

"Are you saying she was *dating a roadrunner*?"

"Well, in a manner of speaking. I don't know that there was much holding hands involved," said Grandma. "Look, I'm not saying it was *that* kind of relationship. There might have been more to it, or less. But Amelia thought everybody deserved to be loved and maybe she was right about that, but she had a habit of trying to see to it personally, if you get my drift. Works when you're taking in a kitten or a couple of orphaned chicks. Doesn't work so well on spirits that ain't used to human company. Snake-Eater took a liking to her and he didn't know how to let go and Amelia was no good at telling him no, you understand?"

Father Aguirre came back before Selena could even begin to process that. He had a bottle of some clear liquid, without a label, and three mugs.

"Fill 'er up," said Grandma.

"Not on your life," said the priest. "I don't have any shot glasses, or I'd use them." He poured out a fingerful for himself and Grandma, a slightly smaller amount for Selena.

It was raw and potent and had no flavor beyond burning so far as Selena could tell. She gulped it much too fast and sputtered, and he had to bring her a glass of water as well.

"So what do I do?" she asked, when she could breathe again. She felt as if coughing had knocked something loose, in either her esophagus or her soul. "I have to do something! Will those things come back?"

"These won't," said Father Aguirre. "I'll burn them in the morning. It'll be quite a stink, but nobody'll be using them again."

"Snake-Eater's a day creature, puts his head up under his wing at night." Grandma nodded to Selena. "You're pretty well safe from anything but scaring after dark. Assuming it *is* him, of course." She considered. "Not much to be done tonight, in any event. I'll think on it. There's bound to be something."

Selena chewed on her lower lip. *Bound to be something* did not sound promising. But what could she do? She couldn't very well demand that her friends come up with a way to scare off a rogue spirit that might or might not have been a friend of her aunt's.

"We'll work something out," said Father Aguirre kindly. He squeezed her hand. "Worse things have come up out of the desert. It may be as simple as finding the . . . person . . . responsible and explaining that there's been a misunderstanding."

Misunderstanding was a good word. Selena felt the heat of the liquor in her stomach. Misunderstanding. She could fix a misunderstanding.

"You mind putting us up for the night, Father? I don't think I'm up for the walk back myself."

"Certainly," said Father Aguirre. He downed the rest of the contents of the mug. "Right this way, ladies. It's not much, but it'll do."

Chapter 12

Selena woke to sunlight streaming through a window. It was coming from the wrong direction and she stared at the square of light lying across the bed, puzzled, until she figured out why.

I'm not at home. I'm at the church. Yes.

The events of last night hung in the back of her head, but she did not have to think about them just yet, so she didn't.

She was in a whitewashed room with bare wood floors. There was a cross on the wall opposite her, beside the door. It was made of cholla ribs cut and fitted together.

A month ago, she would not have recognized what they were. She felt absurdly, transparently proud that she could look at the cross now and think, *Of course, that is made from the cholla cactus,* as if knowing this was no surprise at all.

Copper's hind end was sticking out from under the bed. She was on her side, her belly pale against the wooden floor. She was snoring.

Selena sat up and the bed creaked under her. The snoring stopped.

After a moment, the dog emerged, making champing noises. She put her muzzle on Selena's knee and looked pleased with herself.

"Good morning," said Selena, rubbing the dog behind the ears. "If it's still morning, which I don't think it is. The sun's too high."

Copper sighed deeply and rolled over to have her belly petted, which meant that she began to slide slowly down Selena's legs and eventually landed on the floor.

"You're ridiculous."

Selena got up. Her clothes were on a chair in the corner. Beyond the chair, the cross, and the bed, there was nothing in the room but a hook on the door with a much-faded robe on it.

She wasn't sure if she was supposed to put on the robe—did it belong to Father Aguirre? Was it there for someone to use, or just hanging there out of the way? Would it look strange if she showed up wearing someone else's robe?

She pulled on her clothes instead. They smelled like sweat and there was dust streaking the legs of her jeans.

Well, after the night I had, a little sweat and dust probably means I got off lightly . . .

And then she could no longer put off thinking about it. The memories came crowding back, as if they had simply been waiting for her to get dressed. The fetches, and Snake-Eater, and her aunt. Grandma Billy with the shotgun. Walking through the dark pushing a wheelbarrow full of owl skins.

She couldn't remember very much of that last. She knew it had happened, but the images seemed strangely small and far away, seen through the wrong end of the telescope. Grandma Billy and Copper had been with her.

The gap in her memory seemed very much like the gaps when her mother had died. She knew what she had been doing the entire time, she knew that things had gotten done, but when she tried to remember what it had been like, she had only fragments where she could see herself doing things.

Well.

Is there anything there that I need? Do I really need to remember it all vividly, step for step? Is it enough to know that it happened, and I got through it?

It seemed like it might be, at that.

She took Copper's collar in her hand and led her toward the kitchen, and the smell of coffee.

Father Aguirre was wearing a faded T-shirt as he cooked. Selena checked for the Roman collar automatically, didn't see it, and felt briefly confused, as if the priest were somehow in disguise.

Copper had no such concerns. He was cooking bacon, and therefore in Copper's world, he was her dearest and oldest friend.

He looked up and smiled at both of them. "Good morning. Do you want some breakfast?"

The script for this was "Thank you, I'd love some if it's not too much trouble." Selena got about half of it out and then her brain overrode her mouth, so that she ended up saying, "Thank you I'd love *is this really happening?*"

"Try that again, maybe?"

She took a deep breath. "Is this really happening?"

Grandma Billy would have said, "What, breakfast?" but Father Aguirre was a more sympathetic soul. He nodded instead.

"It is. I know, it's hard to believe at first. There's coffee in the pot."

"But how? *How* is it happening? How is there a—a—*roadrunner spirit* behind this? How are there spirits at all?"

She poured herself some coffee. Father Aguirre flipped bacon onto a plate with a sizzle and moved on to other breakfast foods—eggs and chorizo and thin green peppers. "First of all, we don't know that's who did it, regardless of what Grandma Billy thinks."

"And how are there spirits?"

"Now, *that's* a complicated question," he admitted. "Let's start with solid Catholic doctrine and move on to the heresy, shall we?"

Selena wasn't sure if that was a joke or not, so she didn't laugh.

"If you put enough human cells together, you get a human body," he said, sitting down across from her. "And when you get a human body, it quickens, by which we mean that a soul comes to live in it."

This seemed like a strange way to put things, but Selena nodded.

"Same with dogs," he said, ruffling Copper's ears. "Put enough dog cells together and you get a home for a dog soul. Are you with me so far?"

"You think animals have souls?"

"Heavens, yes. A God that watches each sparrow's fall wouldn't bother if they didn't matter to Him in some fashion."

Selena ate a piece of bacon, wondering if God also watched owl monsters swarming the houses of agnostics, and what He thought of the matter.

"Now," said Father Aguirre, "as for spirits . . . well, there's a lot of options. I'm told the Koran says that God made djinn out of fire. In the Middle Ages, they thought fairies were angels that had remained neutral during the Fall. Me . . ." He spread his hands. "My pet theory is that they're not that different from you or me. Except that instead of cells, they're made up of things."

Selena looked blank.

"I'm explaining this badly. Okay. If you put a bunch of buildings together, you get a city, right?"

"I guess . . . ?"

"And I don't know about you, but I think some cities have souls." He laughed abruptly. "Which is probably heresy, and I am not entirely sure how one might arrange to make sure that a city is saved. But presumably God has planned for that already, and there are others more equipped to deal with it than I am."

Possibly it was the coffee, but Selena was beginning to relax a little. "Maybe some cities are missionaries to the others."

"Now *there's* a thought." Father Aguirre grinned into his coffee. "Urban sprawl, explained at last. At any rate, to get back to spirits—the sort of spirits we deal with here—I have always thought that perhaps one gets a spirit by simply . . . err . . . having enough things of that sort about. If a city is made when you have enough buildings to get a soul, and a human is made when you have enough cells to provide a home for a soul, perhaps when you reach a certain . . . um . . . critical mass of things, *they* get a soul. A thousand crows cause a crow spirit to quicken, or a thousand roadrunners, or a thousand rattlesnakes."

"A thousand squash plants," said Selena, thinking of the green-skinned man at the bottom of the garden.

Father Aguirre gestured with his coffee cup. "Exactly. And just as you can influence what the human cells that carry you around do, at least on a very large scale . . . well, maybe a squash spirit can influence the plants that caused him to quicken."

"Is this how it works?" asked Selena. "This is what makes spirits?"

He sighed and sat back in his chair. "Sometimes? Maybe? I think it might be something like that, but there's so much that I *don't* know. If I grow ten thousand squash, do I make one really big spirit or a dozen smaller ones or none at all? Do spirits quicken the way that humans do? Was the spirit always there, and it only took the thousand . . . things . . . to give it form? If I introduced a new animal here, would it make a new spirit in time, or would it bring an old one from somewhere else? Could you kill a spirit by eradicating enough parts of it, and would it go to heaven if you did? Are there spirits of—of dodos and passenger pigeons wandering around the halls of heaven? And why do some *places* seem to have souls of their own? For that matter, what are we to make of spirits that beget children, as some of them do?"

He snapped a piece of bacon in half and stared at it glumly. "I don't know. I've lived in the desert my entire life, except for my time in the seminary, and I'm no closer to understanding it than I was twenty years ago. Sometimes I think perhaps it was meant to be unknowable, and I cannot come to it except by faith." He smiled ruefully. "Although the Jesuits who taught me would be quite put out, and probably tell me that I'm not trying hard enough. But I am not quite willing to experiment with lives that seem to be so much bigger than my own."

Selena digested this. It was interesting, to be sure, but she wasn't sure how much it had to do with her current situation.

Then again, if Snake-Eater was a spirit made of a thousand living beings . . .

"Would that mean that a *bunch* of roadrunners are mad at me?" she asked. This was an alarming thought. She wasn't sure how you made amends to a pack of furious snake-eating birds.

"I hope not!" Father Aguirre let out a crack of not entirely amused laughter. "There are very few animals in the desert that I would like to tangle with *less*. Everyone gets very concerned about rattlesnakes and Gila monsters, but you can outrun those. Roadrunners are like . . . small dragons."

Selena had an image of hundreds of small, feathered dragons swarming the doors of Jackrabbit Hole House. It seemed laughable. Then she thought of the roadrunner that had come into the house and thought that maybe dragons would be preferable.

"I don't think it's likely, though," the priest assured her. "No more than individual cells of your body might be mad at someone."

Selena sighed. "My individual cells are never mad at anyone," she said. "Mostly they're just tired."

"It's a good thing that you're more than the sum of your cells, then."

"Am I?"

"Of course." For a moment Father Aguirre was all priest, despite the lack of collar and the bacon grease on his fingertips. "You are a soul who has a body, never forget."

"I don't know if I believe that," admitted Selena.

"That's all right," said Father Aguirre, smiling. "Fortunately, some things stay true whether we believe in them or not."

Copper lifted her head a moment before the door banged open, and Grandma Billy came in. "Morning, all," she said. "Morning, puppy dog. Is that bacon?"

"It is."

Grandma hooked her ankle around a chair, pulled it out, sat down, and looked up expectantly.

Father Aguirre slid the plate over. "If you'd been awake an hour earlier, there would have been more."

"I been awake for hours," said Grandma cheerfully, taking the last three pieces and holding them like a hand of cards. "Went back home to feed the chickens and check on Am—Selena's place. Everything's fine."

"You went back by *yourself*?" said Selena, half rising out of her chair. "What if there had been more of those fetch things?"

"I'd've put the rooster on 'em," said Grandma, unruffled. "Fetches just look scary, they ain't got any real power." She took a bite of bacon.

"What if there had been something worse?"

Grandma's lips thinned. "I may be old, but I ain't dead yet. I ain't gonna lie down and let Snake-Eater run over top of me."

Selena recoiled, thinking, *I've gone too far, now she's mad, I didn't mean to . . .*

"I'm sorry," she said hurriedly. "I didn't mean . . . I mean, you can . . . I just . . . please don't be mad!"

The old woman's expression smoothed. "Oh, hon, don't worry about it." She leaned over and patted Selena's arm. "I'm not mad at *you*. But I've been living with Snake-Eater out in the desert for a long damn time, and that's enough time to get a grudge going."

"Assuming it *is* him," said Father Aguirre.

"Well, yeah. Assuming. If it ain't, I'll make my apologies and take my lumps."

Selena put her hand down to Copper's head and rubbed the dog's ears.

She knew already that she would have to go back to Jackrabbit Hole House. The knowledge had come to her in the night, perhaps, or maybe she'd always known it.

The alternative was to stay at the church or with Grandma Billy. Grandma would take her because she was a friend, and Father Aguirre because he was a priest, but she would still be imposing on them.

For weeks. Maybe months.

Without the garden at Jackrabbit Hole House, she had no way to earn money. If she couldn't earn money, she couldn't get a train ticket back to the city. And that meant she'd be staying even longer, taking advantage of other people's hospitality . . .

The thought made her chest knot with shame, even though she hadn't done anything yet.

No. I'm broken, but I'm not useless.

I definitely need that Hard Worker Fallen on Hard Times card.

If *they'd* needed *her* help, it would have been different. She'd stayed with her friend Katie once for a month, just after college, before she'd moved in with Walter. Katie's grandfather had been a hoarder before he died, and it had been a long month of pulling out box after box, making sure that her friend ate and that the parts of the house they were living in were kept spotless. Selena had run errands and done paperwork and priced out cleaning services. It had been a *job*, if not the sort of one that you put on your tax forms.

But Grandma Billy and Father Aguirre had their lives very well in order. They didn't need her. Even if Father Aguirre said he was relieved that she was there, it wasn't quite the same thing.

And anyway, she *had* a job. Her job was to take care of the garden. So that meant that she had to face this . . . even if it meant staring down a spirit.

She swallowed. "Will you come back to the house with me?"

"'Course," said Grandma.

"Certainly," said Father Aguirre.

Selena hadn't expected the priest to volunteer. "You will?"

Grandma nudged her. "Don't turn down a priest's help. Well . . . not this one's, anyhow."

"I wasn't, I just thought—well, isn't he busy?"

Father Aguirre grinned. "There are not too many sick or sorrowful to minister to at the moment, fortunately."

"You never minister to me," said Grandma Billy. "I had a cold a coupla months ago and you just showed up to make sure I wasn't dead. You didn't sit by my bedside and read or anything."

"You'd throw a book at my head if I tried to minister to you, Grandma."

"Yeah, but that woulda cheered me right up."

"At *any* rate," he said, turning back to Selena, "there's little enough I can do but pray. But prayer never hurts anything."

"Besides," said Grandma Billy practically, "we can make him push the wheelbarrow."

Jackrabbit Hole House looked no different than it ever did. Copper went right up the stairs and flopped down with a *whumph!*

Selena's heart lifted a little when she saw it—*home, I'm home, I can go sleep in my own bed and shut out the world*—and then crashed down again, because *monsters there are monsters.*

Someday, she thought wearily, *I will know exactly how I feel about something and it will not be complicated and I will not have to keep going back and checking to see if I still feel the same way.*

Both Father Aguirre and Grandma Billy looked at her. Selena took a deep breath—*my job, this is my job*—and opened the front door.

Nothing jumped out at her. The inside was cool and dim as ever.

She took a step inside. Copper's tail thumped on the floorboards behind her, but the dog clearly didn't think there was anything worth investigating inside the house.

She went into the bedroom and it was exactly as she had left it: rumpled bed, bathroom door ajar, gloriously tacky toilet.

She heard fierce whispering from the next room.

"Ow! Fine! Er, bless this house in the name of the Father, the Son, and the Holy Ghost . . . Did you have to poke me so hard?"

"Silent prayer! What good is *that*?"

"God hears everything, you know!"

"Yeah, but Selena doesn't, and this is about making her feel better."

"I can certainly hear *you*," said Selena, fighting a wild urge to laugh.

Grandma looked unrepentant. "Don't know what good a Catholic priest is if he's gonna act all demure and modest. Might as well get a Unitarian."

"Some of my best friends are Unitarians," said Father Aguirre. "That nice young man who comes in from the Fair Trade Association is Unitarian."

"Which one?"

"The one you keep ogling."

"Oh, him! Man, I gotta convert."

Father Aguirre leaned against the fireplace. "It is a tenet of faith that trials endured in this life will be rewarded greatly in heaven," he told the ceiling. "Another twenty years in a town with you, and surely I will stand among the saints."

Grandma Billy squinted at him. "What're you implying?"

Selena suspected that they were hamming it up a bit for her benefit, but she was grateful anyway.

She went out on the back porch. A scorpion perched at the edge, raised its claws briefly at her, then scuttled over the side.

"Oh . . . hello . . ." she said to it.

"Something there?" asked Grandma, poking her head over Selena's shoulder.

"Scorpion," she said. "A big one."

"Big ones are better. Not much more than a beesting."

"So everyone keeps telling me. It went under the house."

"Oh, well, out of harm's way there."

Father Aguirre cleared his throat and both women looked up.

At the far end of the garden, a roadrunner stood on the rock wall.

Selena took a step back.

It looked nothing like a cartoon. It looked like a dinosaur.

The roadrunner turned its head to look at Selena out of the other eye. She thought of reptiles, lizards, dragons. Its long tail swept up like a sword.

"Please don't be mad at me," said Selena out loud. Her voice was shaking, but she had to say it.

This part was easy, even if she hadn't rehearsed it. She had a thousand scripts for apology, well worn as river stones.

"Whatever I've done to offend you, I'm sorry. It wasn't my intent. Please let me know what I can do to make it up to you. I'm Amelia's niece. I . . . I want to be on good terms with anyone who was a friend of hers."

"Huh!" muttered Grandma Billy. "Ought to be apologizing to *you*, not the other way 'round—" and then Father Aguirre shushed her.

The bird stared at her. It turned around and stamped again.

Selena took a deep breath and stepped down off the porch. She could feel her shoulders hunching up, but that was fine, that made her smaller, and now she wanted to be small and harmless, she wanted this desert spirit to accept her apology and leave with nothing left owing between them.

"I'm sorry that we got off on the wrong foot. It was probably my fault. I didn't mean to offend. If I can make it up to you somehow, I will."

She stopped halfway down the path. This close, she could see the bare skin behind the roadrunner's eye. It was shockingly blue at the top, shading to a deep carmine near the back of its head. The claws on its feet were wickedly curved.

The bird turned one more time, tilting its beak to look at her.

It spread its wings.

Selena swallowed, thinking, *If it jumps for me, protect my face, try to get away, maybe Copper can pull it off me before it gets my eyes . . .*

The roadrunner dipped its head to her, crest flattening, like a courtier bowing, then leapt down from the wall and was gone into the desert.

Selena's breath went out as if she'd been struck. Her legs felt suddenly weak.

Copper, released from Father Aguirre's custody, came up and shoved her skull under Selena's hand.

"Was that it?" she asked. "Did it work?"

"Who knows?" asked Father Aguirre. "But it was a good sign, I think."

"Jeez, you apologized enough," said Grandma Billy. "Don't know what more Snake-Eater wants."

Selena thought about explaining that apologies were the best tool she'd ever found for making something be *over*. If apologizing meant that fetches in the window were a thing that *had* happened and not one that was *still* happening, she would cheerfully apologize for everything up to and including being born.

She had a feeling that Grandma wouldn't feel the same way. Grandma had made a different sort of peace with the universe.

But she was still a good friend to have. "Will you sleep here tonight?" she asked. "I mean, you can have the bed, I just . . . in case there's something . . ."

"Sure," said Grandma. "Planned to. We'll drink mojitos and play cards."

Father Aguirre smiled. "If you need anything, yell," he said. "And Selena—the house seems quite happy to have you in it."

Selena blinked.

He waved, patted Copper, and went off down the road back to town.

Grandma Billy went back to her house to get blankets and another pillow. She checked three times to make sure Selena was okay being alone for a few hours.

"It's fine," said Selena. *Is it? It must be, or Grandma wouldn't let me stay alone.* "It's broad daylight."

"Broad daylight's when the desert gets you," said Grandma. "But I won't be a minute." She paused. "Honestly, might be that I'm more trouble than I'm worth with your . . . um . . . friend. He and I were never close."

"I'd still rather you came back," said Selena. "But I think I'll be okay."

Grandma went off in a flurry of skirts and bangles.

After she was gone, Selena made a cup of tea and stood at the back door and looked at the spot where the roadrunner had been.

There was no sign of where the dead fetches had fallen. She'd expected rags or something left on the porch, but nothing. Either Grandma had cleaned them up or there had been nothing left or . . . well, something might have taken them away.

The roadrunner had seemed to accept her apology . . . *And that I am even thinking this is completely mad. Walter would shout and stomp around the house, or accuse people of drugging him or . . . something.*

Walter would probably think I was in a cult.

She considered this dispassionately yet again. Grandma Billy and Father Aguirre, ringleaders of a strange little desert faith in the middle of Quartz Creek. Possible? It wasn't like her judgment of character could be relied upon. It was possible that they were both diabolical masterminds. It was possible that this was all drugs and special effects and . . . something. Hypnosis, maybe.

But she still found herself thinking that Grandma Billy would be the worst cult leader imaginable.

And Copper likes them both. So there's that.

On the other hand, Copper had tolerated Walter with the cheerfulness that the Lab displayed toward anyone who filled the food dish, so it wasn't like Copper was entirely reliable either.

She sat down on the front porch and draped her arm over her unreliable dog.

If Snake-Eater doesn't bother me again—if this was all a misunderstanding—would I still want to stay?

She dug around in the hollow space under her sternum and found that the answer was probably *yes*.

Until I get a train ticket, anyway.

The thought of the train seemed distant and unimportant. What did she want to go back for, anyway? To go to yet another strange place. To an apartment that wouldn't be hers, and probably she'd have to share with another person, and that meant finding a place that would take Copper. Hard enough when you already had someplace to live, let alone when you were sitting at a train station making phone calls.

And then a strange job. Having to learn all the new scripts for the new work and the new people. Dashing home at lunch to take Copper out.

Copper was much happier in the desert, that was for sure.

The house seems happy to have me in it, Father Aguirre said.

Cicadas rattled in the paloverde trees. The air shimmered with heat, but nothing more.

Does that make three of us, then? Me and the dog and the house, happier together?

She searched, and found that the answer, once again, was probably yes.

Chapter 13

Grandma Billy was back before sunset, carrying a load of blankets slung over her back and holding a pitcher that dripped with condensation.

"Should we really be drinking?" asked Selena, staring at the jar. She could smell sage and alcohol from here. "What if something comes out?"

"Told you, the stuff at night is just to scare you," said Grandma. "Get enough of this in you and you won't scare easy."

"I may be more scared of the mojitos than the monsters," said Selena dryly, but she got two mason jars from the cupboard anyway.

They sat down on the back porch together with the pitcher between them, the way they had several times before. Selena kept looking for the roadrunner, until it got too dark to see more than dim shapes.

Are there more fetches out there? Am I going to turn my head and one will be standing next to me?

"So tell me about this husband of yours," said Grandma, more or less out of the blue.

Selena blinked. "Eh? What? Walter? He's not my husband, just my partner. I mean, we didn't get married." That was one of the few sensible things she'd done, not marrying him. It made the split so much easier. "Why do you ask?" He wasn't fun to think about, but it turned out that thinking about fetches suddenly appearing was even worse.

"'Cause I'm nosy."

"Oh. Uh." She glanced at Grandma, but the older woman had a faint, interested smile and nothing more. "Well, I lived with him."

"We all make mistakes."

Selena snorted. A mistake. God. If she could stuff Walter into a neat little box labeled *mistake*, the world would be so much easier!

"He wasn't a mistake at first," she said cautiously. "I mean . . . I was in pretty bad shape from my mom and he understood all that, and he was okay with it. It was good at first. But then . . . well . . . *you've* been married . . ."

She stared into her mason jar. She still wasn't entirely sure about this "desert mojito" thing. It tasted like sagebrush smelled, or at least what sagebrush would smell like if it were grown in the middle of a distillery.

"You know what it's like," she said finally. "When you have to live with somebody."

"Eh, yeah . . ." Grandma Billy poured herself another slug of mojito. "The first one was pretty, but not worth much. Fun to date but awful to live with. 'Course, that was back in the day, when they were still calling me *sir* instead of *ma'am*, and I wasn't thinking too straight myself."

"Sir?" said Selena blankly.

"It's ma'am now, of course."

"No, I mean, of course it's . . . wait . . ."

There was a lengthy pause while the light dawned. "Um," said Selena. "I. Um."

She flailed for a script and couldn't find one. For some reason, all she could see in her mind was the employee handbook from the deli, which had a page on addressing transgender employees. *It is very important to address the employee by their preferred pronouns. Failure to do so will be grounds for a Human Resources complaint.*

That line had been highlighted. *Oh god, I didn't misgender her, did I? That's bad—you* don't *do that, that's the thing you don't* ever *do—I mean, I didn't know, but oh god, have I said "man" or "dude" or called her a wise guy I can't remember—*

She had a sudden panicked feeling that if she turned around, someone from HR would be standing behind her *right this minute.*

Except it would be even worse because Grandma Billy was a *friend* and not an employee, which would mean there was an HR for *friends* and . . .

"Close your mouth, dear, you're gonna catch moths," said Grandma Billy, much amused.

"I'm sorry," said Selena. "I haven't said anything horribly offensive to you, have I?"

"You insulted my rooster. I haven't forgotten that. That rooster may not look like much, but his sire was Dynamo, who once went six rounds with a javelina and sent that pig crying back to his mommy. That rooster has hidden depths."

"Grandma!"

She grinned. "Lord, you're fine. It ain't any kind of secret. It's been forty-seven years since I made the switch, all the hard bits got knocked off a long time ago."

"I didn't know," said Selena meekly.

"No reason you should. Never met a person so resistant to gossip." She shrugged. "Had to stop getting the shots when I hit seventy. That was a bitch. You ever have a hot flash in a desert?" She took another slug of mojito and shuddered theatrically.

The silence that followed was awkward but companionable. A white moth spiraled raggedly toward the yucca flowers.

I guess that sort of explains why Billy's mother thought grandkids weren't on the table. Although they could have adopted or had a surrogate, so she was just being awful. In addition to the bit with the dead rats. "So anyway, you've been married . . ." said Selena, trying to pick up the thread of the conversation again.

"Oh yeah. Couple times."

"Anyway, once Walter and I had lived together for a while, it got . . . not good." She tried to fit words around it. "Like, he knew I have a hard time talking to new people. So then if we hired someone new at the deli, and I told him about it, he'd start asking if I'd screwed up, if I'd offended them.

And if I hadn't worried about it before, then I started to. And it went from a thing that I was worried about to a thing that he *made* me worry about."

"You ain't bad with new people, you know," said Grandma. "I mean, you said it tires you out, and I believe that for sure, but you fake it as well as anybody."

"Do I?" Selena rubbed her hand over her face. "I keep worrying I've said something horrible . . ."

"Lord, no. I think people are more worried about offending *you*."

This was a sufficiently novel thought that Selena had to pour herself another mojito.

"He wasn't all bad," she said, feeling guilty. Walter had gotten her away from her mother. It was just that there had been nobody left after that to get her away from Walter.

"Hardly anybody is," said Grandma Billy.

"He didn't hit me or anything."

"That's a damn low bar to clear."

"Yeah." Selena sighed. "Yeah, it is. And . . . yeah, okay, it was pretty bad. But I was so tired working at the deli and then coming home and getting picked apart—and he just wanted to *help*, I know he wanted me to be *better*, maybe he just wasn't very good at making people better . . ."

Grandma said nothing. Selena heard the glass rattle as she drank.

"And you know, there's that point where you're like, 'I love you, but you're loading the dishwasher wrong'?"

"Twenty-seven years with Billy," said Grandma, snorting. "Twenty-seven years, and every damn dish had to soak for three days. Not that we had a dishwasher, but he'd leave things in the sink." She glared at her mojito. "I miss him something fierce, even now, but by *god*, my sink is clean."

Selena grinned, but it faded. "Maybe it was just that. He loved me. I'm just not good at things, and it bothered him."

"Maybe. But I didn't nag Billy about dishes in the sink for twenty-seven years either. I realized it wasn't going to change and I learned to deal with it."

Selena nodded gloomily. "Anyway. A point hit where . . . well, some stuff at work was hard and my mother was being exhausting and Walter was trying to help, I guess, and then it all just got to be too much. I had a bit of a nervous breakdown."

Grandma did not respond to this with shock or horror. "Huh. Never had one myself. Always thought they sounded interesting."

"It wasn't. I couldn't stop crying for three days. I got so tired of it. I wasn't even crying at anything. I'd make a sandwich and cry. I'd drive and cry at stoplights. I wasn't even sad, you understand, I just . . . *couldn't.*" She swallowed, remembering the sheer banality of it all, that apparently she was now just a person who cried all the time for no reason. Walter had tried reason and logic and all she'd wanted was to just be left alone long enough to stop crying, but he just kept coming in and talking to her as if he could somehow argue her out of it and she finally snapped and said, "*I'm* not crying, my *face* is crying, it's got nothing to do with me." She'd come out of it feeling unable to trust her own brain, which had, after all, failed her spectacularly. Everything had gotten worse after that. It left her obsessively memorizing her scripts because she couldn't be trusted to act normal on the fly, as if all her hard-won skills at simply being around other people had fallen by the wayside. "Anyway. Walter tried to help, and I know he meant well, but . . ."

"Sounds like you're well out of it," said Grandma Billy. "Having people picking at you all the time is hard enough. Acting like it's for your own good, that's just too damn much."

"Yeah." Selena lifted her glass in toast to her absent mother. "That was the last good turn Mom did me. She died, and I had to go deal with things. Walter couldn't. He couldn't get away from work for that long. And we were sure I'd screw it up, but it turns out it's easy. I mean, there's lots of paperwork, but there's a system, you know? You just go down the list. And everybody expects you to be broken up, so it was okay if I had to stop and be alone for a little while. That was *normal.* It was like closing the deli at night. I just had to do the things and check the boxes and it went . . . fine."

"That's good."

Selena nodded. "And the thing was . . . I was staying in my mother's house and he wasn't there and . . . oh god, it was so *easy*. At first I thought that it was horrible of me and I must hate my mother because I was so relaxed now that she was dead. But then he'd call and I'd get tense again and I realized it wasn't her, it was *him*, and that I was calm because I didn't have to listen to him pick apart my day over and over . . ."

"Christ. No wonder. That'd drive a body to more than drink."

"I was going to go back. It hadn't occurred to me not to go back. But then I was sitting there looking at flights and I suddenly thought, *What if I don't?*" She shook her head. She didn't think she could explain to anyone, even Grandma, what that moment had been like. How the whole world had stopped around her and the thought had rung inside her skull like a bell, leaving great tolling echoes behind. "There was only a little money left from Mom's insurance—I didn't dare take any out of our joint account, he'd have known right away—and I told him I had to stay an extra day to talk to the Realtor and then I just got on the train. Mom hadn't thrown away Aunt Amelia's old postcards. I knew the address. And at the first stop, I used a pay phone and I called the deli and told them I had to quit." She sighed. She still felt guilty about leaving them short-handed.

She stared dry-eyed into the mojito. Her last act before she'd gone out of cell service had been to send Walter an email saying that she was sorry but it was over, and she needed time before she talked to him again. Then she'd turned off her phone because he was going to call her and talk to her and he would talk to her until he wore her down and she came back.

"Well, you got out here eventually," said Grandma. "That's the important thing." She raised her glass. "Good job, you."

It was full dark. The stars blazed overhead. Copper snored at Selena's feet.

"We should probably turn in," said Grandma.

Selena slugged back the last of her drink and followed obediently.

It occurred to her, as she made up a nest of blankets in front of the fireplace, that she had not thought about fetches after Grandma had asked her about Walter.

And nothing bad had happened.

She went to sleep with Copper curled up warm against her back and nothing bad continued to happen for the rest of the night.

Selena got up in the morning and the world was still there. Copper ambled outside and peed on a bush that looked dead, and then sniffed around for rabbits. Finding nothing immediately interesting, she came back up the stairs and dropped on the porch with a *whumph.*

Grandma was on the porch, sitting in a rocking chair. Selena grunted and went into the bathroom to splash water on her face.

"Are you to take her place?"

"What?" She looked over her shoulder. "What did you say?"

There was no immediate answer. She wiped her hands off on her jeans and went to the door. "Sorry, what did you say?"

"Eh?" said Grandma. "Didn't say anything."

"I'm hearing things," said Selena.

"Well, that happens. The desert's full of voices."

Still half asleep, she thought. *That must be it.* Maybe it had been a leftover fragment of dream.

Maybe I'm losing my mind, she thought, almost reflexively. Normally she would worry about that, but she had thought it so many times recently that there didn't seem to be much point in rehashing it so soon.

Instead she had coffee and went out to work in the garden.

Grandma left at midday. "I'll stay another night if you want," she said, "but I'm guessin' you'd rather get some time without somebody chattering at you. I gotta go feed the chickens, but you know where to find me."

This was true on multiple counts.

She did not see the squash god or the roadrunner. She saw a scorpion and shut Copper in the house, then scooped it up with the shovel and carried it out of the garden.

Afterward she thought, *I just took care of that and nobody helped. My hands didn't shake at all. I am a person who can roust scorpions by myself.*

Walter couldn't have done that without freaking out.

She cooked herself dinner and ate it all while Copper crunched her dog food under the table. She washed the dishes and dried them, then dropped onto the couch and stared at the bookcase. She'd been trying to ration out her aunt's journals, since when she finished those, she was down to such page-turners as *Field Guide to Minerals of the Southwest*, but it occurred to her that if Amelia had been involved with Snake-Eater, she might have written about it. She began pulling down journals and checking dates, wishing that her aunt had been a bit better about shelving things in order.

The stars came out over the garden wall. Insects made skittery, chattery noises. DJ Raven announced that they had been personally contacted by aliens, who had said that the invasion was underway and, in the meantime, the alien government had some requests, which Raven was choosing to ignore because the aliens had lousy taste. Instead Raven played Black Sabbath, Hank Williams, and Handel in that order, then did a dramatic reading from *Old Possum's Book of Practical Cats*.

Halfway through "Growltiger's Last Stand," Selena had located the last three journals. She started with the earliest one, flipped past a trip to Iceland, which looked spectacular, and found several pages of sketches of mountains.

Been in a hiking mood lately, Amelia had written next to one. *Went down to the Superstitions last week, but hate that arcology looming like it's going to fall on you. Headed north instead. This is more like it. The mountains aren't as good but at least the sky's clear. Thank god for historic zones.*

From what Selena could gather, scanning the pages, her aunt had been in the habit of taking water, a compass, and a backpack and simply strolling out into the desert, often for several days at a time. It seemed wildly dangerous to Selena, but Amelia treated it as if it was a perfectly ordinary pastime.

She was almost at the end when she found a note, above a drawing of three rocks leaning together, that said, *Came across a local while out hiking. S was grumpy at first, but warmed up after we talked a bit.*

Could it be? Selena held her breath, turned the page . . . and found a drawing of a roadrunner.

That's him! S has to stand for Snake-Eater! But . . . grumpy? Selena had had plenty of grumpy customers at the deli. She'd never had one send monsters to stare in her windows.

Also, her aunt was awfully blasé about meeting a local that happened to be a minor god.

It seems you had hidden depths, Aunt Amelia.

She kept reading, hoping for more information, but there wasn't anything of interest. Just more drawings of mountains, and some notes on the weather, and a pasted-in photo of a sunset. DJ Raven spun up a mournful gothic cover of "(I Can't Get No) Satisfaction."

Frustrated, Selena grabbed the next journal. Her aunt went to Mexico, drew pyramids, drank tequila, got food poisoning. It wasn't until the two-third mark that she wrote, *Went to see S today. He was very happy to see me. I think he's lonely. I should come back more often.*

"Don't do it," Selena groaned, feeling like an audience member watching a horror movie.

But Amelia did. She went back multiple times, and then apparently it became so common that she stopped writing it down. Selena saw pictures of the same three rocks, and dozens of little roadrunners, along with comments on the weather.

When she came across a doodled cartoon of a roadrunner with heart eyes and the comment *Spent the night with S. Wow!* she didn't know whether to laugh or cry.

It wasn't until the third journal that the tone began to shift. *Haven't been traveling much,* her aunt noted. *S gets very anxious when I leave. I tell him I'm fine but he still just freaks out. I know he's just afraid to lose me, but it's a good thing he's cute.*

Then: *S came to visit the house today.*

Then: *Needed a nap again today. Must be from S keeping me up all night.*

Then: *So tired these days. All I want to do is sleep. GB keeps nagging me to see a doctor. Even if she's right, I'm tired of it. S has been very sweet, though.*

Then Selena turned the page and found the next one blank.

She sat on the couch, the blank book in her lap, and wept the last few tears that she had left for Aunt Amelia. Then she carefully slid it back among the other journals on the shelf.

"Well," she said. "Well."

On the radio, a song was abruptly interrupted by DJ Raven announcing that the aliens had been in contact again and they had agreed to postpone the invasion if Raven played more Alice Cooper. "I have agreed to this deal for the good of civilization," DJ Raven announced. "Here's 'Poison.' You're welcome, Earth."

Selena snorted and stood up. "Tomorrow I'll go borrow a book from Grandma," she told Copper. "I bet she's got romances full of dirty bits."

Copper opened one eye, moved her tail a few inches, and closed her eyes again. In a few minutes she began to snore.

I just had a normal day, Selena thought, with a deep sense of relief. She locked the doors to Jackrabbit Hole House and went to sleep.

Chapter 14

The next morning, Selena was pulling weeds—where were they coming from? They didn't look like anything she'd seen out in the desert—when a voice said in her ear, "You are her kin."

She jerked back, landing on her heels, just in time to see the roadrunner leap up onto the stone wall.

She would have wondered if the voice she'd heard was real, and if so, was it related to Snake-Eater, but she was immediately distracted by the fact that the roadrunner was carrying something. For a wild moment, she thought that it had a whip, and that made *no* sense, but Selena was pretty sure that she'd abandoned sense the first day the squash god came down to her garden.

The roadrunner stamped its feet and turned its head to look at her, and Selena finally realized that the long ropelike thing in its mouth was a dead snake.

Snake-Eater. Yes, of course.

The reptile was at least three feet long and its head was a bloody ruin. The thin tail, with its line of rattles, was very much intact.

"Oh," said Selena. "Oh, that's . . . um. Very . . . big. Yes. A big snake. That you killed."

The roadrunner spread its wings and snapped them back in, then bowed and laid the dead rattlesnake across the low stone wall. It stepped back and bobbed its head in her direction.

"Oh. Is that a . . . a gift?"

It spread its wings and snapped them back in again. The wings briefly gave it bulk, and there were patterns of light and shadow on them like winking eyes.

There was absolutely nothing less in the world that Selena wanted than to go pick up a dead snake that might not be all the way dead, but she stepped forward anyway. One, you didn't refuse gifts just because you hated them. Two, Snake-Eater was apparently bringing her a peace offering, and she definitely didn't want to reject that. So she steeled herself and reached out and put her hand on the snake's bone-colored belly. It was the same temperature as the air and it didn't move.

"Thank you," Selena made herself say, and bowed back to the roadrunner. "It's very . . . ah . . . impressive."

It let out a low string of mechanical sounds, clicks and whirs, like a piece of clockwork. Selena felt her eyes go wide. Then it nodded, as if it had concluded some important piece of business, hopped off the wall, and scurried away into the desert.

Selena looked down at the dead rattlesnake. If she threw it away, would that count as rejecting the gift?

Well, I'm certainly not going to eat it!

She sighed, placed the dead rattlesnake gently on the porch, and went to get the shovel to bury it next to the house.

Six days passed. She borrowed two books from Grandma and read them both. They were indeed romances and the dirty bits were very impressive. She returned them and got another two, which were equally impressive, and then Grandma took her to the town library, which was not at all impressive, but had a room full of dusty paperbacks. It turned out that Gordon, the elderly bird-watcher, was also the librarian. Selena filled out a form and he gave her her own library card. She stared at the little square of card stock and tried not to think about how this was one more thing tying her to Quartz Creek.

There was an internet connection at the library. She thought of going online and seeing . . . what? All the news of world events that she couldn't change, celebrities whose names she couldn't remember. *Sorry,* she told the world silently. *I can barely manage to take care of myself right now. Maybe later.*

Instead she looked up information on roadrunners. There wasn't much, which surprised her. On some level, she expected every species to have been painstakingly analyzed and cataloged by science, but apparently not. Most of what she got simply confirmed what Gordon had said—they mated for life, they ate practically anything, and they hunted rattlesnakes. The only surprising fact was that they wept salt tears, like humans. The website said that it was a desert adaptation and used less water than excreting it via the kidneys.

Nothing about what to do if your aunt had been dating a god of roadrunners. Well, that was probably beyond the Cornell Lab of Ornithology's purview.

After a lot of internal dithering, she logged on to her primary social account. There were ten messages from Walter. She hovered over them, decided she couldn't handle it right now, and sent him a message instead. "I'm fine. I'm doing well. I'm sorry that I'm not responding to messages, but I don't have reliable internet. Please feel free to give away or donate my stuff if you haven't. I hope you're moving on with your life."

She collected her bounty of romance novels and added a book on gardening in the desert. It was a trifle embarrassing handing the books to Gordon, but he held up the first one and said, "Oh, *When a Scot Ties the Knot,* that's a good one," and recommended two others in the same vein, which left Selena relieved and slightly confused.

She took her books and went home with Grandma Billy, where the peacock screamed at them both.

Selena harvested the first tiny green sprouts of lettuce from the shaded side of the garden. She saw the squash god and raised a hand in salute, but did not approach him. She read more books and returned them and checked out more. She spent a little more of Aunt Amelia's credit and bought a new pair of jeans from Connor's store. Lupé promised to take her to a thrift store in the next town over for more T-shirts the next time she went out that way.

And nothing terrible happened. The tiny nerves along Selena's spine began slowly to stop their jangling, and when she looked at the screen door, she did not expect to see monsters.

Another week passed, then two.

The most stressful thing that happened was actually Grandma Billy deciding that Selena needed to learn how to use a gun.

"But I don't want to shoot anyone," Selena argued, knowing that it was futile but feeling as if she should make a token effort.

"What about them fetches the other night?"

"Well . . ."

Grandma Billy's eyes narrowed shrewdly. "What about if something came after Copper?"

"That's a low blow," muttered Selena, but shouldered the bag that Grandma handed her and followed the old woman out into the desert.

"I thought cans on the fence were traditional," Selena said, eyeing the bank of orange dirt with a pair of faded targets leaned against it. One was shaped like a deer and one like a human. The ground was littered with brass.

"That's fine if you plan on gettin' attacked by a can." Grandma sighted down the barrel of a rifle. "But if it's a person, I'd rather you knew what part to aim for."

"What if it's . . . err . . . not a person?" Selena thought of the roadrunner.

"Shotgun," said Grandma. "But we'll start you out on a rifle, 'cause it scares people less."

Selena felt plenty scared enough. The gun felt like a scorpion, something that you could handle safely but would punish you if you got careless for a second. "Can I shoot at the deer-shaped one?"

"Sure, if it makes you feel better."

It did. Otherwise she was pretty sure she'd be picturing Walter on the man-shaped target and the thought made her feel both guilty and exhilarated in some hard-to-define fashion.

Grandma ran her through loading and unloading. "This here's a cartridge, but if you call it a bullet, I don't mind. And this is the magazine, but plenty of people call it a clip, and the only people who get pissy about the difference are a pain in the ass at the range."

"What do you call those?"

"I call 'em earplugs. Put 'em in."

When Selena had loaded and unloaded to Grandma's satisfaction and mastered the safety, she wedged the rifle hard against her shoulder—"No, harder than that"—aimed, and was finally allowed to pull the trigger.

"Not bad," said Grandma after a moment. "Might do even better if you kept your eyes open."

"It's loud," said Selena meekly.

"Yep, and you know it's gonna be loud, so you flinch. That's why we're using a little bitty .22 to work the flinch out of you first."

Selena thought glumly that life had been instilling a flinch in her since birth and it was gonna take a lot more than an afternoon with a rifle to get it back out again, but tried again.

And again. And again.

When she finally hit the faded red bull's-eye on the side of the deer—not the center, but at least one of the inner rings—she was astonished at the sheer *glee* she felt. "I hit it. I really hit it!"

"You sure did," said Grandma. "If you're hunting a deer, that'll do the job, assuming you've got a proper deer rifle."

Selena paused. "*Are* there deer here?"

"Yep. Mule deer, mostly. Some whitetail. Pronghorns too, but I never could stand the taste. Like chewing sagebrush. Even javelina's better—and do *not* go shooting a javelina." Grandma's frown woke all the wrinkles in her face. "You see a javelina around here, you can yell at it, but don't you point a gun at it, you hear?"

"I wasn't going to. Err . . . what's wrong with the javelina?"

"Never you mind." Grandma nodded to the target. "Now let's see you hit that again."

Selena's right shoulder was sore and her hands had a slight buzz when they got home. Grandma had threatened her with another round of training later in the week. She wasn't sure how she felt about that. On the one hand, it probably didn't hurt to know, but on the other, it was impossible to imagine herself pointing at a living being and pulling the trigger.

She didn't feel like going out to the church for a meal, even though the alternative was yet another omelet for dinner. (Selena was starting to suspect that Grandma Billy was using her as a dumping ground for excess eggs.) But there were green things in the garden that could go into an omelet, even if they were mostly herbs and a few leaves of spinach.

An unexpected glimpse of yellow winked at her from the far end of the garden. Selena approached and saw the golden trumpet of a squash blossom, and let out a cry of delight. She'd been so busy the past few days, what with the . . . well . . . everything . . . that she hadn't even seen the bud form. She picked up Copper's front paws and did an impromptu dance with the Labrador. "It flowered! The squash flowered!"

Of course it did, said the Walter in her head. *It's a plant. What did you expect it to do, explode?* She ignored him, dropping to her knees to inspect the flower. There were ways to eat squash blossoms, she knew, but she didn't want to remove it and stop it forming an actual squash. Summer squash sliced and fried would make a nice change from omelets, even if she'd probably be sick of squash too by the time the season ended.

"Thank you, squash god!" she called, and went inside without considering that she was already thinking like she was staying until the end of the season.

◆ ◆ ◆

There was a man in bed with her, but this time Selena knew that she was dreaming. That was good, because if it was a dream, she didn't have to be afraid or even ashamed. She could turn over and wiggle closer, feeling hands stroking down her waist and up over her hip, feel his mouth closing over hers in a hot, hungry kiss, feel the tension gathering low in her belly and starting to burn.

"Yes," said a voice in her ear, and it was the voice of the man she was kissing, but that was fine because it was a dream and it didn't matter that real people couldn't talk and kiss at the same time. But she did open her eyes and draw back a little, trying to make out his face. It was too dark to see anything but his eyes, which were golden brown with a white ring around the pupil. That reminded her of something, but he kissed her again and she forgot, and now his hands were sliding over her thighs . . .

"Woof!"

Selena sat bolt upright in bed, the dream fraying around her. Copper was also sitting up, and her next bark was practically in Selena's face. Then she seemed to notice that her person was awake and gave her a desultory swipe with her tongue, attention elsewhere.

"Goddammit." Selena was wide awake and remembered just enough of her dream to be frustrated, and a little embarrassed. She didn't often have dreams like that. *Must have been the books I've been borrowing from Grandma.*

Copper was still looking around the room, her nose working and ears twitching, as if to catch an elusive scent. Then she shook herself and hopped down, stretched, and looked at Selena as if to say, "Since you're up already, why not feed the dog?"

Selena sighed. It was barely after dawn, but she didn't think she'd be getting back to sleep. She went to the bathroom to splash water on her face. Her lips looked slightly swollen in the mirror.

Even after breakfast, Selena felt restless and wanted to walk . . . somewhere. It was still early enough that the desert was cool.

She had not been to her aunt's grave since the first time. You were supposed to visit graves. That was a normal thing people did.

"Right," she said out loud. "Let's go visit Aunt Amelia."

Copper was puzzled but generally willing. She ambled along beside Selena. A line of quail scurried away from them and a pair of doves erupted from the bushes with a whir of wings. Copper strained briefly at the leash after the quail, then subsided with an air that said chasing quail was beneath her.

Selena saw the large saguaro looming ahead and smiled involuntarily. It was a beautiful . . . she searched for a word, since *tree* clearly wasn't right, and finally settled on *plant*. Although there was something very un-plantlike about the saguaros. The way they held their arms up made her think of people. *People, but not human people.*

That was a lot easier to accept about the saguaros than about Snake-Eater.

When she reached the clearing, though, she paused. Was this the right place? She'd been sure she recognized the cactus, but Amelia's grave marker should have been right over there, and it wasn't.

Did I get turned around? It was strangely easy to do in the desert. All the bony little shrubs looked like each other, and even though she could look down and see the town, she couldn't be sure if it was from the same angle it had been when Father Aguirre brought her here.

No, this has to be right. I recognize *the saguaro. It has the big arm off to one side and the two little ones just starting.*

She walked around the clearing, peering into every nook in case she'd simply overlooked the marker. Halfway around the perimeter, she finally found it.

". . . huh," she said.

The wooden cross had been ripped out of the ground and flung aside. Selena could see the deep hole left by the foot of the cross. She realized that she was probably standing on Amelia's remains and hastily stepped aside. "Sorry," she said reflexively, even though her aunt was long past caring. *And wouldn't have cared anyway, judging by those journals.* Her aunt had been a carefree woman, slow to take offense and quick to forgive. *Which probably explains why she was still talking to my mother. And why she got on with Snake-Eater, come to that.*

I wonder if he ever brought her *a dead snake.*

Selena picked up the cross, which was mostly intact. The lower part was stained red orange from the earth. She slid it back into the hole and put her weight on it, trying to reseat it again. It still wiggled a little when she was done, but it was better than nothing.

I wonder how that happened. Wind, maybe, or some animal? She had experienced one of the rare desert thunderstorms a week ago, a great howling fury of lightning and wind, gone almost as soon as it had begun. Copper had barely had time to climb under the bed before it was over.

Selena studied the cross, which leaned slightly despite her best efforts. The *W* in WHERE IS SHE? had filled partly with pale sand, and she tried to flick it out, then gave up.

The storm could have done it. Or one of those javelinas that Grandma Billy's always talking about. She'd yet to actually *see* a javelina, but she gathered they were little gray piggy things, and the reason that you didn't have trash cans outside.

Oh well. Set to rights now. Selena faced the marker and tried to think of what to say to her aunt. "It's been a strange few days," she said finally. "I met . . ." She remembered what Grandma and Father Aguirre had said about Snake-Eater not liking his name in people's mouths. "I met an old friend of yours. The one you called S. We, um, had a misunderstanding. It's ironed out now, I hope." She looked past the grave to the saguaro, studying the small holes in the trunk and the scaly gray patches that formed around them. "I like living in your house," she said finally. "It's been good. Really good. I don't want to go back to the city."

Her words echoed in her ears long after they should have faded away, like a crow's caw. As if the desert was listening to her.

As if she ought to be listening to herself.

Unsettled, she gathered up Copper's leash and said, almost in a whisper, "Come on, girl. Let's go home."

When she got back to the house, in a pensive frame of mind, there was a dead rattlesnake on the doorstep.

"Oh, for the love of . . ." Selena hurried Copper inside, which was difficult because Copper was very, very interested in what appeared to be a supremely long chew toy. Selena had to practically carry her over the threshold, like a furry wiggling bride.

She went back out, got the shovel, and poked the snake a few times to make sure that it was really dead, then scooped it up, looked around to make sure that no roadrunners were watching, and buried it in the compost heap. *I know you're not supposed to compost meat, but if Snake-Eater is going to keep leaving dead rattlers for me, like a cat bringing home dead mice, damned if I'm digging a hole for each of them.*

"I hope this isn't going to be a constant thing," she muttered. "For the local snake population, if nothing else." Selena had no particular love of rattlesnakes, but it seemed like a waste. Still, that was one less rattlesnake for Copper to step on. She came inside, gave the Labrador a treat, and washed her hands, then flopped down onto the couch and stared at the ceiling.

I don't want to go back to the city.

Had she meant what she said?

She had friends in the city. Well, coworkers who she liked. But her old job was probably filled now anyway, and they hadn't been close friends. Not like Grandma Billy had turned out to be.

My mind has been easier since you've been here, Father Aguirre had said. As if maybe she wasn't completely a burden, even in this strange, isolated place that seemed to exist out of time, so far from the gleaming steel of the city. And if Grandma Billy was right—if she did manage to earn money from selling something as exotic as rare heritage corn smut and chiltepins—maybe she'd be less of a burden yet.

What if she didn't spend it on a train ticket? What if she bought more dog food and chicken feed for the chickens that Grandma Billy had threatened her with? What if she just . . . didn't go back?

She tried to think of all the things she'd miss. The internet, obviously. Though she'd mostly only gone on social media to admire pictures of people's pets and put up her own photos of Copper. Probably no one had even noticed that she'd stopped posting.

Movies, definitely. Though the librarian had said that there was a movie night every Friday. And access to the internet too, if she decided she missed it.

It was weird how much she didn't miss it.

But what did I ever do with it? Get the news, which I mostly couldn't fix, or look at pictures of people's dogs. Look things up, sometimes.

She could probably use the library computer if she needed to look anything up, like how to stop roadrunners from leaving dead snakes on your doorstep. *I'd want to get my phone sorted out so that I could still take pictures with it, but I'm sure someone in town can help me do that.*

Selena closed her eyes, trying to think of other things she'd miss. *Good Vietnamese food. Mindless games on my phone. Not having to walk everywhere.*

It didn't seem like much of a list. The fact was that she hadn't really *done* anything most days. She worked, she came home, she watched TV or read books, she slept. Get up, rinse, repeat. If she went back, that was what waited for her.

Or she could live here, at least for a while. She didn't have to decide now, forever. The city wouldn't go anywhere. But Jackrabbit Hole House might not be waiting when she came back.

She'd told Walter to get rid of her stuff. She wasn't the sort who kept photo albums and she couldn't think of anything she wanted enough to give him her new address. She'd brought the good shoes that she could stand in for eight hours at a stretch, and as for the rest, if she hadn't missed it by now, she probably didn't need it.

She had stopped buying frivolous things after a while. Walter had a way of looking at them that made them turn ugly. Selena remembered a vase in a deep, gorgeous oxblood red. She saw it in a little boutique shop and fell in love with it at once and it was beautiful all the way home, and then Walter saw it. "Lovely shape," he said. "Shame they didn't have it in another color." And then she looked at it and how it didn't match anything in the house at all, which was all white pine and sleek chrome. The oxblood color turned garish and embarrassing. She returned it to the shop the next day.

Sitting in her aunt's house with all the cheerfully mismatched furniture, Selena thought that if she had the vase now, she'd put it on the mantel and let the rich red color glow against the white walls. It would look beautiful there. Maybe where the statue of Snake-Eater was. She hoped that wouldn't offend him.

Copper yawned and stretched and got to her feet. She scratched at the door and looked expectantly over at Selena.

"You like it here, don't you?" Selena said, opening the back door for her.

Copper answered with a brief wave of her tail, ambling down the steps to sniff around the garden and find the single correct spot to anoint.

"I like it here," Selena said, more quietly. At the far end of the garden, the little green god shimmered into existence. "I even like you," Selena told him, though quietly. She still wasn't sure about the supposed "thin place" in the garden, but it hadn't done anything suspicious in the last few weeks, so she was starting to think of it like a septic system—potentially troublesome and expensive, but not an immediate threat.

She didn't have the money to fix the septic system here, if it went bad, but Grandma had mentioned in passing that historic zones had a fund for any repairs that Samuel's oldest couldn't patch up with spackle and a new fuse. Maybe if the thin place went bad, Father Aguirre could do the spiritual equivalent of spackle.

She'd miss Father Aguirre if she went back to the city, and Grandma Billy and everyone at the church potluck and even DJ Raven with their bizarre choice in programming.

A terrible hope was starting to fill her, and the most terrible thing was discovering that she'd been feeling it for a while now.

Don't, she told herself, trying to forestall it. If she didn't hope, then the disappointment couldn't crush her. *It can't be that easy. It's a historic zone, there's bound to be mountains of paperwork. They want people who have historic skills to live here, like weaving and gardening and raising sheep. Nobody thinks operating a deli meat slicer is a historic skill.*

Selena shook her head. It was better to rip the bandage off quickly. She called Copper in and fetched her leash. "Come on," she said. "Let's go talk to Mayor Jenny and find out it's impossible."

Chapter 15

"Of course it's possible," said Mayor Jenny. "I was hoping you'd decide to stay."

"What?" asked Selena. She had been bracing herself for disappointment and having it yanked away left her suddenly off balance. "How? But this is a historic zone, isn't it?"

"Yep," Jenny said. She was sorting the mail, which mostly looked like junk, shot through with the narrow white envelopes that meant either checks or bills. "And relatives of people in the zone get first placement. You get grandfathered in because of your aunt."

"But . . ." Selena leaned against the counter. It didn't seem possible that you could get what you wanted simply because you *asked.* That wasn't how the world worked . . . was it?

Jenny sighed and set down the mail. "Selena, hon, if you haven't noticed, people aren't exactly clamoring to live out here. It's hot and it's dusty and it's poor and there's no theaters or restaurants or shopping malls. Most of our young people grow up and move out. The only people who move *in* either grew up in a zone or are wild-eyed back-to-the-land types, and those sort don't last." One corner of Jenny's mouth crooked up. "Well, except for the folks out at Rivendell Ranch, and they're harmless."

"Rivendell?"

"Yeah, you should meet Galadriel sometime. Actually, I think she's coming to the crucifixion party this afternoon."

And here it is, Selena thought. *This is where I find out that everyone's actually in a cult.* "Crucifixion party," she said, with what she thought was the right amount of mild interest.

Jenny grinned. "Lupé's hosting. It's good fun. Bring some interesting twigs. And fill out this change of address form while you're here." She slid a sheet of paper across the counter. "And . . . let me print out one of the occupancy forms . . ." She vanished into the back.

"Crucifixion party," Selena said to Copper, who thumped her tail happily.

The *crk-whirrrr* of the printer preceded Jenny's reemergence with a small stack of papers. "Sign here," she said. "It says that you realize this is a historic zone and you won't sue if anything historic happens."

"Historic?" asked Selena faintly, wondering if crucifixion counted.

"Like getting kicked by a sheep."

"Ah." She scanned down the form, which said the same thing in more complicated language, initialed twice, agreed to binding arbitration, then signed her name at the bottom. Jenny signed as witness, then stamped it with a notary seal. "What else?" Selena asked.

"That's it."

"But there's got to be more paperwork than that."

"Sure," said Jenny. "I'll go fire up the computer tonight, click through about ten screens, and tell the government that I approved your application. Then somebody will come out to interview you—it's only a formality, just to make sure you exist—and in maybe six months, you'll get another form where they ask you about your net worth to make sure you're not using the zone as a tax haven, and then in about a year someone will get around to sending you a form letter saying that you haven't been accepted, and I'll send another official request, and then they'll send out a form letter saying that the requirements have been waived as long as you stay for at least five years. Which I hope you do."

"Oh," said Selena. "Me too."

"Get on to Lupé's," said Jenny, not unkindly. "I've got to lock up here."

Still slightly numb, Selena scoured the churchyard and surrounding bushes for some dry bits of wood that might be considered "interesting." Copper attempted to help, although Copper's definition of *interesting* was a lot different than Selena's.

Even as her hands were busy, Selena's brain was silent. It seemed to have gotten stuck on one thought.

I can stay.

I can actually stay.

It was impossible. It had been too easy. It had come like a gift, not like something she had earned, and Selena was too used to gifts having strings.

And yet . . . and yet . . .

I can stay.

"No," she said out loud, looking at her dog. "*We* can stay."

It turned out, when Selena arrived at the café, that "crucifixion party" meant making decorative crosses. Half the people from the church potluck nights were there, including Gordon, along with a few women that Selena hadn't met yet.

"Authentic folk art," said one of the women, a big, sturdy matron with hips like empires. "Insomuch as we're folks." She grinned at Selena, who smiled tentatively back. "From a historic zone, no less. City people pay good money for stuff like this."

That was pretty much it. Lupé broke out beer and a couple bottles of a cheap, too-sweet wine, which tasted better the longer the afternoon went on. Selena learned to tie twine around two twigs to hold them in place—it wasn't hard—and secure it with a dab of superglue. That was the simplest type to make, but people had brought all kinds of odds and ends—horseshoe nails and spotted chicken feathers and banded stones and bits of old leather—to get progressively fancier. Lupé tagged each one with a label before boxing it up. "The cooperative will send the money to Connor's place once these sell," she explained, "and you can pick it up as cash or put it on credit if you want."

"How much money do they make?" asked Selena.

Lupé held up one of Selena's better efforts, which had a little leather swag draped over the crosspiece, held in place with tacks. She'd glued small flat stones to the tack heads and the result was actually rather nice. "This one's probably worth at least seventy-five, after the commission."

"But it only took me like twenty minutes!"

The stout woman, who, as it turned out, was Galadriel, burst out laughing. "I told you, hon, it's authentic folk art. We get together a couple times a year and make up a whole pile like this, then the galleries sell 'em a few at a time."

Grandma killed the last of the too-sweet wine. "You can make 'em at home too," she said, "but it's more fun like this."

She wasn't wrong. There was a festive, almost giddy air that reminded Selena of making holiday cards in grade school, albeit with less glitter and more alcohol.

It didn't occur to her to wonder what Father Aguirre might think about crucifixes as commercial art until the door to the café opened and he came in, all in black, Roman collar just visible over the box he was carrying.

"Contribution to the cause," he said, grinning, and set down the box.

It was full of pieces of the strange, weblike wood that Selena had learned came from cholla. Galadriel let out a whoop of delight and descended on it. "Oh, this is the *stuff!*"

Selena, after finishing her own glass of wine, decided that she quite liked Galadriel. "Yes, that's my real name," the woman said, heaving a sigh. "My parents were the worst sort of hippies, and they all wanted to go back to the land. Turned out they weren't all that good at it. But by the time they figured it out, I'd fallen in love with . . . well . . ." She made a sweeping gesture that took in the whole world of sand and sage and desert outside. "It gets in your blood, out here."

"Yeah," said Selena. "Yeah, it does." She frowned, remembering something. "Didn't you call in to the radio a while ago? About a weird energy?"

"Yep," said Galadriel, as matter-of-fact as if she was discussing the weather. "I got a touch of the sight. There was something churning away northeast of here. Still is, though it's settled down a bit."

It occurred to Selena that here was someone who would take a god in the garden absolutely in stride. "What *kind* of energy?" she asked. "What does it mean?"

Galadriel shrugged. "Felt like a Santa Ana wind. Dry and hot and makes you itchy and jittery and short-tempered. Just hanging there, not really doing anything. That's all I know."

"But what causes that sort of thing?"

Galadriel gave her a considering look. "Desert's full of spirits," she said finally. "Pretty sure one got woke up. For all I know, some kids went drinking and pissed on the wrong rock and riled somebody up good."

Someone like Snake-Eater? Could she be feeling him? She tried to think of how to ask, but the sentence would have started with "Okay, so my aunt was sleeping with a roadrunner god . . ." and she couldn't put the script together. She went back to making crosses.

Father Aguirre had settled into a corner, and after a few minutes, Selena couldn't stand it anymore. "Does this bother you?" she asked him in an undertone. "People aren't being very . . . um . . . respectful about crosses." Her mother would have tried to throw the devil out of the whole building several times over by now.

The priest chuckled softly. "What do you think Jesus's greatest miracle was?"

"Uh." Selena hadn't been expecting this question. She racked her brain, trying to remember Sunday schools past. "Raising someone from the dead?"

"Which was certainly very impressive." Father Aguirre folded his hands on one knee. "There's not a wrong answer, but for my money, it was the loaves and fishes. People were poor and hungry and He fed them, because He knew that it's hard to listen to a sermon when your stomach is growling." The priest made a small gesture that encompassed the busy room. "Perhaps this is a modern equivalent. People are poor, but the symbol of the cross, in a roundabout way, will feed them. And I do not believe in a God who would be more offended by jokes about crosses than by the system which has made them poor."

Selena couldn't help but contrast Father Aguirre's God with her mother's. She wasn't ready to worship either of them, but she certainly knew which one she preferred.

By the time dusk came and everyone was gathering up their things, Selena had put nearly five hundred dollars' worth of "authentic folk art" into Lupé's care. It would have been a week's salary at home, done in a few hours. *Granted I can't do that every week, but still. That'll keep Copper in dog food for quite a while.*

Selena tried to do math as she steered a somewhat inebriated Grandma Billy home, a task not made any easier by the fact that Grandma had begun singing the Marines' fight song. *If I can do that every quarter, and if the garden stuff sells as well as Grandma claims . . .*

"From the haaaalls of Montehhhzuuuuma . . . !"

Food's a lot cheaper out here than it was in the city too, and potatoes and beans hardly cost anything, so if I save my money . . .

". . . to the shores of Tripoleeeee . . ."

Merv the peacock yelled a greeting from the roof as they reached Grandma Billy's house.

"We will fight our country's baaaattles . . ."

"We're here, Grandma."

"In the land, on air, and—wait, what?"

"How much wine did you drink?"

"It was terrible wine," said Grandma with dignity, "so I felt obliged to save the rest of you." She pushed the door open. Selena made sure that she got inside safely, then led Copper toward home.

This could work. This could actually work. *At least until I figure out something that might work better.*

Behind her, faintly, she could hear a cracked voice warbling, "They will find the streets are guaaaarded . . . by United States Marines!"

Chapter 16

It was dark in the room, but there was a low red light coming from somewhere, the light of banked embers or the memory of a fire. The man who held her had a long, angular face and his skin was brown, but not the way that human skin was brown. It was mottled with white, the color of dust, and when she ran her hand down his arm, it felt sleek as feathers.

This was familiar. This was right. They'd done this before, hadn't they? He wasn't a stranger, certainly.

He kissed her, and that was familiar too, and very good. Except . . .

There was a thought inside her head. She tried to ignore it, to lose herself in the heat of the moment, but it was as prickly as a cactus spine, working its way deeper, desperate to be known.

She didn't want to think it. She wanted this to last a little longer, this frisson of skin against skin, answering a craving she'd almost forgotten she had. But the thought was insistent and at last she drew back and looked up and met her lover's eyes.

They were brown and gold, with a moon-white band around the pupils.

Selena stared into them and it finally clicked where she'd seen eyes like that before.

She swallowed, the heat in her blood turning cold and sluggish.

"Snake-Eater? Is that you?"

◆ ◆ ◆

Her dream lover cocked his head to one side, birdlike, lizardlike, and Selena knew that she was right even before he said, "Yes, of course." His voice was familiar in her ears, as if she'd heard it before, though she couldn't remember where.

"Ah." Now that she was looking, of course, it was obvious. That sleek mottled dust skin and the inhuman angularity of his face. The moon-banded eyes.

She inched back on the bed. Was it still her bed? She could feel the blankets under her fingers, but the red lighting was strange and indirect and Copper was no longer at the foot of it.

This no longer felt entirely like a dream.

"Selena?" He drew her name out in a caress. No one had ever said her name like that before, with a growling note to it. "What is wrong?"

What's wrong is that you're a . . . a god of large birds! I am not fucking a bird god!

. . . *Again?* She could only remember the edges of other dreams, but she had a horrible feeling that it might be *again.*

I suppose Aunt Amelia did say that he was lonely, she thought, and had to choke off the urge to laugh hysterically.

Snake-Eater reached for her again. Selena put up her hands to ward him off. "Ah—uh—so you knew my aunt Amelia, then?"

He cocked his head the other way. There was a streak of color at the corner of each eye, and she suspected that if the light had been different, it would have shown blue. "Yes, of course. I loved her, but she has gone away and would not stay with me. But now you have taken her place, as her kin, and I love you instead."

That, as one of Selena's past therapists would have said, was a lot to process. She inched back again, hoping to find the edge of the bed, but it seemed to keep going. "Ah. Hmm. I'm . . . err . . . flattered, but . . . I don't really know you?"

Snake-Eater looked blank. "What else is there to know?"

Maybe if you were a god of roadrunners, you didn't have much time for hobbies. She cast around desperately for something to say.

"My aunt . . . um . . . said that you were very sweet when she was ill. Maybe we could share some memories? Of her?" said Selena hopefully.

Sweet was not really the term she wanted to apply to the figure in front of her. Actually, she could see the appeal. Snake-Eater had a body that could have come off the cover of one of Grandma Billy's romance novels. He looked very, very male.

Very. Extremely.

I didn't know birds even had *those parts.*

"She was not ill. Her strength wore away," said Snake-Eater.

"Wore away?"

He shrugged.

Selena was starting to get a very bad feeling. *Great. I will put that with all the other bad feelings.* "Did you . . . err . . . ?"

Snake-Eater bristled. Literally bristled. His hair lifted in a feathery crest and Selena fell back on her elbows. "She gave it freely," he growled. "She should not have given so much strength away. *You* will not give yours away."

"Uh . . ."

Snake-Eater reached for her again and she retreated.

"What is wrong?" he asked again.

"I'm sorry," she said. "I can't do this."

Snake-Eater stared at her. A clicking noise started all around her, a sharp, thin sound like a snapping beak. It seemed to arise from the darkness and Selena dug her fingers into the blankets, wondering what was out there and if it was still Snake-Eater or more of Snake-Eater or whether this man was some kind of illusionary body overlaying something different and far more alien.

"But I love you now," he said, as if that was the answer to any possible question.

"Yes, but I . . ." The only thought in her head was *can't fuck a bird,* but she was pretty sure that would not go over well, so she settled on the script that had served her for the better part of a decade. "I'm sorry, you're very attractive but I'm seeing someone."

A membrane slid down over the moon-band eyes, a blink as slow and cold as a lizard's. "What?"

"Engaged," said Selena. "Um." She twisted her engagement ring on her finger. She'd been thinking of getting rid of it, but now it might be what saved her. "Sorry."

"But you accepted my courtship gifts."

"What courtship g—you mean the *dead rattlesnakes*?"

"What else?"

"But that's—"

The moon-white band suddenly thinned as Snake-Eater's pupils dilated. Selena cut herself off in mid-word. "I didn't realize that they were, um, courtship gifts. I thought it meant that you, uh, wanted to be friends."

"Yes." Snake-Eater swept a hand down in a gesture that took in her entire body. "That is their *purpose*."

It occurred to Selena that maybe roadrunners didn't have friends in the sense she understood. *They don't form flocks, I guess, so maybe they don't have friends, just mates and children?* "Oh. Um. I didn't realize what you meant. Humans, uh, do it differently?"

"And you are already mated," said Snake-Eater, in tones of deep disgust. The clicking sound started up again. "Where is he? I will kill him and it will no longer be a problem."

Selena spent one glorious moment imagining unleashing a bird god on Walter, then brought herself back to earth. "I'm afraid he's far away. You can't kill him. You and I just, uh, can't be friends. Not friend-friends. Not in the way you were with my aunt. Sorry."

Snake-Eater rose to his feet in a single abrupt motion. The sight of his smoothly muscled, almost-human body in motion made Selena realize yet again why Aunt Amelia had been willing to overlook the bird bits.

But even if he wasn't a roadrunner god, I'm still not sleeping with anyone who just decides he loves me. That seems like a recipe for nine kinds of disaster.

The look he turned on her no longer seemed loving. His pupils shrank until the white bands were full moons with a dark spot across them, and he flexed his hands back and forth. His nails were diamond shaped, like claws.

"You deceived me," hissed Snake-Eater. The red light got redder and the white moons began to expand until they filled Selena's field of vision, until it seemed as if they might engulf the world. "You lied to me. *I no longer love you.*"

Something shoved her, hard. Selena fell for an instant that felt eternal, Snake-Eater's voice ringing in her ears, and jerked awake in bed, with the sun streaming through the window.

"What a dream," muttered Selena, holding her head. Her temples throbbed. "Christ, I hope that was a dream."

She had a horrible sinking feeling that it might not have been. She stumbled into the bathroom to splash water on her face.

Dreams aren't real.

Neither are monsters.

She shook herself, like Copper coming out of water, and went to make coffee. She drank too quickly and scalded the roof of her mouth, but it helped chase away some of the cobwebs. *Had* it been a dream? It had the hazy edges of one, but she could remember Snake-Eater's words so clearly.

I no longer love you.

"What the hell?" she muttered.

Copper scratched at the door and Selena followed her outside. At the far end of the garden, the little green squash god shuffled between plants. *He's real. And Snake-Eater is real. Did I just mortally offend him? Again?*

The dog found an important spot to sniff, and Selena watched the squash god, which was why she saw the roadrunner.

The bird came up on the stone wall at the end of the garden, froze for an instant, and then, lizard-quick, launched itself at the squash god.

Selena heard herself yell a warning too late. The bird landed on the god's back and drove its long beak down in a single savage thrust.

The god threw his head back in a soundless scream. He staggered forward, as the bird struck again, stabbing his neck with the same killing force that it would strike a snake.

"No!" Selena yelled, already off the porch. "No! *Leave him alone!*"

The god vanished. The bird dropped to the ground, then leapt back onto the wall. White-moon eyes stared into hers, pitiless and cold.

Selena didn't realize that she'd grabbed the shovel until she was swinging it in front of her, still shouting.

The roadrunner dodged her blow with contemptuous ease, jumped down into the desert, and was gone.

Still clutching the shovel, Selena went to her knees where the little god had been. There was no blood, but who knew if gods even had blood? Had he vanished to get away, or had he been hurt? The roadrunner's beak had gone in at least an inch. A human stabbed in the neck like that would be horribly injured or worse.

"I'm sorry," Selena said wretchedly. "I'm so sorry." Snake-Eater had done it to get at her, no question, and it was all her fault, she hadn't known, she hadn't *understood—*

A wet nose prodded her shoulder. Selena dropped the shovel and threw her arms around Copper.

Amelia had thought that Snake-Eater was lonely, but this wasn't loneliness. This was something dark and deep and dreadful.

The cool prickle of adrenaline subsided, but left a deeper cold behind. If Snake-Eater had gone for the little squash god, what would stop him from going for Copper? If he wanted to hurt Selena, there was no quicker, surer way.

"Shit," Selena said, getting to her feet. She locked her fingers around Copper's collar. "Come on, girl. We've got to go *now*."

"Oh shit," said Grandma Billy. "Shit, shit, shit. This ain't good."

"I didn't realize what he was doing!" wailed Selena. She had come straight to Grandma Billy's at a run, stopping only to grab a leash and pick up the shovel again. "I didn't mean to—they were *dead rattlesnakes*!" It was all her worst nightmares, the unwritten rule that she should have known but didn't, except this rule came with talons behind it. Not even Walter could have known *this* rule.

"No shame on you," said Grandma Billy. "Doubt anyone who wasn't a bird would've realized it." Her eyes unfocused and she stared briefly into the distance, drumming her fingers on the porch railing. "Huh! Wonder if that's how it went with Amelia."

"Bringing her dead snakes?"

"And thinking that the only way to be friends is fucking. Although that's a lot of men's problem, not just his." She spat over the side of the railing.

"Is it all going to start up again?" Selena asked miserably. "The fetches and everything?"

"No idea, but I ain't suggesting we sit tight and hope for the best. Snake-Eater ain't happy being crossed."

"What do we do? Is there anything we *can* do?" *Please have an idea,* Selena pleaded silently. *Please tell me there's a way to fix this. Please tell me I don't have to start running.* She had only just decided to stay, and now it seemed as if that might be snatched away.

"Well—" Grandma Billy started to say, and then a massive ruckus kicked off in the chicken yard behind the house.

Grandma Billy ran through the house and threw the back door open. Selena grabbed Copper's collar as Grandma Billy stepped out onto the porch.

The roadrunner was back.

Loose feathers filled the air. One hen lay dead already, and the rest were huddled in the far corner of the pen. But it seemed that this time, Snake-Eater's minion was meeting resistance.

Merv the peacock was bloody and listing to one side, but he stood between the roadrunner and the hens like an iridescent blue wall. Grandma Billy cursed.

The roadrunner danced from side to side, striking out at the peacock's head. Merv was just a fraction too slow and staggered sideways. Selena sucked in her breath to yell.

The bantam rooster came out of nowhere and hit the roadrunner from behind like a very small tornado. Snake-Eater's minion spun, trying to lash out, but this enemy was much more agile and armed with spurs. Feathers flew.

Outmatched, the roadrunner jumped high in the air and came down running, with the bantam in hot pursuit. The roadrunner leapt onto the wall surrounding the yard, paused for a heartbeat—then exploded.

Grandma Billy lowered her shotgun. Selena hadn't even seen her pick it up. The bantam flapped a few times, outraged, then stalked over to his hens.

"Bastard," Grandma said, almost conversationally. She put the gun up and went to Merv. "Ah, hell."

The gallant peacock had collapsed into a heap of ragged blue. Grandma Billy knelt down and stroked his side. "He did a number on you, didn't he?" she murmured. "But you did good. You saved the ladies."

Selena bit down on her knuckle, tears springing to eyes. Another casualty of her own foolishness and Snake-Eater's malice.

"Right," said Grandma Billy. She sat back, sighed deeply, then hefted the peacock's body in her arms. His long neck dangled lifelessly over her wrist. "First we're gonna bury Merv. Then we're gonna get Father Aguirre, and then I aim to fuck up Snake-Eater's shit but good."

Chapter 17

"A noble cause," Father Aguirre said an hour later, when Selena and Grandma Billy had finished recounting their story. "Obviously I'll help any way I can."

They were seated around the table in the rectory, with Copper dozing underneath. Sunlight streamed through the window and it was all so normal that it felt impossible to believe that the horrors of the morning had actually happened. If not for the raw red patch across Selena's palms, from the shovel they'd used to dig a peacock-sized grave, she would have thought she'd dreamed the whole thing.

But I didn't dream it. It all happened. Snake-Eater attacked the little squash god and killed Merv and he's not going to stop. She rubbed her thumb across the sore spot. "I'm going to have to leave, aren't I?"

"Eh?" Grandma Billy looked over at her. "Leave? Why?"

"So that more people don't get hurt." There was a lump in her throat at the thought, and yet a strange relief, as if the world had snapped back into a more recognizable pattern. Of course she didn't get to stay. She'd always known it was impossible, hadn't she?

"Snake-Eater's mad at me, not at you," she tried to explain. "If I leave, he'll probably go away."

"Hell with that," said Grandma Billy. "You don't gotta leave unless you want to. Tell her, Father."

Father Aguirre raised a mild eyebrow. "Do you *want* to leave? I know you've been saying this was a temporary stay. And all this . . ." His gesture somehow took in the desert and roadrunners and their gods. "All this is a lot to deal with."

Selena bit her lip. Now that it seemed like she couldn't stay, all her wavering had fallen away. She *didn't* want to leave Quartz Creek. She wanted to stay here as long as she could.

She pictured the pitifully small grave they'd dug for Merv and knew that time had come to an end.

"I wish I could. I don't want to go back." She pinched the bridge of her nose, willing the tears back. "Father, can you . . . could you . . ." It was the hardest thing she'd ever done, harder than facing the fetches outside the windows, harder than leaving her old life behind her. "Can you take Copper?"

"What?" She could hear the surprise in his voice, even if her eyes were closed.

"I'll have to go to a shelter, I think," she said to the backs of her eyelids. "And they don't let you have dogs. I can't do that to her."

"To hell with all of this," said Grandma Billy savagely. Her fist thumped on the table, accompanied by a jangle of bracelets. "I'm not gonna see *my* friend and Amelia's *kin* driven out of her home by that nasty, jumped-up little road bird. We're gonna find Snake-Eater and tear his ass-feathers out, that's what we're gonna do."

Selena opened her eyes in time to see Father Aguirre's lips twitch. "I might not have phrased it quite like that," he said, "but I agree with the sentiment."

Selena gulped. "I don't want you to get hurt, Grandma."

"Feh. Bigger things than him have tried."

"But . . ." Selena racked her brain, trying to think of a script that would make them understand. "I don't . . . *I can't* . . ."

"I've had about enough of this *I can't* nonsense," said Grandma Billy sharply. "I swear to God, you and Amelia both. You'd think there wasn't a scrap of spine between you."

Selena gaped at her, not used to Grandma Billy's sharpness being turned on her. "But—"

"But *nothing.* Stand up for yourself, girl! Look, you had a job in a deli, right? Ran things, didn't you? So pretend I come into your place and start messing things up."

"Uh . . ."

Selena started to look to Father Aguirre for help, but Grandma Billy snapped her fingers. "Don't you look away from me. I'm in your place, knocking shit over. What're you gonna do about it?"

It was the most ridiculous scenario imaginable and yet suddenly there were scripts in Selena's head that had been hammered in by years of work. "I ask you to leave," she said.

"I tell you to go to hell. I throw one of them rotisserie chickens at your head."

Someone had actually thrown a plastic container of macaroni salad at Selena's head once, during the rush when a woman in a sweater that said PEACE ON EARTH had discovered that you could not order a full turkey dinner on the morning of Thanksgiving. And Selena had ducked and it had splattered on the wall and she'd turned around and faced the woman and yelled—

"Come on," snarled Grandma Billy, right up in her face. "I'm throwing the fancy cheese around and wiping my ass with the ham."

"GET OUT!" Selena roared, at a volume that shocked her and sent Copper to her feet with a worried bark.

Grandma Billy blinked, clearly taken slightly aback, then broke into a broad grin and sat back down. "*That's* what I'm talkin' about," she said. "You gonna let some stupid roadrunner mess up *your* place, where you live?"

Selena leaned down and hugged Copper until the old dog settled down. She cleared her throat, somewhat embarrassed, and looked over at Father Aguirre.

"Oh, don't mind me," the priest said. "I'm still trying *not* to picture somebody wiping their ass with a ham."

"You'd want to slice it first," Selena said, and that set all of them off laughing, while the dog looked at the three humans as if they were losing their minds.

Father Aguirre leaned back, wiping his eyes. "Mercy. I promise, we'd much rather have you around than Snake-Eater."

"Hear, hear," muttered Grandma Billy.

The Selena that Walter had known wanted to run away, run away and not let anyone get hurt on her behalf. But there was another Selena in there too, one who had handled customers and cleaned up messes and had very calmly wrapped the newest hire's hand with a towel when he'd hit an artery after forgetting basic safety with the meat slicer. *That* Selena knew that running just meant somebody else had to clean up the mess later.

It was profoundly absurd that being the assistant manager at a deli would prepare you to fight a god. But it was profoundly absurd that there were gods in her garden and that a roadrunner would turn out to be a frightening little dinosaur of a bird and that your best friends would turn out to be an elderly chicken lady and a Catholic priest.

"Okay," Selena said. "Okay." She couldn't believe she was saying this, but Grandma Billy was grinning so hard that it was the only thing she could say. "Let's go kick Snake-Eater's ass."

"The only problem is that we don't actually know where to *find* Snake-Eater."

"We don't?" Selena asked.

The priest shook his head. "We don't know where his home ground is. Ah . . . some spirits are bound to a specific place and stay there. Others have a kind of home territory, but may be anywhere within it. But even with those, their home ground is the spot where they're most . . . them."

He smiled ruefully. "You could say that Our Lady of the Palo Verdes is my home ground. The place where you feel most like yourself."

Selena tried to think if she had such a place. The deli had probably been the closest, back in the city. That was where she could be her own self, not her mother's daughter or Walter's partner. Now . . .

"Mine's wherever Copper is, I think." Though the image of Jackrabbit Hole House lingered, the back porch where she sat and read books and sometimes saw the little green god.

Father Aguirre shook his head. "And it's probably possible for someone or something to be someone else's home ground too. It's another one of those things I haven't figured out yet. I suspect that Snake-Eater has a home ground of his own, but I don't know for certain."

"No, he's got a place," said Grandma Billy, unexpectedly. "Amelia said she met him when she wandered into it."

"Did she say where it was?"

The old woman's lips pressed together. "No. And it could have been anywhere. You know what she was like for wandering in the backcountry. Never saw a hole or a draw she didn't want to explore."

"A hole or a draw . . ." Selena said slowly. Something in her brain was yelling for her attention. "What are they?"

Father Aguirre raised his eyebrows. "Parts of the landscape. Draws are like a little valley that runs into a ridge. Sort of like an arroyo, except that draws don't necessarily carry water, although some of them do." He waved his hand. "Confusing enough?"

Her brain was yelling louder. "And a hole?"

"It's an old name for a valley. You still see places out here named that—Jackson Hole, Red Clay Hole—"

A topographic map, with its tiny handwritten notes, flashed into Selena's mind. The map that Aunt Amelia had hung in the bedroom of the house named . . .

"Jackrabbit Hole House." Selena stared at Father Aguirre. "You told me that she'd changed the name a few years ago. But jackrabbits don't live in holes."

"Oh shit," Grandma Billy said. "Oh shit. That was just a few months after she started talking about Snake-Eater."

Selena got to her feet. "I've got to check the map, but I will bet you anything that Aunt Amelia wrote it down. And that Jackrabbit Hole is the name of the place she met Snake-Eater."

Getting back to Jackrabbit Hole House was unexpectedly fraught. Grandma Billy had been all set to walk back in a knot and shoot anything that looked at them funny. Father Aguirre was not terribly happy with this plan and kept saying things like, "Innocent bystanders" and "Collateral damage."

Finally the priest held up a hand. "After we get the map, we'll have to go out in the desert, correct?"

Grandma Billy allowed as how this was so. Father Aguirre heaved a great sigh and said, "Then I suppose we'll have to take my truck."

Grandma let out a whistle. "Can I drive?"

"Over my dead body."

"You have a truck?" Selena asked. She'd only ever seen the priest walk places.

"He's got a *classic*," said Grandma Billy.

Father Aguirre led them to the small locked building next to the church, paused for a moment with his hand on the garage door and said something brief and heartfelt in Latin. Then he pushed up the metal door, revealing a large dustcover with wheels.

With a flourish like a magician yanking away a tablecloth, the priest pulled the cover off and revealed an ancient pickup truck with a rounded hood and a cab that looked as if the corners had melted. It was deep green and someone had lovingly polished every part of it until it blazed like an emerald in the shadows of the garage.

"If I was wearing a hat, I'd take it off," said Grandma Billy, gazing at the vehicle with wistful avarice.

Selena had managed to go her whole life without learning anything about cars, and wasn't about to start, but still knew what was required of her. "It's beautiful. But what *is* it?"

"That," said Father Aguirre in equal parts pride and despair, "is a 1950 Ford F-1 pickup truck."

"But that's over a hundred years old!"

"It was my great-grandfather's," the priest said. "They made them to last in those days." He heaved another sigh. "And now I am about to drive it through the desert, probably off anything resembling a road. Saint Christopher have mercy upon my paint job."

"It'll love it," Grandma Billy assured him. "Truck like this wants to be used, not sit around in a garage all day. The other trucks'd laugh at it if they knew."

Father Aguirre took the keys from a hook on the wall. "Give me ten minutes to pack. And *don't touch the truck.*"

Grandma Billy waited until the priest had vanished back into the rectory and then immediately began touching it. "Look at this baby," she said, opening the passenger door. "He drives it around at Thanksgiving and Christmas, deliverin' all the food packages, and takes it to the parade in Jerome once a year. I ain't never been inside it." She hopped up into the cab. "Oooh . . ."

"Are you sure you should be touching that?" asked Selena, more because that was the script in her head than because she had any hope of stopping Grandma Billy from doing whatever the hell she wanted.

"Can't ride in it without touching it," the old woman pointed out. She rubbed one bony hand across the dashboard, which was the same green metal as the outside of the truck. "Man, forget what the father said about the church being his homeplace. It's this truck right here."

I am asking a man to drive the place of his heart through the desert to get scratched and dented and maybe break. Selena closed her eyes briefly.

Copper took advantage of her distraction and jumped up into the cab after Grandma Billy, who obligingly scooted over. Unable to beat them, Selena climbed up to join them on the long bench seat, which was made of faux leather in a questionable shade of burnt orange.

When Father Aguirre came back out of the rectory, carrying a heavy pack under each arm, he didn't seem at all surprised. He tossed the packs into the back, then went back inside and came out with two five-gallon jugs of water that sloshed as he walked. "Right," he said, setting the jugs in the back of the truck. "Let's go."

There was a brief pause when, after leaving the garage, he stopped the truck and took the keys out of the ignition before going back to close the door. "You don't trust me?" asked Grandma Billy, oozing wounded innocence.

"Not even a little," said Father Aguirre.

The drive to Jackrabbit Hole House was much shorter than the walk. That was good, because the truck jounced and rattled over the washboard road so violently that Selena thought her tailbone was going to separate from her spine.

"I guess the suspension's from 1950 too, huh?" said Grandma Billy snidely.

"On the contrary," Father Aguirre said pleasantly. "The suspension is barely seventy years old. Someone told me that's not old at all."

Grandma Billy opened her mouth, closed it, gave the priest a glittering glare, and muttered, "Practically new, then. Mechanic must have robbed you." Father Aguirre's smile would not have shamed the Mona Lisa.

He parked in front of Jackrabbit Hole House, pulling far over to one side, as if there was really going to be an unexpected stream of traffic going by. Selena opened the front door, remembering all of Grandma Billy's stories about disemboweled zombie squirrels, and got ready to leap out of the way.

No squirrels. No roadrunners, for that matter. Nothing appeared to have changed. Apparently Snake-Eater hadn't had time to send out a minion capable of working a doorknob.

She sighed with relief and gestured everyone inside. It was a little embarrassing having them all crowd into her bedroom—she hadn't made her bed, and there was dirty underwear on top of the hamper—but no one commented.

"Jackrabbit Hole . . ." Grandma Billy muttered, kneeling on the bed and tracing her finger over the map. "Jackrabbit, jackrabbit . . . a*ha*!" She jabbed a nail at the paper. "Right there!"

Selena, who had only just had time to start worrying about whether she'd been wrong, let out a sigh of relief.

"That's a full day of walking," said Father Aguirre, peering at the map. "Amelia may have made camp in Snake-Eater's home ground and that's what brought her to his attention."

"Oughta take the map with us," Grandma Billy said.

"I can take it down and fold it up," Selena offered. She tried to reach the thumbtacks at the top corner and realized that she was about an inch too short. "Err . . . let me get a stool . . ."

There was a soft, familiar click. Father Aguirre looked up from his phone and said, "What?"

"You have a cell phone?" Selena said. She was astonished, although she couldn't really say why.

"We *have* coverage in town, you know," the priest said. "We're not complete barbarians."

"Yes, but . . ." It occurred to her belatedly that she hadn't even checked for signal, or thought to buy a burner at the general store. She'd just been keeping her phone off so Walter didn't find her, and had gotten out of the habit of checking it every five minutes.

"*I* don't have one," Grandma Billy said loftily. "The government can track you through it. And also those cell plans are highway robbery."

"I have *told* you," said Father Aguirre wearily, "that if you will get a new phone, I will show you how to set it up."

"It's still highway robbery."

"There are discount plans for seniors—"

"Are you calling me old?"

Father Aguirre's exhale came from his toes. "Let me just get a close-up of the map, please."

He took several more photos, traced lines over the map with his fingers, and finally grimaced. "Some of these roads are more like suggestions, but I can get us pretty close. I think."

"Stop by my place first," said Grandma Billy. "I want to get my shotgun."

Selena would have questioned whether you could actually shoot a spirit, but the memory of the exploding roadrunner was still vivid. When Grandma Billy came back out of her house, she was carrying the gun, a backpack, and a coffee can full of eggs.

"Here," she said, handing Selena the coffee can. "We'll want dinner eventually."

Selena clutched the can between her knees as Father Aguirre executed a three-point turn that was more like nine, then set off down the road and into the desert.

Chapter 18

They drove through the desert for hours. Father Aguirre picked the most cautious of paths, which meant that the roads were only washboarded instead of washed out, but the farther they drove, the rougher the surfaces became. Selena could no longer feel her tailbone and at least one egg had become scrambled on the bottom of the coffee can.

The only two people who were enjoying themselves were Grandma Billy and Copper. Copper hung her head out the window, grinning hugely, with her tongue dangling like a peculiarly meaty pennant. Grandma Billy was not so much a backseat driver as a backseat heckler: "You coulda made that!" "I bet this thing can do twenty miles an hour, if you really push her." "C'mon, Padre, you drive like my old granny and she's *dead*."

Father Aguirre did not respond to any of this provocation, but he *had* been muttering to himself in Spanish for the last five miles.

At last they reached the end of the road they were on, and it was, quite literally, the end. The ground fell away into a dry streambed and the other side was overgrown with gnarled shrubs that were already starting to lose their spring flush of leaves. Father Aguirre parked the truck, got out, and looked both ways.

Selena took advantage of the pause to stretch her legs and rub her tailbone. Copper found something to pee on. Grandma Billy joined the priest at the edge of the dry wash.

"We can make it," she said. "And there hasn't been any rain in the mountains for a week."

Father Aguirre consulted the map on his phone, looked at the wash, and consulted his phone again. "We could go back about an hour, and try to come in from the east side."

"Can't imagine it'll be any better than this."

"This is a terrible idea," the priest said. "If we get stuck and it *does* rain . . ."

Grandma gestured at the sky, which did not have even the suspicion of a cloud. "C'mon, Padre, didn't the Lord promise something about floods?"

"He promised not to destroy the *world.* Individuals are still expected to get to high ground."

"Then I guess we better get getting, huh?"

"Lord Jesus Christ, Son of God, have mercy upon me, a sinner," the priest muttered. "Never do this," he told Selena, then got into the truck, started it, and bumped down the drop to the broad floor of the wash.

"What could happen?" asked Selena meekly, getting in.

"Flash flood," Grandma Billy said. "It rains way over there and the rain comes down and this turns into a river, and turns the Father's granddaddy's truck into a pile of junk." She grinned and slapped the dashboard. "Which means you better step on it, eh?"

Father Aguirre grunted, but pushed the gas pedal down another fraction of an inch.

Travel down the wash proceeded in fits and starts, as clear stretches gave way to clusters of boulders. Father Aguirre had stopped swearing in Spanish and begun swearing in Latin. Selena turned on the radio in hopes that it would stop Grandma Billy's running commentary, or at least drown it out.

Raven's soothing voice came over the airwaves, informing them that it was five o'clock and that the DJ had just eaten an edible, and that meant that it was time for some Pink Floyd.

"Wish *I* had an edible," said Grandma Billy.

"I wish you had one too," said Selena, which drew a snort of laughter from Father Aguirre and an appreciative cackle from Billy.

"You got some snark hiding in there, I knew it," the old woman said.

A few miles and most of *Dark Side of the Moon* later, Father Aguirre found a place to get the truck up the other side of the wash. "We're going to have to stop soon," he said. The sky was already turning orange. Selena couldn't imagine trying to navigate the nonexistent roads at night, at least not in the car. But still—

"Isn't Snake-Eater weaker at night?"

"Sure," said Grandma Billy. "But I ain't looking to fight him on an empty stomach."

Father Aguirre found a flat spot a little farther on and was reaching to shut off the engine when Selena stretched out her hand.

"Hmm?"

"Listen."

On the radio, DJ Raven was saying, "What's that, caller? I'm sorry, it's the edibles . . ."

The voice of Galadriel came on air. "I *said*, that weird energy started up again, and it's a lot worse this time. Feels like something's going to get broken." Selena pictured the big, practical woman and could almost hear the scowl. "Whatever's going on northeast of town, it's pissed off but good."

"That sounds bad," Raven said, after a moment of dead air.

"You bet your ass it is. If anybody listening to this is messing around northeast of Quartz Creek, either stop doing it or do it a lot harder, because it's starting to get on my nerves."

She hung up. "Huh," Raven said, and a moment later, the opening strains of something called "Aura Biscuit" started up. Father Aguirre turned the key and they sat in silence in the cab of the truck for a moment, in a clearing northeast of Quartz Creek.

Ten minutes later, the smell of frying eggs and bacon filled the air, as Grandma Billy expertly wielded a fry pan over a small fire. Father Aguirre had grumbled about the fire too, and insisted on clearing away anything even remotely flammable within ten yards.

"Could build it in the truck bed if you like," said Grandma serenely, which only evoked more irate Latin.

Father Aguirre's packs contained camping gear, as it turned out. After they'd wolfed down their bacon and eggs—Copper received two burnt eggs and sighed deeply when the rest were cooked without incident—the priest unrolled sleeping bags in the back of the truck.

"Are we sleeping?" asked Selena, who was tired but so keyed up that she couldn't imagine falling asleep.

"No," said Father Aguirre. "But if we succeed, we'll be so tired when we get back here that we'll be glad we don't have to unroll them, and if we fail, it won't much matter either way."

Selena's heart sank. "Do you think we're going to, erm, fail? I mean, what do you think our odds are?"

"I haven't the least idea," said the priest. "Anything I've done like this in the past has been with . . . let us say, other individuals of a spiritual persuasion. It may be extremely easy or far beyond my powers. I truly cannot say."

"The odds are fifty-fifty," Grandma Billy said. "Either we win or we don't."

"That is not how odds work," Selena said.

"You ever won any money gambling?"

"No?" Selena's mother had been so antigambling that she was half convinced that if she put a coin in a slot machine, she would immediately become a compulsive gambler.

"Well, I have, so I say that's how the odds work," said Grandma Billy and despite everything, Selena found herself feeling irrationally comforted.

Father Aguirre poured water into canteens while Grandma Billy strolled off into the brush to "take care of some personal business." He filled a dish for Copper and offered a canteen to Selena. "Drink now," he said, "and I'll fill it up again."

Having already learned how quickly the desert could dry a person out, Selena drank until she felt like she was going to slosh. She handed it back, and asked, "But what are we going to *do*, exactly?"

Her voice sounded plaintive in her own ears. *I'm sure he's heard much worse in confession,* she told herself firmly.

"Well," the priest said, refilling the canteen, "we are going to find Snake-Eater's home ground, and I will try to bind him to it. And then, while he is there and we are there, we will call upon those spirits who might be kindly inclined toward us to . . . ah . . . enforce a restraining order, as it were."

"And they'll do that?"

Father Aguirre shrugged. "We'll find out."

Selena stared down at the canteen as water dripped over her fingers. "Grandma Billy said your mother was a god," she blurted, then winced.

"I prefer to think of her as a spirit," said the priest, unruffled. "Otherwise I would have to be a demigod and even the Jesuits would have a hard time with that. But yes, she is a spirit. She took human form as it suited her and loved a human man and gave him a son, but she was always a wild thing."

When Selena looked up, there was an odd smile on his face. "I grew up in a trailer well south of here," he said. "My father was a day laborer. My aunts actually raised me. My father came when he could get away and my mother came when she remembered to be human."

"And you became a priest," said Selena, trying to imagine Father Aguirre as a young boy and not entirely succeeding.

"Aunt Consuela felt the best way to counter any devil in my blood was to send me to a very Catholic school." He grinned abruptly. "And unlike what you hear about many Catholic schools, the nuns there were exceedingly kind and saw that I was very timid and liked to read, so they gave me as many books as I wished and the Sister Librarian—her name was really Sister Theresa Francis—would talk about them all with me.

She was an absolute treasure. I learned later on that the money had run out for my schooling in my second year, but she went to the diocese and told them that it would be a sin against God to turn me away for lack of money. When I wanted to go to seminary, she helped me get every scholarship I could."

"She sounds wonderful," Selena said.

Father Aguirre nodded. "She was. When she passed away, God rest her soul, the line of mourners wrapped around the block. She helped more people than I suspect she knew. If beatification was left up to me . . ." He coughed. "Sister Theresa was one of the few people who knew about my . . . ah . . . parentage."

"And she believed you?" asked Selena, amazed. "When you told her?"

"She didn't have much choice." He paused, looking as if he were about to commit a severe social faux pas and not sure how to go about it. "I suppose I should show you, so it's not a shock later."

"Oh, this'll be a treat," said Grandma Billy, returning.

"What will be?" asked Selena, by now completely at sea.

Father Aguirre sighed. "Half a moment," he said, loosening his collar. He went around the far side of the truck and began undressing. Selena watched in absolute astonishment as he laid his clothes neatly in the bed of the truck, underwear last. "Please don't be alarmed," he said. His skin was very white in the dimness.

Then he bent down and vanished from sight. A moment later, something large came around the back of the truck.

Something *very* large. Also very bristly.

It looked like a pig, if pigs came in salt-and-pepper gray with black manes. But it was also strangely narrow, despite being twice the size of Copper.

The giant javelina pawed at the ground and dipped its head to Selena.

Copper yawned, got to her feet, and strolled over to the javelina without any apparent concern. She gave the beast a good sniff, wagged her tail, then went back to her spot by the fire.

Selena realized that her mouth was dangling open and shut it again with a snap.

"Father Aguirre?" she croaked, her mouth suddenly dry despite all the water she'd drunk.

The javelina nodded its head up and down and snorted.

Half of Selena said, *Oh, of course,* and the other half was screaming that this was insanity and hallucination and she had really cracked this time because this was impossible, there'd been drugs in the fried eggs, there was no other explanation. But that half sounded like Walter, and Walter wouldn't have survived ten minutes out here, so Selena shoved it away and focused on a much more pressing issue.

"Oh my god," she said, "you were eating bacon!"

The giant javelina cocked its head to one side and snorted. Selena could swear that it was a laugh.

"Javelina ain't pigs," said Grandma Billy. "It ain't cannibalism. They're somethin' else that just came out looking like pigs. There's a fancy term for it."

"Convergent evolution," said Selena, reaching back to a college biology class and finding the words waiting.

"Sure, if you say so. Anyway, nobody makes bacon out of javelina. They got no fat on them. You want the hams."

The javelina snorted explosively and prodded Grandma with his nose. "I'm talkin' in general," she grumbled at him. "Ain't nobody gonna eat *your* hams. You got no ass, Father, no matter what species you're being."

He turned small, dark eyes on Selena, and whatever species he was being, the long-suffering expression was pure Aguirre.

With a shake of his head, the javelina trotted back to the other side of the truck and a moment later, Father Aguirre stood up and began pulling his clothes on.

"Gonna take care of more business . . ." Grandma Billy said, getting to her feet.

"You take care of that business over that way," Father Aguirre said. "There will be no ogling."

"You take all the fun out of being a dirty old woman, Padre." Grandma Billy shook her head. "You'll be old someday, just you wait, and anything you drink will go right through you." She ambled off into the dark again.

"And you can just *do* that?" said Selena. It took her a minute, because there were absolutely no scripts for discovering that your friend could become a two-hundred-pound peccary. "Turn into an animal? Whenever you want?"

"More or less." Father Aguirre came around the truck, buttoning up his shirt. "It takes effort. I have siblings who could do it as easy as breathing, but they were born in that shape, and when they become human, they're only about yea big." He held up his hand to indicate someone the height of a child. "Conservation of mass seems to apply to spirits too. And I can't be too far from the desert either."

He sat back down by the fire. Selena was still trying to imagine being a were-pig. *Were-not-pig. Were-convergent-evolution-pig.* She heard a wild giggle forming in her throat and shoved her hand into her mouth to stop it. *Walter would . . .* Her thoughts stopped there, because Walter would already have dropped dead of shock weeks ago. She was in a world where Walter no longer applied. "Don't you worry?" she asked. "That, like, the government will find out and put you in a lab or something?"

One corner of the priest's mouth crooked up. "I used to," he admitted. "But as I said, I can't be too far from the desert. I didn't change all the years I was at seminary. I think if anyone tried to put me in a lab, I wouldn't be able to change, even if I wanted to. Which I have decided is for the best." He nodded firmly, as if convincing himself. "No matter how much I might wish to know what exactly happens and what it would look like if I was in an MRI tube, it's not worth it if the wider world became aware of the existence of people like me."

"*Are* there more people like you?"

"I don't know of any other javelina. There are three women I know who can become deer, and I met one, many years ago, who claimed that she could become a snake. I had no reason to doubt her."

Selena stared into the coals that were all that remained of the fire. "So, werewolves . . . were they . . . ?"

"Mostly people with porphyria, I expect. Though I do wonder about the Beast of Gévaudan." At her look of noncomprehension, he waved his hand. "Never mind. I'll loan you a book when we get back to Quartz Creek. It's interesting reading."

"Huh." Selena reached out and rubbed Copper's back. The dog groaned and stretched. *Copper still likes him.*

And anyway, this was Father Aguirre, who sometimes drank one too many glasses of wine at the community dinner and would sing hymns *very earnestly* and everybody smiled and sang along because, well, it was *Father Aguirre.*

And he was risking the paint job of the truck that he clearly loved to help her. *Also we might all die, but I think for him the paint job is the important bit.*

There was a script for this sort of thing, as it turned out. "Thank you for showing me," Selena said. "I know that couldn't be easy."

He smiled at her. "We're friends," he said. "And it's probably good that someone other than Grandma Billy knows my secret. You know, in case something were to happen." He flicked his fingers, indicating a whole wealth of potential misfortune. Selena, with her finely tuned anxiety, didn't have to work to picture it. *If he got very sick, maybe delirious, would he change shape on accident? Or if someone drugged him, maybe, or—*

Copper lifted her head suddenly, fur spiking along her back. A growl rose in her throat and she got to her feet, staring out into the dark.

"Something wrong, girl?" Selena asked. *The way the last half hour has gone, I wouldn't be surprised if she answered me.*

Copper barked once, querulously, an old dog sensing something she didn't like, then slowly settled back on her haunches, though her hackles didn't go down. Selena strained her ears, but all she could hear was the *zeet-zeet-zeet* of small insects in the brush.

"Where's Grandma Billy?" asked Father Aguirre abruptly.

"She went to . . . but that was . . ." Selena tried to think how long it had been. Too long, even for an old woman's digestion.

Father Aguirre stood, scanning the landscape. So did Selena. The coals of the fire made an orange island in a sea of darkness, and she could see nothing.

The priest cupped his hands around his mouth. "Billy!" he called. "Billy, you out there?"

The little calling insects fell silent, but there was no other reply.

Father Aguirre tore his clothes off and flung them at Selena so fast that she barely had time to register that she was seeing a lot more of a Catholic priest than the church would perhaps have condoned. Then he seemed to fall down on all fours and the big javelina went running into the darkness, snout to the ground, huffing furiously.

Not knowing what else to do, Selena followed, her arms full of Father Aguirre's clothes and Copper's leash wrapped around her wrist. She could almost hear her old dog trainer chiding her. *Never do that, she could break your arm if she decided to bolt.*

Oh yes, if someone comes along in the middle of nowhere and decides to throw a tennis ball, I'll be in real trouble.

Then again, she was carrying a priest's boxer shorts while following a giant peccary who was doing its best impression of a bloodhound, so god only knew what counted as likely or unlikely any more.

The javelina continued snuffling along, a darker shadow on the thicket of black cutouts left by branches. It found a particular spot and halted for a long moment, then began slowly tracing a widening circle, making little huffing snorts as it went.

After about five minutes, while Selena stood and watched and petted Copper and felt useless, the javelina went behind a bush and Father Aguirre stood up. "May I have my clothes? Thank you."

"What did you find? Where did she go?"

It was too dark to read the priest's expression, but his voice sounded heavy. "She came out here, used the facilities, then went about five steps northeast. Then vanished."

"Vanished? Vanished how?"

"I don't know. But since I didn't hear a car and I doubt she's been abducted by aliens, I think we have to assume Snake-Eater took her."

"*Took* her?" Selena pictured a gigantic roadrunner lunging out of the dark like a Tyrannosaurus rex and snatching Grandma Billy up in its beak. "You mean grabbed her and carried her off?"

"I suppose that's possible, but I think it's more likely he pulled her into the spirit world."

Selena curled her fingers around Copper's collar. "The spirit world," she said, pleased with how calm she sounded. "You mean there's another *world* somewhere?"

"Eh . . ." The black cutout shape of Father Aguirre made a maybe-yes maybe-no gesture. "That's a matter of some philosophical complexity. The Jesuits—no, never mind. Not important now. Yes, another world, although it is tied very strongly to this one, and there are gaps and passages. It's where your little squash god is from, and where it goes to. Spirits move through both worlds, but most can't actually appear here physically. That's why Snake-Eater has to work through his intermediaries. But apparently we're close enough to his home ground that he was able to pull Grandma Billy through." He paused and added, almost to himself, "I didn't expect him to be this strong . . ."

Selena gulped, feeling nauseated. One of her friends was gone. It was exactly what she'd feared, but she'd let Grandma Billy goad her into facing Snake-Eater anyway. "Is she . . . do you think she's . . . ?"

"Dead?" Father Aguirre turned and began to make for the truck. "I don't think so."

Relief drenched Selena so strongly she almost cried. "You don't?"

"Knowing what I do of Snake-Eater, no." They were close enough to the fire that she could make out his expression, which was wry and unhappy. "If he's doing this to hurt you, he won't kill her until he's sure you're watching."

Bushes slapped at the sides of the truck, scraping the paint off in thin shrieking lines. Father Aguirre ignored them. Bugs fluttered in the glare of the headlights, but Father Aguirre ignored them as well. The priest had his foot jammed firmly on the gas pedal, DJ Raven was singing along to Johnny Cash, and Selena's only thought, as she tried to keep her bones from bouncing right out of her skin, was that it was a damn shame Grandma Billy wasn't there to see it.

"I am going to have to do so much penance," Father Aguirre said, as calmly as if he wasn't hunched over the wheel, rattling over rocks and shrubs and leaving a trail of wreckage behind. "You should never drive like this in the desert." Something thudded against the undercarriage and Selena clutched Copper tight. "It takes years for tracks like this to heal." He swerved around a saguaro as if it were a pedestrian in the road. "Still, needs must."

"Are we going to have to go to the spirit world?" asked Selena, and marveled at how calmly she said something so absurd.

"That is very possible, yes." The priest didn't take his eyes off the ground in front of him, which did not resemble a road in any sense of the word. "If we do, we must try very hard not to get separated. It could be dangerous."

"As dangerous as this?" Selena asked, burying her face against Copper's ruff as the truck slalomed through another thicket.

"We're much more likely to die here." The truck slowed as it began to climb a hill. "But we're much more likely to have our lost souls wander for eternity over there. I know which one I'd prefer."

"That was not reassuring."

"It wasn't meant to be." He considered. "If we do get separated, be polite to whatever you meet, but don't offer them your name. If they offer you anything—food or water or help or directions—ask what the price will be first."

"Like fairyland?"

Father Aguirre frowned. "Not exactly. Most of the spirits here are not actively malicious. But they are also wild and don't behave like humans expect them to behave." He freed one hand from the steering wheel long enough to make a fierce gesture. "This is not a cash-and-carry world. You can't buy your way out. But a debt or an obligation is a binding tie, and the echoes could go on for a long time."

Just what I need, Selena thought miserably, *another set of social rules.* She slid down farther in the seat. Her tailbone complained.

"The man in black, everyone," Raven said from the radio. "And now let's keep it going for our travelers tonight, with 'I've Been Everywhere.'"

The engine whined as the truck climbed higher, their forward motion converted into a series of upward lurches. They were in hilly country now, but they hadn't gone straight up a hill before. Selena wondered if she should offer to get out and push. Then, quite suddenly, they were bouncing downhill, and then Father Aguirre put on the brakes and stopped. He clicked off the ignition, interrupting Johnny Cash's recitation of states, and they sat together in the cab for a minute, in a silence at once companionable and terrified, listening to the engine ping as it cooled.

"Right," Father Aguirre said. "Saint Christopher, holy patron of travelers, protect us and lead us safely to our destiny."

He got out. Selena did not much like the sound of destiny—destiny sounded like a thing that would ultimately include death at some point—but she got out too.

"That," said Father Aguirre, pointing downward, "is Jackrabbit Hole."

Jackrabbit Hole didn't look like a den of evil spirits. It didn't look like much of anything. There was a steep slope downward, some large stones and a small copse of desert willow at the bottom, and a steep slope up the other side. The whole valley wasn't more than a quarter mile across, if that.

"That's it?" asked Selena.

Father Aguirre gave her a quick, puzzled look, then laughed. "Ah. Of course, you can't see—well, never mind. That, down there, is Snake-Eater's home ground. The place he is most powerful."

"But why here?"

The priest spread his hands. "Perhaps he found it and liked it. Perhaps he was already here and people came along and found water at the bottom and gave thanks, and their gratitude strengthened him. Perhaps this area simply has a lot of roadrunners. As I've said, I really don't know how this all works."

Selena looked down into Jackrabbit Hole a moment longer, went to the car, and picked up Grandma Billy's shotgun. She loaded it as the old woman had taught her, but kept it broken in half—there was a word for that but she'd forgotten it—and slung it over the crook of her arm. "All right," she said. "I'm ready. Let's go."

Let's go turned out to be somewhat optimistic. Parts of the slope were sheer rock walls, so they had to pick their way downward through narrow bands of scrub. Even though Selena's eyes had adapted to the dark, it was a nerve-racking journey, made worse by carrying a gun and having Copper's leash wrapped around her wrist. She grabbed for bushes to slow her descent, and lost track of the scrapes and gouges across her hands.

Copper, surefooted, kept looking back over her shoulder at Selena as if to see if this was some odd new game. "I wish I had four feet," Selena muttered. She watched Father Aguirre skid down the slope below her. He could have had four feet if he wanted. She still didn't know how to feel about that, or if she had any right to feel anything about it at all.

The priest held up a hand to call for a rest. Selena gladly halted. The shotgun was digging into her arm in a horribly uncomfortable fashion. She shifted it carefully to the other arm, secretly convinced that even broken in half, the gun would fire if she looked at it wrong.

"Stupid of you to come here," said Snake-Eater's voice in her ear. "This is *my* place. I will unmake even your bones."

Selena jerked, sending an avalanche of grit down the slope. Father Aguirre looked up at her, startled.

"I heard him. Snake-Eater. Talking to me." She waited for him to say that it wasn't real and words couldn't hurt her, and that she should just ignore it. She even knew what she'd say in response—"I'll do my best."

Instead the priest said, sounding resigned, "Only a matter of time, I suppose."

"I'll d—what?"

Father Aguirre negotiated a tricky bit of slope above a jojoba bush. "We are quite close now. Speaking should take him no effort at all."

Snake-Eater's laughter ran in her ears. Judging by Father Aguirre's expression, he was hearing it too. "So close. What did you hope to achieve, coming here?"

"I hope to ask the other spirits to contain you," said Father Aguirre to thin air. "Though if you don't return our friend unharmed, we may have to take stronger measures."

"You?" Another round of mocking laughter. "Liar. Mongrel. Child of Dirt Pig. What do the three of you hope to accomplish against a god?"

"¡No mames!" said Father Aguirre in a conversational tone.

The world rippled. It wasn't quite like an earthquake or a migraine or the wavering of heat coming off baking asphalt, but it wasn't unlike them either. Selena stumbled. She had a sudden feeling that something was rushing toward her, something vast, like a wall of water or an oncoming train. When she looked up, she couldn't see anything but it was still there, picking up speed, and stranger still, something inside her rib cage was rising to meet it and when the two smashed together . . . what then?

"Lord have mercy upon us," said Father Aquirre, grabbing for Selena's hand.

The warning not to get separated was still strong in her ears, and she reached back. Their fingers slid along each other for an instant, then Copper barked.

And lunged.

The leash that Selena knew she shouldn't have wrapped around her wrist yanked taut and jerked her away. Father Aguirre said something in Spanish that sounded incredibly rude and her last thought as the invisible wave crashed over them was that she would have to ask Lupé what it meant.

Chapter 19

The world was black and silver, sand and brush, and it went on forever. So did she. She had been walking since the beginning of time and she would walk until the end of it. Perhaps her legs should have been tired, but it did not seem strange that they were not. Walking was what she did, what she had always done, threading her way between the black branches of creosote bushes, under a sky that blazed with alien stars.

Once or twice, the thought came to her that there was something she was supposed to be doing, someone she was supposed to be concerned about, but it faded quickly. There was no one else to worry about. There might be no one else living in the entire world.

Strangely this did not concern her. The purpose of the world was to be walked through, and she was the one who did that. There was no need for anyone else.

She had been walking for decades or heartbeats when she came to a saguaro that loomed like a monolith over the landscape. She went around it. Then there was another one, a young one without any arms, and she went around that too. Then came a particularly tall one, arms upraised, riddled with holes. Something looked out at her from one of the holes and she took a step back, startled, and a creosote bush behind her tapped her wrist like a friend trying to get her attention.

Her wrist burned. She looked down, startled, and in the silver starlight, she saw raw lines seared across it. *Oh,* she thought, *of course, that's where I had Copper's leash—*

Copper.

Like a key in a lock, her memories unfolded. Her dog. Her friends. Her own name, which Selena had not realized that she had forgotten.

Snake-Eater did this to me. Did something to my brain. Where am I?

She turned in a circle but could see nothing but the desert in all directions. The ground did not seem to rise or fall in any direction. The creosote bushes made a labyrinth with a thousand passages, and when she looked behind her, the ground had not taken any of her footprints.

Is this the spirit world?

What had Father Aguirre said? Something about lost souls wandering for eternity?

Dear god, how long have I been walking?

"Copper," she called. Her throat should have been dry, but it wasn't, despite her not having drunk anything for what felt like centuries. "Copper? Where are you, girl?"

There was a panicky thought in the back of her skull that maybe she really had been wandering for eternity, and that Copper and Grandma Billy and Father Aguirre had died of old age. Maybe if she stumbled out of the spirit world, centuries would have passed.

No, that's fairyland. This isn't the same. Except that I'd probably know more about fairyland. I don't belong here. This is not my place. Surely this endless black-and-white landscape was meant for someone else—for the Native people who had lived here since the beginning of time and knew the shape of the spirits, for someone like Father Aguirre who was part spirit himself. Even for someone like Grandma Billy, who knew about magic, and who seemed to bend the world around her. But not for shy, neurotic former assistant managers. Wherever she belonged, it certainly wasn't here.

"I didn't mean to come," she said out loud, to the saguaro, who seemed a little like a god itself. "I'm sorry. Snake-Eater brought me. I know I shouldn't be here. I just want to find my friends."

The saguaro was silent.

"Thank you. I think you, um, snapped me out of . . . whatever that was. I'm sorry to bother you."

There was movement inside the hole again, and something inched forward. Selena saw starlight reflected in two round, unblinking eyes, and a body smaller than her fist.

"You're an elf owl," she said. She only knew what that was because she'd seen them on a page of desert birds when she was looking up roadrunners. "Aren't you?"

The elf owl bobbed its head, then launched itself into the air, circled the great saguaro twice, then winged its way into the desert. For lack of any other direction, Selena followed.

The owl was so small that she lost sight of it frequently, but then it would pop up again, a dark shape crossing the stars.

I hope it doesn't think I'm chasing it.

She had been following the owl for perhaps a quarter of an hour when she heard a distant bark.

"Copper! Copper, is that you?"

The barking started again, closer, and now she recognized it. *"Copper!"*

The Labrador hurtled out of the dark, starlight shining on her coat. "Copper!" Selena ran to her and dropped to her knees, then realized, mid-hug, that her dog wasn't alone.

The other was a medium-size yellow dog with dark eyes and a curved tail. It wagged its tail when it saw Selena, and drew back lips in a canine grin.

"Oh, you made a friend." Selena held out a hand cautiously. "Who's a handsome boy?"

"I certainly am," said the yellow dog.

Selena yelped and snatched her hand back. "Oh my god!" *Of course the dog talks, you're in the spirit world now, you* knew *that,* why *did you think it would be a normal dog?*

The yellow dog grinned even more broadly, showing black lips. Selena put a hand on her chest and reached for one of the scripts that almost always applied, even if she'd only ever used it on humans before. "I'm sorry," she said. "I didn't mean to be rude."

"No worries," the dog said. "Copper said you startled easily." He walked up to her and nonchalantly shoved his head against her hand. Selena scratched automatically behind his ears.

"You can talk to Copper?" she said weakly.

"Of course. I'm a dog god," said the yellow dog. "That's a palindrome, incidentally."

Copper had rested her head on Selena's shoulder, where it was rapidly becoming heavy enough to be painful, but Selena didn't care. This was an opportunity she'd never even dreamed of. "Can you . . . can you tell her that she's the best dog in the world? And I love her?"

The yellow dog lifted his head and gazed searchingly into her face. "Dogs don't really do abstract concepts like 'best in the world.' And she already knows you love her."

Copper turned her head and licked her human's face. Selena gave a shaky laugh and wiped her cheek with her sleeve. She was pretty sure that she was crying for no reason.

"Ye-e-e-s . . ." said the yellow dog, drawing the word out. "Yes, I think I'll help you."

Selena swallowed. "Wait. If you help me—I was told—I'm supposed to ask you about the price?"

The dog grinned again. "No charge for Copper's human. You already scratched behind my ears." He stretched. "Come on, then. I'll take you to the others."

"Thank you. Err—" She climbed to her feet, then paused, suddenly remembering the owl that had led her here. "There was a saguaro and a little owl . . . ?"

"There usually is," said the yellow dog cryptically.

"Is there some way I can thank them? I think they saved me."

A canine shrug. "Be grateful."

"I am."

"I mean in general." The yellow dog's face was clearly made for grinning. "Now come on. You don't want to keep the gods waiting."

The world changed as she and Copper followed the yellow dog, although Selena would have been hard-pressed to say exactly when. They were still in the creosote-lined desert, but also they seemed to be walking through a long enclosed hallway that grew narrower and narrower around them. The stars were still bright overhead, but one particular star on the horizon grew closer and closer, and then it was not a star at all but a campfire ringed with figures. Selena tried to make them out as she approached. First they seemed like elderly men and women seated around the fire, their faces as lined as Grandma Billy's, but then one would turn their head in a particular way and the shadows would stretch out and Selena would catch a glimpse of feathers or thorns or a coyote's vulpine smile.

Spirits, she thought. *Gods.* She could not tell how many there were. The fire didn't look big enough for more than a dozen people, but she looked from face to face and never seemed to reach the end. Some of them wore what looked like blankets or robes, while others had faded work shirts, and many seemed to wear nothing but their own painted skin.

"Brought her," said Yellow Dog, flopping down beside the fire and scratching vigorously behind his ear.

"We can see that," said one of the old women acerbically. Halfway through the sentence, her head became a hawk's, beak open in a soundless scream. "What do you expect us to do with her?"

Yellow Dog's tongue lolled. "Ask her yourself."

"Well?" The hawk-woman turned a hard golden gaze toward Selena. "Why are you here?"

"I'm sorry . . ." Selena began automatically.

"Have you done something to be sorry for?" asked another of the people. Selena had an impression of lizard quickness and blue-black lines, like a skink.

"I'm not sure," Selena admitted. She swallowed. "I came with my friend Father Aguirre. He was the one who was going to speak to you. I don't know what to say."

"Start with the truth," said Hawk.

"Yes, of course." Selena couldn't imagine a lie standing up to those piercing golden eyes. She wondered if mice often felt inadequate before Hawk ate them. "I—I came because Snake-Eater sent me here. He's been harassing me. He killed Merv. He was, um, a peacock." She looked from face to face but saw no one gaudy and blue. Perhaps there weren't enough peacocks in the area to make a god, if Father Aguirre was right about how things worked.

"Oh, *Snake-Eater*," said someone else, sounding unimpressed. "Snake-Eater's no trouble."

"Not for *you*," hissed a scaled spirit with an old man's face.

"And he took my friend Grandma Billy. Dragged her here, I think. I mean, to the spirit world. I just want her back safe. And for him to leave us alone."

"So you want us to do something about it?" asked Hawk.

"Yes?" said Selena. "If it wouldn't be too much trouble?"

One of the spirits snorted explosively. She had ocotillo branches for hair. "I don't love Snake-Eater but this one apologizes too much."

"Sor—oh, *damn*," said Selena, which sent a few of the spirits into gales of laughter. Yellow Dog fell over on his back, snickering, and Copper took this as an indication to play and pounced on him. Selena didn't know whether to laugh or cry. She'd expected the desert gods to be solemn and terrible, not bickering like old people at church bingo night. "If my friend Father Aguirre were here, he could explain it better."

"Oh, the javelina child," said Ocotillo. "He's with his mother."

"Probably getting yelled at," added Skink.

Selena spread her hands helplessly. She'd had a vague mental image of Father Aguirre praying, probably in Latin, formally invoking the desert spirits, but it was hard to reconcile that with the people before her.

"Why don't we just ask Snake-Eater what he's doing?" asked a long-faced woman with a sheep's square-pupiled eyes.

"Musssst we?" asked Old Man Rattlesnake on a long hiss.

"I'm sure *that* will be enlightening," said a new voice, which sounded oddly familiar. Selena looked for the speaker but couldn't find them in the shifting circle of faces.

"Bring him here and let them fight!" said a high, thin voice with a buzz in it. "Put out each other's eyes!" Selena didn't even need to see the bright flash of red on the man's throat to know that was Hummingbird.

"No one is putting out anyone's eyes," said Hawk. "At least not yet. Jackrabbit? Will you call him?"

Jackrabbit stood. He looked very human, but his eyes were wide and staring, and he wore only a loincloth. He raised his hands and began to sing.

His voice was low and eerie, rising in unexpected places. The other spirits joined in, making a crooning chant, with edges that seemed to waver into invisibility. Selena could not have begun to describe it, and suspected that parts of it were beyond the range of human ears to hear.

Jackrabbit raised his hands higher and now the song became insistent, calling, demanding an answer, demanding that someone come closer and closer still. Selena took an involuntary step forward, even though the song wasn't directed at her. Copper cocked her head as if listening.

Jackrabbit clapped his hands together abruptly, and the song stopped. For a long, fraught moment, there was no sound at all, not even the crackle of the fire, and then Snake-Eater stepped out of the shadows and into the circle of light.

Unlike the other spirits, Snake-Eater did not look old. He looked as he had in Selena's dreams, the ones she remembered and the others she was starting to. Tall and strong-featured, like a hero off the cover of one of

Grandma Billy's romance novels, with a presence that seemed stronger than anyone else's there.

It's because we're on his home ground, I expect. Oh Father, why did you ever think this would work?

The bird spirit's gaze swept over the shadowy figures gathered around the fire, then landed on Selena with sudden heat. "So," said Snake-Eater coldly. "You cannot best me on my home ground, so you think to run to other gods, like a child carrying tales?"

"Where's Grandma Billy?" Selena demanded. "Where did you take her?"

Snake-Eater smiled. His teeth were very white against his tanned skin, but the shadow of a massive beak hung over him like a sword. "You were coming to confront me, were you not? I simply took her where she was going."

"If you've hurt her—"

"If I've hurt her, it was my right, and there is nothing you could do about it if you tried."

Fury and terror mingled and briefly canceled each other out. "*What* did my aunt see in you?" Selena blurted.

The laughter from the assembled spirits included both Yellow Dog and the half-remembered voice. Snake-Eater rounded on them, flushing. *Some men can't bear to be laughed at.* Someone had told Selena that once—a therapist probably. They hadn't been wrong.

"Enough," said Hawk. "Snake-Eater, this person has come to ask for aid against you. What have you done? Speak only the truth to me."

"I need not lie," he said coldly. "I courted her kinswoman and loved her, but she went away and left me behind—"

"She died!" Selena interjected.

Ocotillo looked at her as if death was a human failing, and one in poor taste at that. Selena clenched her fists. "She died," she repeated, "and you're responsible, aren't you?"

Snake-Eater stared at her, unblinking. Selena tried to feel her way through the next words, aware that she was taking a terrible gamble.

"You said she shouldn't have given so much of her strength away. But she gave it to *you*, didn't she?"

"Is this true?" asked Hawk.

For a moment, Selena thought that Snake-Eater wouldn't answer, but then he said, grudgingly, "It was freely given and freely taken. Why would she give so much away, if she did not have enough to spare?"

"Because she *loved* you, you asshole!"

A little silence fell. Selena felt hot, then cold. Had Amelia even known that Snake-Eater was taking strength from her? Surely she would have stopped if she'd known.

Or maybe, like Selena herself, she had thought that her place was to give and give until there was nothing left of her at all.

Hawk's shrug was a ripple of feathers and unseen wind. "Her choice was her own," the god said, and Selena knew that there would be no help from that quarter. Beings that could barely conceive of death would hardly care about such human frailties. "Go on, Snake-Eater. Say what you mean to say."

"Then this one came and took her place. I watched her until I knew that they were kin, then gave her the traditional courtship gifts. *Which* she accepted."

A murmur went up from the spirits. Selena's stomach clenched. "You left dead rattlesnakes on my doorstep! I didn't *know* what they were!"

"But gifts were given and accepted?" Hawk asked.

"I didn't know I was accepting them!"

Another, louder murmur. Clearly ignorance was no excuse. It was Selena's worst nightmare made flesh: a place where she did not know the rules and had violated them and would suffer the consequences.

"Hardly seems fair," said Yellow Dog. "If somebody leaves food lying around and you come along and eat it, who's fault is that, really?"

"That is true," said a tall woman with the bald red head of a turkey vulture.

"And then," said Snake-Eater, ignoring that, "when the courtship was complete, when it was time for joining, she turned in my embrace and told me that she was already mated!"

This time the murmur was clearly disapproving. Even Yellow Dog seemed a bit taken aback. Hawk turned to stare at her, looking far less human than before, like an Egyptian god with an animal's head. "And is this true?" she asked.

"Yes—sort of—but I didn't *know*!"

"Snake-Eater's people mate for life," Ocotillo said coldly.

"So do mine," said the familiar voice. "But we generally choose mates that know what's happening to them."

Snake-Eater made a hostile sound in the speaker's general direction. Selena racked her brain, trying to remember where she'd heard that voice before, but all she could think of was "Now it's time for some Pink Floyd . . ."

"DJ Raven?!"

The spirit grinned at her. They had glossy blue-black hair that ruffled like feathers, and Selena was pretty sure that she could see a ragged Nirvana T-shirt underneath their robes. "Oh, are you a fan?"

"I . . . yes, I listen to you all the time, but *how* . . . ?"

DJ Raven beamed. "I love radio," they said happily. "You talk and people miles away can hear your voice."

"Of course *you'd* like that," muttered Ocotillo. "You never shut up."

"Focus," said Hawk, sounding less like the incarnation of a thousand birds of prey and more like a harried grade school teacher. "Raven's point is fair, Snake-Eater."

"Her kinswoman knew," said Snake-Eater. "If she did not pass down that knowledge, the fault lies with her, not me."

Horrifyingly, the spirits seemed to find this a fair argument. Selena dug her hands into Copper's ruff, trying not to burst into tears.

"Seems like a lot of work for a lady that doesn't want you," DJ Raven murmured. "Clearly you ought to have brought more snakes."

A ripple of laughter went up at that. Snake-Eater flushed an ugly color, streaks of red and blue smearing across his temples.

"Will any of *you* speak against me?" he sneered. "Will you really put yourself out for a human who broke faith with me? Not even one of the first people, whose voice might be worth listening to, but an interloper?"

"I always forget how obnoxious you are," DJ Raven said.

Hawk sat back. "Snake-Eater's question is fair. Does anyone actually wish to defend this human and her friends?"

"I will," said Yellow Dog.

"You'd defend *every* human if you could," said Ocotillo.

"Still counts."

Snake-Eater folded his arms and looked down on Yellow Dog with clear contempt. "*You* can hardly stop me."

"Not without help, I suppose." Yellow Dog glanced around the circle. "Anyone?"

Selena's heart, already in her toes, seemed to sink into bedrock. When Father Aguirre had spoken of getting the aid of the spirits, this wasn't what she'd expected. Not knowing the rules and then asking strangers for help were two of her worst nightmares rolled into one.

"Please?" she said. Her voice came out as a dry croak. "Please, I just want my friends back."

Silence, except for the crackle of fire. Snake-Eater's smile grew slow and wide.

Then:

"I do not love humans," hissed Old Man Rattlesnake, climbing to his feet with sinuous grace, "but I love Snake-Eater even less."

"But *I* love *you*," said Snake-Eater, with malicious pleasure. "Your children taste so sweet." Old Man Rattlesnake spat on the ground.

"His creature injured one of my sons," said a man wearing familiar green stripes.

Selena knew that she shouldn't interrupt, but she couldn't help herself. "Is he okay? Will he be?"

The striped god looked at her thoughtfully, though she could not see his eyes. "Our roots are strong," he said, which she hoped meant *yes*.

"You're ridiculous," said Ocotillo. "Humans are only good for destroying our roots. *I* stand with Snake-Eater."

"What would the saguaros say?" asked the striped god.

"This child is no kin of theirs," snapped Ocotillo.

No one else spoke for a long moment. The fire crackled. *Not enough,* Selena thought. *They aren't enough.* She felt intense gratitude toward all three, even the rattlesnake god, but it was not going to be enough.

"*I* might." DJ Raven examined their nails. "If you want one of my fans, get your own show."

Selena was surprised to see Snake-Eater take a step back from the dark-feathered spirit. Then he seemed to gather himself, and the fire cast a saurian shadow behind him. "Elsewhere, you might be stop me," he said. "But this is my home ground, my territory, not yours, for all you might pass overhead. In this place, I am still stronger than you all combined."

"Barely," said the striped god.

"But enough."

Hawk stirred. "There is no point fighting a battle with a foregone conclusion. Then, if that is all—"

"I will speak," said a small voice.

The spirits drew back from a strange person, no larger than a child, who matched the voice. They were very pale, with soft, bloated flesh and hands, and when Selena gazed into their face, she seemed to see too many eyes. Her instinct was to recoil. There was something dreadful and alien about that face, something that went directly to her spine and whispered *enemy*, like the buzz of a rattlesnake's rattle.

And yet Old Man Rattlesnake was, for a moment, her ally, and so was . . .

"Scorpion?" asked Ocotillo.

"Defending a human?" Snake-Eater seemed genuinely nonplussed. "They kill your kind whenever you meet. It is the way of things."

"This one has not," said Scorpion, in that small venomous voice. From the way they peered around, Selena thought that they were nearly blind, despite their many eyes. "And you, Snake-Eater, have eaten many of my kind, have you not?"

"It is the way of things," Snake-Eater said again.

"If a human can change the way of things, perhaps so can we."

Snake-Eater stamped the ground and his shadow grew. "You are a small god," he said. "You will not be enough either."

Scorpion smiled gently at him. "If I am so small," they said, "come closer."

Yellow Dog began to laugh. So did DJ Raven. Old Man Rattlesnake smiled, showing white gums.

This can't be working, Selena thought. *The god of scorpions can't be helping me just because I kept taking those scorpions outside instead of squashing them.*

"Well?" said Hawk, her golden eyes fixed on Snake-Eater. "Now what?"

With an inarticulate cry, Snake-Eater seemed to spin in place, shedding even the appearance of humanity. What remained was all sharp points and savage claws, streaked with red and blue, a distillation of bottomless hunger and blinding speed.

The spirit lunged toward Selena. Before she even had time to register it, other spirits pushed between them, one sinuous and streaked with lightning bolts, one sending long green tendrils up from the ground, and the largest by far, arching over all of them on long black wings.

Is this what they truly look like? Were they all just appearing human for my benefit? Or was my mind doing something so I could understand them at all?

Only Yellow Dog seemed to retain his own shape. He bounded into the fray, barking, and plunged his muzzle into Snake-Eater's shadow. Selena put her hands over her mouth.

It was impossible to tell what was happening within the roiling mass of spirits. Selena saw claws pierce scaled flesh, saw Yellow Dog's teeth ripping out feathers, saw beaks clashing like swords.

With a bark of her own, Copper charged. Selena snatched for her collar too late. "No—!" The black dog joined the yellow one, darting in and out, teeth snapping. Selena would have flung herself after, but she lacked sharp teeth or claws and even Grandma Billy's shotgun had vanished or been lost somewhere on the way to the spirit world.

"She chooses to fight for you in her own way," a voice said in her ear. "Would you ask strangers to fight for you, but deny your friends?"

"I don't want her to get hurt. I don't want *any* of them to get hurt!"

"Would you bear her hurts if you could?"

"Yes, of course!"

A soft, maternal chuckle. "Then grant her the same thing. You cannot stop others from loving you, you know, or from being noble about it."

Selena tore her eyes away from the melee to see who was talking. It was a woman, late middle-aged, and although there was nothing overtly inhuman about her, Selena had seen features like hers stamped across the face of a friend.

"Are you Father Aguirre's mother?"

The javelina spirit chuckled. "*Father* Aguirre. I suppose that makes me a grandmother. Yes."

"Is he—"

"Oh, my son is fine. Smarting a bit from a talk we had, but it was long overdue." Javelina nodded her head toward the battle. "And it appears that your friends are winning."

Selena jerked her attention back. The writhing shadow of Snake-Eater seemed much smaller now, as if it was diminishing into the distance. Both the striped god and Old Man Rattlesnake stood off to the side, panting. Scorpion stood a little apart, hands folded, waiting.

With a sudden scream, the clawed shadow broke away. Two dogs, one dark, one light, gave chase. Selena stood, arrested. She recognized that scream, that call of infinite sorrow and loneliness that had troubled the desert. *Not a fox after all . . .*

DJ Raven—she could not seem to stop thinking of them as *DJ*—was suddenly standing by her side, inspecting new rents in their Nirvana T-shirt.

"You just can't get these anymore," they said mournfully. "Not the real thing."

"I'm sorry," said Selena automatically.

"I begrudge nothing for a fan." They nodded to Javelina. "Madam."

"Raven."

"Is this it?" asked Selena wonderingly. "Did we win?"

"More or less." DJ Raven poked a finger through a hole that looked like a stab wound, though the flesh underneath was unmarred. "Snake-Eater won't venture out of his home ground for quite some time."

"There is nothing most spirits hate more than looking like a fool," Javelina agreed. "Present company excluded."

DJ Raven grinned. "Someone has to be the fool."

"It's usually Coyote."

"We take turns."

Selena looked around. The circle around the fire seemed empty now, as if the other spirits, having seen the outcome, had left. Old Man Rattlesnake and the striped god too were fading away.

"Wait!" Selena said, as Scorpion began to do the same.

Small and pale and fragile-looking, the scorpion spirit turned toward her, blinking myopically. "Yes?"

"Thank you," said Selena. "I never thought, when I was rescuing the . . . the little ones . . ."

Scorpion smiled. "It was a small kindness you did," they said. "But you and I are both small creatures, are we not? So the kindnesses feel larger."

"I think you are much larger than I am," Selena said.

"Compared to the size of the world, we are both very small indeed," Scorpion said, and then curled inward and became a tiny white creature that scurried into the darkness.

Selena was still looking after the spirit when two dogs came trotting out of the darkness, tongues hanging out, looking enormously pleased with themselves.

"He's been chased out," said Yellow Dog cheerfully.

"Then . . ." Selena looked around the world, black bushes and silver sand and glittering alien stars. "Are we done? Can we go home?"

"Mmm," said DJ Raven. "Not *quite* yet, I'm afraid."

"You still walked into Snake-Eater's home ground like fools," said Javelina tartly. "And you'll have to walk out by yourselves. If you can."

Selena felt her eyes go wide. "You mean—"

"Best get started is what I mean," Javelina said, and put her hand on Selena's chest and *shoved* her out of the world.

Like most people, Selena had had moments, right on the edge of sleep, when she suddenly jerked awake. The javelina spirit's push felt a little like that. She was falling, falling, falling—and then it felt as if her entire *soul* twitched and she was wide awake and standing in a jumble of broken boulders at the bottom of Jackrabbit Hole.

The boulders were much larger than they had looked from the top of the slope. The shortest was still higher than her head, the color of bone in the moonlight. The very largest leaned together, making a rough cave that sheltered a depression which must fill with water from time to time, but which had dried up, leaving only white rings behind. She recognized that cave, and those stones, because she had seen them sketched in her aunt's journals.

Dark marks scored the face of the stones, but Selena did not have time to work out if they were natural or man-made, because the first thing she saw was Snake-Eater and the second thing was Grandma Billy.

"Grandma!"

The old woman sat slumped against the largest stone, clearly holding herself upright by will alone. There was blood and dirt on her face and her breath rattled in her chest.

"Selena," she said, her voice low and raspy. "Don't you worry, hon. I'll be up in just a minute."

"She will not," said Snake-Eater inside Selena's head. "Your miserable little gods may have trapped me here, but you will not get away."

The bird spirit had clearly come off badly in the fight. He was no longer a pillar of clawed and sharp-edged shadows, but a shifting, stunted thing with a shape that barely seemed able to hold together. A bristling crest melted into raw-looking skin and golden eyes turned first human, then reptilian, pupils narrowing into slits. But the monstrous beak was still there, sharp as a sword, and when he began to advance, it was like watching a dinosaur come to life. The back of Selena's brain screamed that she was only a tiny skulking mammal and this ancient beast was coming to devour her.

If Snake-Eater had still had a roadrunner's terrifying quickness, he would have caught her at once and that would have been the end of it. But he moved slowly, clawed feet scraping up furrows of dust, and Selena retreated and then Copper, who was valiant and ridiculous and probably thought that she had defeated this monster all by herself, bounded forward and sank her teeth into the bird-beast's leg.

Snake-Eater roared and kicked out hard, lifting the dog off the ground. Copper was flung away, and struck a boulder with a yelp. Snake-Eater lifted a clawed foot to disembowel his attacker.

"No!"

Selena, who generally ran away from everything, ran *toward* Snake-Eater, yelling. She didn't know what she said, but apparently it was enough. The bird-beast's head swung around and focused on her instead of Copper. He struck out at her and Selena jerked back and felt a puff of wind across her cheek as a beak like an axe blade passed mere inches in front of her face.

If that hit me, she thought, as if from very far away, *it would tear me in half.*

But before Snake-Eater could come at her again, she heard a clatter of hooves and a javelina the size of a man struck Snake-Eater low to the ground and bowled him off his feet.

Snake-Eater shrieked. Claws raked the javelina's sides and Father Aguirre squealed furiously. Selena ignored them both and ran to Copper's side.

The dog was trying to get to her feet but something was wrong with one hind leg. Selena tried to get down on one knee beside her, but there was something digging into her arm.

She looked down and realized that somehow, in this world, she was still clutching Grandma Billy's shotgun.

Good thing I didn't fall on it, she thought absently. *It might have gone off and hit someone. That's why I don't like guns.*

Guns.

I have a gun.

Everything seemed to be moving very slowly. As if in a dream, she heard herself saying, *But I don't want to shoot anyone,* and Grandma Billy answering, *What about if something came after Copper?*

Grandma Billy had been going to shoot Snake-Eater. Grandma Billy was in no shape to do that, but Selena was.

She lifted the shotgun, made sure both halves fit back together, and took aim. It seemed to take centuries. She saw Snake-Eater getting unsteadily to his feet and the javelina shake himself off. "Father Aguirre," she said, very calmly, "you need to get down."

Her voice sounded quiet in her own ears, but somehow the javelina heard her and flung himself down. His legs were so short that this didn't actually do much, but then he fell over on his side and Selena lifted the shotgun.

In her head, she tried out saying, *"Meep meep, motherfucker,"* and possibly that would be amazing and possibly it would be incredibly silly and since she couldn't decide, she said nothing at all and pulled the trigger instead.

Chapter 20

"See?" Grandma Billy said. She had revived enormously after draining most of a canteen of water. "Told you shooting the bastard would work."

Father Aguirre, attempting to arrange what was left of his clothes so that they provided basic modesty, said, "Yes, you did. I should not have doubted you."

Snake-Eater had been reduced to scattered feathers and gobbets of something dark and oily, which was already sinking into the sand and vanishing. There was much less than Selena would have expected from the sheer size of Snake-Eater's body. Perhaps he had made himself look bigger somehow, expanding a roadrunner skin in the same way that the fetches had with barn owls'.

"Is he dead?" Selena asked.

"No," said Father Aguirre. "You can't kill a spirit with a gun, merely . . . discommode him. We should be out of here by sunrise, though. He is a creature of daylight and daylight will see him gaining strength again. But it will be a long time before he stirs from his home ground again."

"Then let's go home," said Selena, feeling suddenly bone-crushingly tired.

It took them a long time to toil up the slope to the truck. Copper was limping, and every time she put three feet down and hopped on the fourth, Selena's heart clenched. Father Aguirre seemed mostly unharmed, but he supported Grandma Billy, who was clearly in pain and pretending that she wasn't.

The eastern sky had started to lighten by the time the truck came into view. Selena opened the door and lifted Copper's hind end to get her up onto the seat, then fell in after her. She had never been so exhausted in her life. She felt as if her bones were made of sand and the marrow was trickling away into the desert.

Father Aguirre helped Grandma Billy into the truck in much the same way that Selena had helped Copper. When he turned on the ignition, DJ Raven's voice came booming through the speakers. ". . . And for a great bunch of fans—you know who you are—here's the late, great Freddie Mercury." The first strains of "We Are the Champions" filled the cab and Selena wrapped her arms around Copper and fell immediately, utterly, profoundly asleep.

She didn't wake up even as they jolted back down the hill and bumped into the dry wash. She didn't wake up while Grandma Billy and Father Aguirre bickered over her head about exactly who had rescued who. She didn't wake up for DJ Raven's in-depth comparison of the lyrics of ten different folk songs about cuckoos. She didn't wake up when the truck broke a headlight on a concealed rock and didn't wake up for the resulting flood of Hail Marys. It wasn't until the truck stopped at an unfamiliar house that Selena lifted her head and said, "Hwuh?"

"Rosa's," said Father Aguirre. "Lupé's sister. You've met her, she comes to the potluck now and again. She fixes up animals, and occasionally people."

"Which do you count as?" Selena asked, too tired to be tactful.

Father Aguirre grinned. "Both, I hope. After all, Copper's a people, right?"

"Definitely." Selena unfolded herself out of the cab. Her joints felt like rusty hinges, and there were aches that she couldn't remember ever feeling in her life.

The house was a low adobe with a cheerful purple door. Rosa opened it up, pushed open the screen door, and said, "Oh Lord."

The four of them limped inside. Rosa, who looked a great deal like an older version of Lupé, put her hands on her hips and surveyed them. "What the hell happened to you?"

It had not occurred to Selena that they'd need a cover story, so she hadn't rehearsed anything. "Uh . . . we fell down the stairs?"

"All of you?"

"We fought a roadrunner god," said Grandma Billy cheerfully. "Kicked his ass too."

Rosa shook her head. "Your first story was better. Right, come around back to the surgery and let's see what we can do."

Copper's leg wasn't broken but two of Father Aguirre's ribs were. He'd also been raked several times by giant claws, which left paired slash marks across his back and shoulders.

"What the hell did this?" Rosa demanded. "If these were any deeper, I'd think somebody came after you with a sword." Her eyes narrowed. "Was this some kind of self-flagellation?"

"Heavens, no!" Father Aguirre looked slightly offended. "I'm not *that* kind of Catholic."

"Hmmph."

She was much kinder to Selena, and only tutted softly as she cleaned out the scrapes and gouges left behind from that hectic descent into Jackrabbit Hole. To Copper she was kindest of all, offering multiple treats and profound apologies for the cone that the dog had to wear for the next week to keep her from worrying at her stitches.

"Don't I get a treat?" asked Grandma Billy.

"You're getting a night of observation and I'm calling in the doctor from Masonville. Falls at your age are dangerous."

"What do you mean, 'at my a—'" Grandma started to say, but Rosa gave her the glare of a woman who routinely wrestled sheep, cows, and the occasional stallion, and Grandma submitted meekly. "Yes'm. Selena, will you make sure the chickens get fed?"

"Yes, of course. You just rest up."

"I think she's probably fine," Rosa told Selena and Father Aguirre in an undertone at the door. "But at her age, when things *aren't* fine, they go bad in a hurry." She gave Father Aguirre a version of the look she'd used on Grandma Billy. "And whatever the *hell* you were getting up to, if she gets banged up like this again, I swear to God, priest or no priest, I'll get out my castrating knife and—"

"No, no, *completely* understandable," said Father Aguirre, in full retreat. "We *truly* didn't set out to do anything dangerous, I swear. It was, err . . ."

"A sequence of completely unexpected events," said Selena hastily. "Never to be repeated. Hopefully."

"Mmm." Rosa clearly wasn't quite satisfied, but accepted this. Selena thought that perhaps when you were primarily a large animal vet, you got used to not knowing how your patient had managed to injure themselves. "I'll keep you posted about her condition."

"I'd appreciate that," said Father Aguirre, who had swung the truck door open and was not quite hiding behind it. "Selena, why don't I take you and Copper home?"

"I'd appreciate that," Selena said. "Very, very much."

She woke into a dream that seemed horribly familiar—a dark place, lit by fire, and another presence beside her. But before Selena could gather her wits to panic, she looked over and saw that it was Yellow Dog, wiggling on his back in the blankets and shedding little tan hairs all over everything.

"Why am I back here?" Selena asked. "I thought Snake-Eater was dead!"

"Dead's a bit of a stretch," Yellow Dog said. "Very much weakened, though. He won't be able to possess an egg, let alone a full-grown bird, for a good long time. A century, at least."

Selena relaxed. She'd be safely dead by then, and presumably beyond such concerns as deranged bird gods. "But why am I *here*? This was where Snake-Eater was . . . um . . ."

"Trying to hump your leg?" asked Yellow Dog, and grinned. "Simple. This wasn't ever his place, it was yours."

"What?"

The dog dug his shoulder blades farther into the blankets, which, now that Selena was looking, appeared to be furs. "Sorry to tell you, but this is where your dreaming mind thinks leg humping ought to occur."

Selena looked around the scene—fire, darkness, furs—and put her face in her hands. *This is what comes of reading* The Clan of the Cave Bear *at a formative age.*

"Eh, don't feel so bad. You'd be amazed what places people dream about. That priest friend of yours has a recurring—"

"No," said Selena. "I don't want to know."

"Fine, fine." Yellow Dog sat up and scratched vigorously behind his ear. Selena suspected that if she ever dreamed about this place again, she'd find fleas in the blankets.

"Thank you, though," she said. "For helping me back there. I couldn't have done it without . . . well, actually I don't feel like I did much. It was all of you. I just stood there and wrung my hands."

Yellow Dog's perpetual smile faded and he gazed at her intently. "Don't do that."

"Don't do what?"

"Don't talk down what you did."

"But I *didn't* really do anything! It was all my friends—I wouldn't even have known how to pull the trigger if Grandma Billy hadn't shown me—"

Yellow Dog snapped his teeth in the air, cutting off her words. "Making friends," he said, very deliberately, "is *doing something.*"

Selena stared at him.

"The tide wasn't turned because you were a great warrior. It was turned because you put scorpions outside without killing them." He stretched, full body, like a cat. "And because your dog loves you. Don't forget that."

". . . oh," said Selena, feeling things shift around inside her head.

"Anyway," said Yellow Dog, "I didn't come here to talk about that. I came to tell you that you probably ought to rename your house."

"Jackrabbit Hole House?"

"Yep. The name made a connection to Snake-Eater's home ground. It was why he was able to come here, so far away."

"And my aunt renamed it three years ago. That was deliberate, wasn't it? So he could come here and be with her?"

"Seems like it."

Selena took a deep breath. "Did he mean to kill her?"

"Eh." Yellow Dog shrugged. "I'm not a doctor, but I doubt it. Snake-Eater did love her, and by all accounts, she liked him well enough. He wasn't quite so bad, you know, until she died and left him alone."

"It wasn't her fault!" Selena said, bristling. "She didn't die *at* him."

"Peace," said Yellow Dog, falling over on his side and showing his belly. She could tell he was laughing at her. "Not all spirits understand how dying works for your people. The ways we die tend to be very different. Snake-Eater very likely expected your aunt to simply come back in another body, and when she didn't, it felt as if she'd abandoned him. And then you showed up, and he couldn't figure out if you were her again or something new."

"And I had no idea why he was leaving dead rattlesnakes on the doorstep." Selena sighed. "If I could have just explained . . ."

"Wouldn't have helped." Yellow Dog bounded to his feet and shook himself. "Birds don't generally have room for more than one thought at a time, and Snake-Eater's not the sharpest spine on the cactus. This would have happened to anybody who moved into that house, I expect." He began trotting away into the dark.

"Wait!" Selena said. "I have so many more questions for you!"

"Too bad, because you're waking up. Remember to change the house's name," he called over his shoulder, and then Selena sat up in bed, feeling the heavy weight of Copper across her feet, and wondering why her sheets were covered in little fawn-colored hairs.

Three days later, she had a gathering at the house. Grandma Billy, using a cane and insisting that she was fine, goddammit, arrived on Father Aguirre's arm. Mayor Jenny and Lupé and Rosa and Gordon all came in Connor's truck. Lupé had insisted on bringing food, of course, and Gordon had a plate of deviled eggs that he said were his secret recipe. ("The secret is bacon," he informed Selena, in a loud whisper.) Selena wasn't going to argue with free food, though she'd spent all afternoon icing a chocolate cake that she'd made from a box of cake mix.

Copper was ecstatic, both from all the people and the fact that her cone had come off that morning. When they were done eating, Selena took down the sign that read JACKRABBIT HOLE HOUSE and put up a new one that Connor's son had carved for her. She took a bottle of wine that she had bought from Connor's store and (after several tries) broke it over the front door as if she was christening a ship. "This house," she said, feeling a little silly but saying it anyway, "this house is called Copper Dog House."

"Witnessed!" said Father Aguirre in a carrying voice, and "Witnessed!" cried the rest of Selena's friends.

"I'll update it in the records," Mayor Jenny promised.

Selena poured out glasses of wine from a second bottle and they toasted the new name and had slices of cake. It was, all in all, a gloriously successful evening.

Father Aguirre was the last to leave, since Rosa had insisted on giving Grandma Billy a ride so that the old woman didn't walk home. "Is that all I need to do?" Selena asked him. "Does it count now?"

"It counts," Father Aguirre said. "It takes a little while for a new name to stick, but people will get used to it. And you're out here far enough that most people in town didn't know what it was called anyway." He smiled. "If I tried to rename Our Lady of the Palo Verdes, it would be a lot harder."

She told him what Yellow Dog had said about the names. And then, over the last of the wine, about Snake-Eater and her aunt.

The priest listened as solemnly as if he was hearing her confession, nodding. "I can hardly speak against unions between spirits and mortals," he said wryly. "And while I have no great love for Snake-Eater, I can tell you at least that I think your aunt was happy."

"It killed her," said Selena. "Eventually. Didn't it?"

Father Aguirre nodded. "It seems likely. He may have been draining her strength to travel back and forth between the house and Jackrabbit Hole. Probably she didn't know it was happening." He paused, possibly debating what to say next, then finally added, "She was very lonely, I think. And some people respond well to being loved so absolutely, above all other things."

Selena dropped her hand to where Copper was lurking under the table, still sulking that she hadn't been allowed chocolate cake. "Well," Selena said, "then she should have gotten a dog."

Chapter 21

Life in Quartz Creek was so divorced from the usual cycles of work and the desert so changeless that autumn crept up on Selena before she even noticed. She spent most of a week at the Rivendell commune helping ready the guest cabins for habitation, and acquired both a decent wage and a reputation for escorting scorpions gently outside. When the tourists arrived, Lupé opened up the café as an actual restaurant instead of an outlet for her relentless need to feed people, and Selena's skills at food service were suddenly useful. She spent the rest of the season making sandwiches for catered lunches as the rich sustainability tourists toured the historic zone, visiting sheep ranches and admiring the way that people lived "so close to the land." Selena felt like a cross between a zoo animal and a total fraud.

"You get used to it," Galadriel told her, during a tour of the commune, while a number of middle-aged ladies in expensively flowy linen admired the gardens and the hoop houses. "And honestly, most of them do mean well. I told one once that my well probably needed to be deepened—just a random comment, you understand—and she left a check for a thousand dollars on the nightstand with a note."

"Wow."

"Right?" Galadriel grinned. "Though for every one of those, you get a half dozen trying to find spiritual wisdom. Lady, my family's from Wichita. I'm good at dry farming vegetables, that's all."

Selena, who had seen a flash of green stripes in the garden early that morning, laughed dutifully.

"Anyway, the bird-watchers will be out next week, and they're a lot easier. Give them a bathroom and a bench and check in every few hours to make sure nobody's got heatstroke and they're happy. And they're much less picky about the sandwiches."

Galadriel was correct on all counts. Selena sliced meat and cheese and made up vast quantities of sandwiches, which were ferried out to various birding spots. Gordon, who made most of his income from leading bird tours, was happier than Selena had ever seen him. "Got an elegant trogon today!" he announced, coming into the café to pick up a cooler full of sandwiches. "This far north! Can you believe it?"

"That's good?" Selena asked, and then there was nothing for it but for Gordon to get out his bird book and show her a picture of a dramatic red-and-green bird that looked like something that belonged in the jungle, not a few miles out of Quartz Creek. She duly admired it, and Gordon went away beaming, while she and Lupé exchanged smiles.

Father Aguirre preached to much larger crowds for the next two months, but otherwise made himself scarce. Selena worried at first that something was wrong, but Grandma Billy laughed. "It ain't that. He's still trying to get the dents outta his granddaddy's truck. That thing needs last rites, if you ask me."

Grandma Billy also enjoyed tourist season, although for entirely different reasons. She would sit in the corner of the café and flirt outrageously with men who came in. Selena teased her about it until one day she came in extremely early, wearing the same clothes she'd had on the night before, radiating smugness on a kilowatt scale.

"Oh my god," said Selena, nearly dropping a plate of tuna on wheat. "You—was it the bald guy with the khaki vest and the funny binoculars?"

"They were Swarovskis," said Grandma Billy, snagging a sandwich off the plate. "Very high-end. You can always tell how much money they've got by the quality of the binoculars." She grinned like a shark. "And his name was Darren. He's a retired actuary, and the sweetest thing."

"Don't go breaking my customers' hearts," Lupé called. "I need the business."

"I'm bringing in repeat business," said Grandma Billy. "Darren'll come back just to see me again, just you wait."

Selena had to wait to slice more provolone until she could stop giggling.

Despite the money, everyone was glad when tourist season finally ended, except possibly Grandma Billy. Selena weeded her sadly neglected garden and was glad for the return of quiet. It had been wonderful to be genuinely useful again, and she'd made more than enough to keep Copper in dog food for months, but hearing so many strange voices had made her tense in a way that she didn't quite understand.

She was listening to the silence and watching to see if anyone would come to visit the planting of winter squash when she heard a screech of brakes out front.

Oh lord, now what? Selena came out onto the porch to see Connor's truck, being driven by Connor's younger son. He waved frantically out the window at her. "Selena! You gotta come quick!"

"What?" She came down off the porch. "Why?"

"Dad sent me. You gotta get into town. There's this weird guy there *asking* about you."

Selena stared at him. It wasn't possible. Snake-Eater was gone. Yellow Dog had said he wasn't coming back. He couldn't be walking around, talking to people. He *couldn't.*

"Dad says you gotta come," Connor's son said. "He's *saying* things."

"Things?" Selena said blankly.

"Like you gotta *leave.*"

Maybe it wasn't Snake-Eater. Maybe someone from the government had come to kick her out of the historic zone. That made more sense. She knew it couldn't have been as easy as Jenny made it out to be.

It didn't matter either way. It had to be dealt with. Selena shook her head to clear it. "Of course I'll come. Just let me grab Copper's leash."

The door to the church was open when Connor's son pulled up in front of it. Copper hopped out and Selena followed. Anxiety was eating a hole under her sternum, and her mind whirled with contingency plans—*if this happens, I'll do this, if that happens, I'll do that instead, if they try to lock me up, I'll ask Father Aguirre to take Copper . . .*

She couldn't imagine that Snake-Eater would come to Our Lady of the Palo Verdes, to Father Aguirre's home ground. Also, it seemed unlikely that he would drive the car with rental plates parked beside the church.

That shut off one set of fears. It must be someone from the government. Jenny had said that the interview was only a formality, but maybe a law had changed or maybe a bill hadn't passed in the faraway halls of government and nobody was allowed to move into a historic zone anymore.

I'll explain about Aunt Amelia. I'll say I'm just taking care of the house until we've sorted out the will. If that doesn't work, I'll ask Grandma Billy if I can stay with her until the historic man leaves. And if that doesn't work, I'll . . . I'll . . . I don't know, go into the church and cry sanctuary if I have to!

She went up the walkway and had just reached the door when she heard a man's voice saying, "Really, I'm extremely grateful for all you've done for Selena. I know she's not always easy . . ." The voice trailed off to a rueful chuckle. "Believe me, I know."

The voice was familiar, and yet for a long moment, she couldn't place it. She *should* know, she *did* know, but her life had changed so much and this wasn't the place where the voice belonged—

Oh shit, she thought. *Of course it's Walter.*

Her first instinct was to turn around and run. Then Father Aguirre said, rather sharply, "Selena's been a great help to have around, actually," and her fingers tightened on Copper's leash and she thought, *I fought a* god, *why am I running from* this*?*

She straightened her back and stepped through the church door. It was cool and dark after the brightness of the desert, but she could make out Father Aguirre standing in the middle of the sanctuary and Mayor Jenny leaning against a pew with her arms crossed.

Another man stood with his back to her, but of course she recognized him. She knew his back quite well. Walter. Her partner. *Ex-partner,* she thought fiercely.

He looked smaller than she remembered. Perhaps it was because the desert was so large and it had seeped into her bones. His hair had always been thin in the back, but it had grown to an honest-to-goodness bald spot.

"That's great to hear," Walter said warmly. She recognized that warmth. It sounded so sincere. It probably *was* sincere. Walter always said that he only wanted what was best for her, and she was pretty sure he believed it.

Hell, she'd believed it.

Father Aguirre's eyes went to her, and relief sparked in them. "Here's Selena now."

Walter turned. "Selena!" he said, taking two steps toward her. "I was so worried!"

"I *told* you it was over," she said, taking a step back. "I told you months ago."

Walter waved his hand as if wiping her words out of the air. "Don't worry about what you said," he said. "I know you were upset after your mother passed away. People do strange things when they're grieving."

He smiled down at her, benevolent and forgiving. That smile flooded her body with relief. It was okay. She hadn't screwed everything up. Walter had forgiven her before she'd even realized she had sinned. It was . . .

. . . a reflex, actually. Something that had been etched into her nerves, year upon year. No different than the way Copper automatically turned around in a circle before lying down.

What if she didn't need to be forgiven?

"How did you find me?" she asked sharply.

Walter's eyebrows went up. "Your name's on a house out here," he said. "Some real estate agent sent a letter offering to buy it. As soon as I got the name of the town, I flew into Phoenix and rented a car."

Oh hell. She'd known paperwork would be what brought her down, she just hadn't expected it to be something so trivial.

Walter must have realized that Selena wasn't reacting the way that he expected, because he reached for her hands. "Selena, it's okay. I'm here now. We can go home."

Selena hastily put both hands on Copper's collar so that he wouldn't have anything to take. Copper, who knew this human and knew that he had fed her, thumped her tail agreeably. Selena sighed internally. Dogs were supposed to be such great judges of character, but Copper was ruled entirely by her stomach.

Mayor Jenny, who had, until now, been watching silently, pushed away from the pew. "I'm not entirely sure Selena *wants* to go home with you," she drawled.

Walter ignored her. "Come on, Selena," he said. "It's okay. It's just another one of your episodes. You've been away so long, and I know it's hard, but we'll get through it." His voice was low and coaxing, as if trying to soothe a frightened animal. And part of Selena *felt* like a frightened animal, felt like she'd been holding herself together for too long, felt like the world had proved itself to be huge and terrible and full of monsters.

If she went home with Walter, she'd never need to worry about monsters again. Snake-Eater and the fetches and the roadrunners would all fade into a hazy memory. And since they couldn't be real, pretty soon, she'd start to think that maybe she'd actually had a psychotic break or something, and she'd be so relieved that she was home and that Walter could take care of things . . .

If she went home with Walter, the world would become a smaller place. No more monsters, but no more vast desert skies. No more Grandma Billy barging through the door with a coffee can full of eggs. No more little green god at the end of the garden, no more potlucks at the church, no more quail for Copper to terrorize, no more radio monologues from DJ Raven, no more drinks on the back porch while the stars blazed endlessly overhead.

She took another step back, shaking her head. "No," she said.

Walter sighed. His expression shifted from coaxing to kindly exasperation. "Selena," he said. "You know you can't stay here."

"Why not?"

He gazed briefly heavenward. "It's a historic zone. They don't just let people move in. And I know people have been very kind, but you can't keep imposing on them."

The words poured through her like water, eroding her foundations. It was everything that Selena had ever been afraid of, summed up in one sentence. *Imposing.* She swallowed hard. She'd done nothing but impose, hadn't she? Grandma Billy and Lupé's leftovers were the only reason she hadn't starved at first and that didn't even get into how she'd brought Snake-Eater down on everyone's head. Poor Merv the peacock had *died* because of her.

"I *know* you don't want to be a burden," Walter said.

"That's good," said a new voice, as the side door slammed back against the wall, "because she ain't."

Grandma Billy came stalking down the central aisle looking rather like a bird herself—not a roadrunner, Selena thought, but one of those big secretary birds you saw on nature shows, the ones that looked like dinosaurs and kicked their prey to death. Her bracelets jangled ominously.

Father Aguirre displayed his finely honed sense of valor and got out of the way. Grandma Billy stalked up to Walter, and even though she was at least two inches shorter and thirty years older, she managed to loom *up* at him.

"And just who do you think you are?" the old woman asked. "Coming in here and telling Selena she's a burden?"

Walter, who had turned to face this new assault, actually retreated a step, then cleared his throat and tried to pretend that he hadn't. "I'm her partner," he said firmly.

"Not anymore you ain't." Grandma Billy poked him—actually poked him! Poked Walter! Selena couldn't believe it—in the center of the chest. "She's done with you and she's said she's done with you, so you got no call to come in here spouting nonsense."

Selena was standing behind Walter, so she couldn't see his face, but when he said, "Ma'am . . ." and spread his hands, she knew that he'd decided on charm. She winced internally.

"Ma'am, I'm very glad that Selena has made such good friends out here, and I assure you, we both want what's best for—"

Poke. "Don't you start telling me what I want."

"Ma'am, I—"

Poke. "And don't you go talking about how she's imposing on me. You don't know the first thing about me, and I don't think you know that much about Selena either."

Walter sighed, a much put-upon sigh, and looked over at Father Aguirre. Selena could have predicted within a raised eyebrow hair the expression on his face. It would be the one that said *You and I are the only adults in the room and do you see what we have to put up with?*

She knew from past experience how effective that look was at getting people on Walter's side. It was like a bizarre personal magic.

But Father Aguirre had a far more potent magic of his own. He kept his eyes on Grandma Billy's figure, and the small smile quirking his lips didn't change.

"Has she killed him yet?" a voice whispered in her ear. Selena jumped, startled, but it was only Lupé, who had just come in the front door. Her dark eyes were snapping with anger and delight.

"Not yet," Selena whispered back.

"Good, then I haven't missed it." She scratched Copper's ears. Behind her, Gordon came in, still clutching his binoculars.

"Ma'am," Walter said, "I'm sorry if I overstepped. But Selena and I have been together for years, and I know that she has these little episodes, and it's important to—"

"Oh, fuck *off*," somebody said.

It took a moment for Selena to realize that somebody was her.

Walter turned, looking rather stunned. She'd never talked back to him like that. She'd certainly never told him to fuck off.

"Selena!"

"I told you, it's over," she said. She wanted to be firm, but her voice shook a little and she hated it, because that meant Walter would hear the shake and not the words. Nevertheless, she plowed forward. "I'm sorry for how I ended it, because I could probably have done that a lot better, but I'm not sorry that it's over."

"Selena . . ." he said, reaching for her again. His hand closed over her wrist, not hard, but firmly. A proprietary grasp, as if it was his right to hold her back.

"I think that's enough," Mayor Jenny said, and something about the way she stood changed. Selena had always known that the mayor was a stocky woman, but she'd never thought about how much of that was muscle. Jenny suddenly looked less like a mild-mannered postmaster and more like a bouncer at a particularly rough bar.

Walter was oblivious to this. *How odd,* Selena thought. *He always picked up all the things I didn't, saw all the people I made uncomfortable. How does he* not *see that Jenny's about to drag him out of here?*

Unless maybe he hadn't seen as much as he thought he had.

Unless maybe he'd been wrong.

You ain't bad with new people, you know, Grandma Billy had said, months ago now, sitting on the back porch, drinking tea. Selena had filed the words away because it was the first time anyone had ever told her that. It had been so novel and so counter to everything Walter had told her that it couldn't be right.

Unless it was.

Something inside Selena's chest unfolded, like a squash blossom opening out of its tight spiral bud. She felt as if her *self* was growing larger, expanding outward, to encompass the sanctuary of the church and the people who stood there, Copper and Jenny and Father Aguirre and Grandma Billy and Gordon and Lupé and even Connor's son, who had poked his head in the far door after Billy, but was obviously afraid to come in any farther.

But not Walter, who stood apart, like a boring beetle on a petal. He didn't have to be part of her any longer.

Mayor Jenny's hand closed over Walter's shoulder. Clearly startled, he dropped Selena's wrist.

"You've said your piece," Jenny said. "Probably time that you clear out, don't you think?"

Whatever Walter saw in her face didn't give him much hope. Still, he tried to rally. "I'll get a hotel room," he said, "and we can talk about this later."

"No hotels in Quartz Creek," said Jenny shortly. "Nearest one's about thirty miles away."

"Then I'll go there." He looked over her head to Selena. "Don't worry, I won't abandon you here. I'll come back tomorrow."

"I think you probably shouldn't come back," Jenny said. "I think Selena's said all she needs to say."

Walter seemed to finally notice the threat exuding from Jenny's sturdy frame. "I don't see how it's any of your business, madam."

"It's definitely my business," said Jenny, "seeing as I'm the mayor." She leaned her head to one side then the other. Her neck cracked like a gunshot.

Walter's eyes went wide. "You can't just force me to leave!" he sputtered.

"Sure I can." Jenny reached into her shirt pocket and pulled out a badge. "I'm also the chief of police."

Selena had the privilege of seeing Walter's eyes go even wider at that. "This is ridiculous," he said. His gaze swept the crowd that had assembled in the church. Lupé stepped in front of Selena defensively and Gordon, who was older than Grandma Billy and a lot frailer, hefted his binoculars in a threatening manner.

"You can't do that, Jenny," said Grandma Billy. "If *you* do it, it's police brutality. Whereas if *I* throw him out, it's just ordinary brutality."

She tried to advance in a threatening manner, and was hastily blocked by Father Aguirre.

The priest cleared his throat. "I think," he said, in his most gentle voice, "that perhaps the house of God is not the place for this?"

Jenny, chief of police, took this as permission to proceed and began herding Walter toward the doors. Everyone stepped back to clear a path, except for Grandma Billy, who was doing an excellent impression of an angry Chihuahua being thwarted by a very resigned German shepherd.

Walter tried to catch Selena's eye over the heads of her friends. "Selena—" he started to say.

"Keep moving," Jenny said, in a voice suited to crowd control and third-grade teachers.

He kept moving. The whole group shuffled out the door after him, and Selena watched Walter go, with many backward glances, to his rental car. Jenny stood in front of it, arms folded, and eventually the car backed up and Walter drove away in a cloud of white dust, and Selena never saw him again.

Epilogue

"I can't believe you actually cracked your neck at him," said Father Aguirre. "I was afraid I'd start laughing and give the whole thing away."

Mayor Jenny grinned. "Remember that time I fell of the ladder and had to have neck surgery? It sounds like popcorn ever since." Her grin turned fierce. "Not that I wouldn't have popped him one if I had to. What a slimy little bastard. Begging your pardon, Selena."

"No, no," said Selena. They had all retired to the rectory and even though her heart had stopped racing, she still couldn't quite believe that Walter had *left*. And not just left, but been *defeated*, as if he were a dragon and her friends had all turned up to help her slay him. "He is slimy, isn't he?"

"Sure is," said Grandma Billy. "All that 'oh, you're just having an episode' talk, trying to make you think you're crazy. I'm sorry Jenny *didn't* punch him."

"I'd have had to arrest myself for assault. It gets awkward, particularly when I have to read myself my rights."

"Wait a moment," said Father Aguirre, giving Billy a suspicious look. "He said all that *before* you came storming in."

Grandma Billy smirked. "Oh, I listened in for a bit. Had to make sure my grand entrance was timed right."

"It was *wonderful*," Selena said. "*All* of you were wonderful."

"I was, wasn't I?" Grandma preened.

"You were pretty wonderful yourself," Lupé said.

"I can't believe I told him to fuck off." A giggle escaped her. Selena put her hands to her cheeks. They felt hot.

"Generally I'd prefer you didn't swear in the house of the Lord, but this time I think it was justified." Father Aguirre went to a cupboard and pulled out a bottle. "I also think this is justified, even though it's rather early."

He passed glasses around and splashed dark red wine into them. Selena took a sip, feeling half drunk before it even touched her tongue. Grandma Billy tried to take two glasses and Father Aguirre took one away.

Only one thing nagged at Selena's euphoria. "Walter wasn't completely wrong," she admitted. "I have been imposing on you all dreadfully."

"Have not," said Grandma Billy.

"You practically ran the catering for the last two months," Lupé added.

"But I have." She didn't want to mention Snake-Eater in front of Gordon and Lupé, and maybe that really hadn't been her fault, but there were other things . . . "I'd have starved those first few months if you all didn't keep feeding me. And if Grandma didn't keep giving me eggs."

"Eggs?!" Lupé drew herself up to her not particularly substantial height. "Grandma Billy, you have *not* been dumping your extra eggs on this poor girl!"

Guilt flashed across Grandma Billy's face, an expression so unfamiliar that Selena froze with her wineglass still halfway to her lips.

"You have! Oh my god, Selena, how many eggs have you been eating?"

"Err . . . well . . . when there wasn't a dinner here at the church, I'd make an omelet . . ."

Father Aguirre put his face in his hands. "Jesus, Mary, and Joseph."

"When you keep chickens," said Lupé, giving Grandma Billy a grim look, "and you don't eat them regularly—"

"They're my friends! You don't eat your *friends*."

"—and you've got a rooster, then you keep getting *more* chickens and those chickens keep laying more eggs. And more. And more. And so from about February on, *somebody* keeps coming around with buckets of the damn things." Lupé's eyes narrowed. "I should have known something was up when you stopped asking me if I'd take 'just another couple dozen' at the café."

Selena struggled to process this information. "But—it was really—I mean, I really was grateful—"

"There, you see?" said Grandma Billy. "Worked out for everybody."

Lupé ignored her. "If she starts giving you summer squash, you come tell me," she said. "We'll hold an intervention."

"There may have been some squash already," Selena admitted.

"Billy!"

"I think," said Father Aguirre, "that perhaps we could use another bottle of wine."

He had just gotten to his feet when there was a hesitant knock at the door. The priest opened it, revealing a skinny young man with a duffel bag over his shoulder. He looked to be about seventeen, at that stage when teenage boys are mostly elbows and Adam's apple. He also looked extremely hungry.

"I'm sorry," he said. "I don't mean to intrude, but I heard on the radio that there was a community meal here?"

"There is," said Father Aguirre. "Come on in."

The young man hesitated. "I don't have much money," he said. "I could wash dishes, maybe?"

"That'd be fine," the priest said. "We were just about to get started." He looked around at the clear lack of food and the presence of the wine. "Ah . . . that is . . ."

"I've got a pan of enchiladas that need eating up," said Lupé. "I'll be back in a second."

"I was going to bring eggs," said Grandma Billy angelically. "Won't be a minute."

Lupé muttered something, but the young man looked like he could eat a dozen eggs without stopping for breath, so she let Grandma go out the door in front of her.

"I'll go get my hot dish," said Gordon happily.

"Dad wanted me to bring some potatoes," said Connor's son.

They all hurried off. Father Aguirre went to fetch silverware, leaving Selena alone with the skinny young man.

"I can work," he said, with a painful earnestness that Selena remembered well. *Hard worker fallen on hard times. I promise I can be useful if you give me a chance.*

"I'm sure you can," she said. "We'll find something for you to do, don't worry."

He set his duffel bag down and, after looking to Selena for permission, petted Copper's ears. Copper leaned against him and thumped her tail.

"Welcome to Quartz Creek," Selena said. "I think you'll like it here."

Acknowledgments

When I started telling people that I was working on a book with an evil roadrunner, one of two things happened. The vast majority of people said, "Like the cartoon?" and I would be left saying plaintively, "No, really, if you've met one, they're like *dinosaurs*."

The other group of people, who were mostly attendees of Bubonicon in Albuquerque, immediately started telling me stories of Horrible Things They Had Watched a Roadrunner Do. Lying in wait at birdbaths so they could leap up and grab sparrows. Murdering baby bunnies in graphic ways, usually in front of small children. If your only exposure to roadrunners is through Warner Bros., you may not be aware of this, but a roadrunner is somewhere between a velociraptor and a chicken with a shiv, and if this doesn't sound alarming to you, you have probably never been attacked by a rooster. This is a two-foot-long bird that routinely kills rattlesnakes. They are a vital and beautiful part of the ecosystem, in much the same way that sidewinders and cactus with inch-long spines are vital and beautiful parts of the ecosystem.

Also they aren't afraid of humans. They know they can outrun us. They are often rather curious about us, in fact. A number of people have befriended their local roadrunners after a fashion, though the only way to get them to a feeder would probably be to pack it with raw meat.

While most are harmless, the murderousness of *some* roadrunners is actually taken from real life, specifically a particularly nasty bird named Carmine who lived in the Sonoran Desert pavilion at the North Carolina Zoo and hated his keepers, killed other birds (including females of his own species), and was generally an absolute jackass despite an entire trained staff desperately trying to figure out how to make him happy. (These are people who built a tiny sex swing for their geriatric elf owl so that he could mate without hurting himself. A more dedicated and creative bunch would be hard to find.) Carmine really did lie in wait and try to drive his beak into the back of the skull of anyone who came in to feed him, and it was hearing this anecdote from one of the keepers and eyeing the size of that beak that made me think, "Man, it would actually be pretty scary if one of those came for you . . ."

This book is one of those that I started and which then sat and percolated for over a decade. I always wanted to finish it, but it took a while for it to find a home. Possibly creepy roadrunners are a hard sell if you haven't actually met a roadrunner in the flesh. Much gratitude to the crew at 47North for taking a chance on a very weird book, and on my agent Helen for not giving up on it!

If I was going to describe the platonic ideal of a Kingfisher horror novel, it would probably be a woman and her dog alone in a house full of creepy family secrets. That was the plot of my first horror novel, *The Twisted Ones*, and I often find books trying to bend in that direction and having to wrestle them back into line. It was a weird relief with *Snake-Eater* to just embrace it wholeheartedly.

I spent a large chunk of my childhood in the Sonoran Desert of Arizona, surrounded by prickly pear and saguaro cactus. They were formative years and I imprinted on the landscape, a fact I didn't realize until decades later when I came back for a visit and felt something unclench because the landscape looked *right* again. This was how the world was *supposed* to look.

There was no help for it. I had to move back to the desert. (The high desert, in Albuquerque in this case, because Arizona is very, very expensive. I do miss the saguaros still, but greatly prefer the weather.) Infinite and unending love to my husband, Kevin, who said, "Sure, let's go," and drove his beloved chickens from North Carolina to New Mexico, eager to embark on a new adventure. (Kevin, not the chickens. The chickens thought it was bullshit.)

Much of *Snake-Eater* was written while packing and wrangling the logistics of that move across the country, but the last pages were finished while sitting in my new office, looking out at the Sandia Mountains and rangeland full of thousands of cholla, and feeling that, like Selena, I'd finally come home.

T. Kingfisher
Edgewood, NM
2025

About the Author

Photo © 2013 J. R. Blackwell

T. Kingfisher is the *New York Times* bestselling and Hugo Award–winning author of fantasy, horror, and occasional oddities, including *What Feasts at Night*, *Nettle & Bone*, *What Moves the Dead*, *Thornhedge*, *A House with Good Bones*, and *A Sorceress Comes to Call*. Under a pen name, she also writes bestselling children's books. She lives in New Mexico with her husband, dog, and chickens, and does not trust roadrunners. For more information, visit www.redwombatstudio.com.

PRAISE FOR T. KINGFISHER

"Kingfisher never fails to dazzle."

—Peter S. Beagle

"T. Kingfisher spins biting wit, charm, and terror into a tale that will make your skin crawl. Poe would be proud!"

—Brom, author of *Slewfoot*

"No one blends humor and creeping dread as satisfyingly as T. Kingfisher."

—Gwenda Bond, author of *The Frame-Up*

"Can horror even be this rollicking, this fun, while still delivering on the creepiness, the dread, the ick? In Kingfisher's hands, it can."

—Stephen Graham Jones, acclaimed author of *The Only Good Indians*

"T. Kingfisher solidifies her place as natural and inevitable heir to the greats of her genre."

—Seanan McGuire

"Kingfisher's trademark wit and compassion transforms 'Sleeping Beauty' into a moving meditation on guilt, grief, and duty, as well as a surprisingly sweet romance between outsiders. There are no false notes here."

—*Publishers Weekly* (starred review)